D1305689

JEANETTE BAKER

Chesapeake Summer

MIRA®

MIRA®

ISBN-13: 978-0-7783-2459-1
ISBN-10:   0-7783-2459-1

CHESAPEAKE SUMMER

Copyright © 2007 by Jeanette Baker.

MIRA and the Star Colophon are trademarks used under license and registered
in Australia, New Zealand, Philippines, United States Patent and Trademark
Office and in other countries.

www.MIRABooks.com

Printed in U.S.A.

This book is dedicated to the memory of my husband, Stephen Farrell, who assured me that he will still be there for everything I write because there would be no heaven without books.

ACKNOWLEDGMENTS

A special thank-you to Officer Rick Hieb of the Long Beach Police Department, East Division, his colleagues in homicide and his wife, Tammie, for their information, their time and most of all, their hospitality.

Thank you to all my friends at Santiago Elementary School for supporting me during this very difficult year.

Thank you to Pat Perry and Jean Stewart, for reading and rereading and then doing both all over again.

Prologue

August had settled over the marshes like a sauna, wet, hot, cloying. Even now, at midnight, breathing was difficult. Movement was impossible. Thick snakes, fiddler crabs, tree frogs, elegant blue dragonflies, cunning, predatory alligators, lay buried beneath the gray mud, hidden below the wild grass and algae-laced water, heat-drugged, motionless, somnolent. The world was silent, human life profoundly absent, except for a single car.

A late-model Cadillac, the windows tinted, the color nonspecific in the absence of sunlight, crawled slowly, without headlights, down the ribbon of highway bisecting the swamp. At a point that first appeared random, it rolled to a stop. Upon closer inspection the site was really a fork, one tine continuing down the highway, the other leading to a pony path, a slim piece of solid ground cutting through the tall grasses and salt-encrusted pines, the birch and willow, an occasional hemlock and pin oak that had, over aeons, adapted to the brackish soil.

For a time, fifteen minutes, maybe twenty, nothing happened. The car appeared to have materialized on its own without a driver or passengers. Then, as if responding to a silent signal, it moved forward again, keeping to the highway, snaking slowly, darkly, down the twisting road until it disappeared into the camouflage of night and swamp grass and trees.

Eight miles away, the residents of Marshy Hope Creek, well into the first few hours of their sleep cycles, the twilight kind of sleep where the senses are still present but pleasantly numbed enough so that nothing much matters, heard a loud, explosive boom. No one cared. But if anyone had, or even paid attention, he would have placed the noise in the direction of the Patuxent River Naval Air Station, along Highway 39.

One

Three days earlier

Verna Lee Fontaine stared at the clock mounted on the wall of her shop and tapped her foot impatiently. Had five minutes ever passed so slowly? Finally, *finally,* the long hand inched its way up to the twelve. It was 5:00 a.m. on the dot, time to flip the Open for Business sign on the window and unlock her door. She'd anticipated this moment for six long months, dropping flyers on doorsteps, taking out ads in the local newspaper, tacking up notices on the library and supermarket bulletin boards and talking to just about everybody in town. Now, it was time to step back and wait…no, pray for customers.

Some would come because they wanted to see her succeed, others because they were curious. A café that offered smoothies laced with vitamin supplements, herbal teas sweetened with honey, egg-white omelets topped with Stilton cheese and oatmeal sprinkled with wheat germ was unheard of in the remote back roads of the Tidewater.

She knew people whispered behind her back. Black folks said that with her fancy college degree and her nine years spent teaching school in California, she didn't really belong in Marshy Hope Creek anymore, not that she ever had. She'd always been uppity and now she was worse than ever, a phenomenon completely unrecognizable in their small fishing community, one of their own and yet, not really, an educated black woman who owned a business.

White folks remembered that Verna Lee Fontaine had always been unusual. She was something to look at, but didn't let it go to her head. She ignored the suggestive comments and blatant invitations, never losing sight of her goal, to leave and never look back. Raised by her grandmother in a small house on the edge of town, she kept to herself, studied hard, ended up number two in her graduating class and earned a top-notch scholarship to one of the best universities in the country. They wondered what brought her back. But she wasn't one of their own and they were too polite to ask.

The thing was, Verna Lee didn't really belong in

either community. Her African heritage was evident in the caramel color of her skin and the full, well-defined lips, which she emphasized with spicy-cinnamon lip gloss. But her pert nose, brook-hazel eyes and the tawny curls framing her face were definitely European. She looked liked someone, but no one could agree on who, except that it wasn't Drusilla Washington, the grandmother who raised her.

Ten minutes hadn't gone by before customers began showing up, first a trickle and then as the sun rose, a steady flow of them, ordering cappuccinos and lattes, foam thickened and cream topped. They sat on her blue couches, spread her yellow napkins, sipped from her ceramic mugs and chatted among themselves, consuming the homemade carrot-cinnamon and blueberry muffins, the peach scones and carob crisps, the apple-nut granola and whole-wheat pancakes. They took away packages of raspberry and peppermint teas, loaves of high-fiber bread and sinfully rich fudge brownies. When it was clear that she couldn't manage on her own, Verna Lee recruited her grandmother to run the blender and refill the cups, to package the to-go orders and wipe down the tables. Four hours later, the shop was empty and Verna Lee's inventory nearly depleted. She slumped into a chair, exhausted but satisfied. "I did it, Gran," she said. "I really did it. I'm a success."

Drusilla Washington wasn't convinced. "It's nine o'clock on your first day of business. Tell me you're a success six months from now when the mortgage is paid nice and regular."

"Killjoy." Verna Lee lifted her head and grinned. "Tell me you aren't as excited as I am."

Drusilla looked at her granddaughter's lovely young face, at the red bandanna holding back the tawny curls, at the golden eyes lit with pleasure, and relented. "You done good, Verna Lee, real good. I'm proud of you."

"Thank you, and you're right." She jumped up. "I won't know this is going to work until I have repeat customers. There's no time to waste. Lunch is only three hours away. Sit down, Gran. I'll pour you a cup of coffee before I start on the chicken salad."

"I hope you put some of that good New Orleans chicory in the coffee, Verna Lee. It cuts the bitterness."

The bell on the door chimed, signaling another customer. Verna Lee, in the act of rinsing a coffeepot, turned to greet the newcomer. Her eyes widened. The man who sat at the window table was a stranger, middle-aged, dressed casually but expensively and, if the Mercedes parked directly outside her window was his, comfortably situated.

She walked over to the table. "May I help you?"

He looked up. "I'd like to see a menu."

Verna Lee's eyes flickered across his face. She was fairly certain she'd never seen him before, and yet he looked vaguely familiar. His accent was a common one around the Tidewater, but she thought she detected a hint of something foreign. Maybe he was visiting family. That was it. He looked like someone she already knew. "The menu is on the blackboard above the cash register. Would you like a cup of coffee?"

"Yes, please." He glanced at the menu. "I'll have a scone and a slice of lemon cake."

Moments later she set the scone in front of him. "Are you visiting or just passing through?"

He sipped his coffee. "This is good. It tastes like New Orleans coffee."

"It's the chicory. My grandmother worked for a lady from New Orleans years ago. Are you from Louisiana?"

He shook his head. "I live in the Bordeaux region of France."

"Really? What do you do there?"

"I'm a winemaker. I own a vineyard." He smiled. "I assume you don't have a liquor license."

"No. But I lived in San Francisco and some wonderful wines come out of Napa Valley, although nothing like your burgundies. You're a long way from home." She rephrased her original question. "Will you be here long?"

"Not too long."

"I'm Verna Lee Fontaine. Welcome to Perks Coffee House. We opened today."

"Congratulations." He seemed to be studying her. "Maybe you can help me. I wonder if I'm in the right place. Is there a Delacourte family around these parts?"

"You haven't told me your name."

"I'm sorry." He held out his hand. "Anton Devereaux."

She took it. "As a matter of fact, you're in the right place. Cole and Nola Ruth Delacourte live a few miles outside of town. If you take the road to the left you'll see their name on the mailbox. The house is on the bay and quite a distance from the road. If you're looking for Cole, it's a weekday. He'll be at his law office in Salisbury."

"I'll keep that in mind."

She felt Drusilla cross the room and stand behind her before she heard her speak. "Where you stayin', Mr. Devereaux?"

"I'm not sure I will be staying."

"Gran." Verna Lee frowned meaningfully, slipping her hand under Drusilla's arm. "I could use some help in the kitchen."

Anton Devereaux watched as the two women worked together behind the counter. The younger one was exceptional, long-legged and full-breasted, a light-skinned black woman who'd inherited the best of both races. There was something about the bones of her face that reminded him of Nola Ruth Delacourte, but that was ridiculous. His imagination was running away with him. She'd called the old woman Gran. Even if she hadn't, the idea forming in his head was absurd. Not in a million years would the Beauchamps have allowed Nola Ruth to have his child, nor would she have wanted to. His deduction was based on what he knew of human nature rather than personal knowledge of Nola Ruth's character. He'd known her only eight weeks and where once he would have sworn on his life that he knew her better than anyone, ten years in a Mississippi state prison cured him of all second-guessing.

He finished his coffee and brought the bill up to the register. "Keep it," he said when Verna Lee tried to give him the change. "The scone was the best I've tasted."

She smiled, a full, warm smile that changed her face, narrowed her lips and showed her strong white teeth. Anton's heart constricted. He couldn't look away. "What did you say your name was?"

"Verna Lee," she replied. "Verna Lee Fontaine."

"Fontaine is a French name. Would you happen to be of French descent, Ms. Fontaine?"

"Not that I know of, although it's possible. There's a large Franco-American community here in the Cove. Washington is my maiden name."

* * *

Six hours later Verna Lee was spraying her front window with a solution of white vinegar and water and wiping it down with old newspaper when she saw the man in the Mercedes once again. A police cruiser dogged his back fender. Verna Lee turned to watch. The red light on the top of the patrol car blinked forbiddingly and Sheriff Grimes, his voice amplified by a bullhorn, broke through the pedestrian conversations. "Pull over immediately. Pull over immediately."

The cream-colored Mercedes, already moving below the speed limit, slowed to a stop. Silas Grimes exited the patrol car, hitched his belt, unlocked the clip on his firearm, rested his hand on his billy club and swaggered to the driver's side of the Mercedes. The door opened and the stranger stepped out. He faced the car, hands and legs spread-eagled while Grimes patted him down.

Verna Lee was staring openly now, the newspaper clenched in her hand.

Drusilla opened the door of the shop and stood beside her. Assessing the taut line of her granddaughter's mouth, she laid a warning hand on her arm. "Easy now, Verna Lee. He'll be all right."

"Silas Grimes wouldn't humiliate a white man like that, not here in the middle of the street. It's because he's black and he drives an expensive car."

"Don't be mindin' anyone's business but your own. No good can come of it."

Verna Lee couldn't hear their conversation, but the stranger wasn't taking his treatment passively. He'd turned to the sheriff. Their faces were very close and they were arguing. The black man was taller by at least three inches.

Sheriff Grimes walked back to his car, pulled out a hand radio and spoke into it. Almost immediately the air was filled with the sound of sirens. Two police cars sped to the intersection and parked in a vee, blocking it completely. Two deputies, guns drawn, approached the black man. A crowd had gathered. Grimes, wielding handcuffs, pulled the man's arms behind his back, cuffed him, laid a punishing hand on his head and pushed him into the patrol car.

Verna Lee watched as they headed in the direction of the police station, a block away. "I'll call Cole Delacourte."

"I'll call him," Drusilla said. "Better yet, I'll call Mrs. Delacourte. She'll get through where we may not."

Verna Lee finished her windows and began closing down the café. She sifted flour, filled the sugar jars and set out recipes for tomorrow's baking. Then she ate a peach, drank a glass of lemony iced tea, drove home, took a long shower, shook out her wet curls, climbed into bed and fell asleep, all before nine o'clock.

The next morning passed much the same as the one before. Customers, many the same faces she'd seen yesterday, lined up for cinnamon bread, poppy-seed muffins, flaky apricot scones and specialty coffees. A few intrepid buyers agreed to shot glasses of vitamin B-12 and wheatgrass in their yogurt smoothies. Once again, the store was empty by nine o'clock, but this time Verna Lee wasn't worried. The lunch rush would begin at eleven thirty and continue until one o'clock. She checked her supplies. She was low on lemons and whipping cream. There was plenty of time for a brief trip to John's Food King.

Nearly every face she saw on her way to the small family owned market at the end of the block was a familiar one. She nodded but didn't stop to chat. Time was cheap here on the Tidewater and conversation an art. A generic how are you was considered an invitation to while away the morning.

"How you doing, Verna Lee, honey?" Mamie Sloane called from her beauty shop across the street.

"Just fine, ma'am." Verna Lee hurried on.

"I'll be in for some 'o those sweet potato muffins. Harley sure did enjoy 'em."

"Looking forward to seeing you." Verna Lee waved and picked up her pace.

Boyd Jessup held the door open for her. "Mornin', Verna Lee."

"Good morning." Picking up a basket she breezed past him, heading for the dairy section.

"You tell Drusilla that my missus is near her time."

"I'll do that, Boyd."

She grabbed four pints of heavy cream from the refrigerator, a dozen lemons from the produce stand, paid cash and dashed out the door, fully intending to let nothing short of a lightning strike divert her.

The scene unraveling across the street at the police station stopped her short. Walking down the steps at a brisk clip was Nola Ruth Delacourte, beautifully turned out as usual. Following in her wake was Anton Devereaux.

Ordinarily, Verna Lee would have come up with a reasonable explanation. After all, Drusilla had called Cole Delacourte on the man's behalf. Nola Ruth was Cole's wife. Maybe he'd sent her to bail his client out of jail, except she knew it would never happen. Cole didn't expect his wife to handle his clients. Nola Ruth frowned on her husband's pro bono work. Not that Anton Devereaux was the pro bono type, not with those clothes and that Mercedes.

Verna Lee pretended she was interested in the contents of her purse. Surreptitiously she watched the man grip Nola Ruth's arm, watched while she pulled away, heard her raise her voice, look around, and then lower it again. It was clear they were arguing. Once again their voices rose.

Fascinated, Verna Lee strained to hear. Their words were disjointed, without beginning or end.

"Ten years, Nola. Your lie cost me ten years of my life. Where were you? Did you care? Maybe you decided you were over your head and made the call in the first place."

"Go to hell," she shot back. "You'll never know what it cost me. I won't give you the satisfaction. Get out of here and don't come back."

There was more, but their voices had dropped to furious whispers. They were drawing attention to themselves. People walked past, stopped at a distance and looked back, while pretending not to.

Nola Ruth was the first to notice she was the focus of all eyes. She walked quickly to her car, climbed in and pulled out of the parking space. Anton Devereaux looked up and down the street. There was no sign of the Mercedes.

Verna Lee was about to cross the road, make her presence known and enlighten the mysterious stranger as to the location of the impound parking lot when she was surprised yet again.

Nola Ruth's Lincoln Continental circled and came back, braking directly in front of Devereaux.

Without a word, as if he'd been waiting for her to do just that, he climbed into the passenger seat. Together, they drove out of town in the opposite direction of the Delacourte's big white house on the bay, taking the Highway 39 turnoff.

Two

The Crab Pot with its spectacular sunset views of the Chesapeake was the kind of restaurant that accommodated anyone with money to spend, no matter how casually or sophisticated he dressed. The bar, for those who preferred golf shirts and slacks as well as a lighter menu, could be found on the first floor. A spiral staircase led to the legendary restaurant on the second level. Complete with flickering candlelight, white tablecloths and the soft dance music of a bygone era, it offered its patrons the same comforts they enjoyed at home: elegance, seclusion and discretion.

Two couples shared the best table on the second floor. Cole and Nola Ruth Delacourte had barely touched their gin and tonics. Amanda Wentworth sipped her sherry. Quentin Wentworth was well into his second martini.

Nola Ruth's eyes met her husband's. The message was clear. *How long do we have to stay?*

Cole barely lifted his shoulders.

Nola Ruth summoned the warm delta charm ingrained in her from birth. "Amanda, tell us about Tracy and Tess. Are you enjoying their stay?"

Amanda was about to open her mouth when the judge intervened. "We'd enjoy it a whole lot more if she planned on leaving anytime soon."

Nola Ruth looked bewildered. "I beg your pardon?"

"Our Tracy has decided to get a divorce. Yes, sirree, a *dee vorce.*" He stretched out the word.

"I'm so sorry," Nola Ruth murmured. "How terrible for her."

The judge leaned forward. "What do you make of these kids, Cole? I've a good mind to deny their request, make 'em get along, tie 'em up together until they're good and ready to come to terms. Divorce." He shook his head. "What's the matter with young people today? Why can't they stay married like the rest of us?"

"Maybe the time for tying up was before the marriage," Cole replied dryly.

"I told her not to hook up with that boy in the first place," Quentin continued. "The Hennesseys are nothing more than dockworkers.'

Nola Ruth bit her lip and remained silent, a Herculean feat considering that Russ Hennessey had courted her own daughter up until he'd gone away to school. That was before Libba had run off to California with Eric Richards, an actor. Nola Ruth shuddered, she still couldn't bring herself to think of, much less utter, her son-in-law's name.

Cole was less inclined to keep his mouth shut. "There's nothing wrong with Russ Hennessey. He's done his family proud. I'm sorry to hear about the breakup, especially since they have a child."

Amanda Wentworth's thin-lipped mouth frowned in disapproval. "Tracy and Tess will be fine." She changed the subject. "You haven't told us about Libba Jane. How long has it been since you've seen her?"

"We flew out to California when the baby was born," Nola Ruth replied shortly. "Libba's in graduate school. We're very proud of her."

"Daughters," snorted Quentin. "More trouble than they're worth. Give me a son any day."

Cole laughed. "We're a bit long in the tooth to be starting over."

Amanda looked pointedly at her husband. "One would think."

A waiter approached the table. Wentworth waved him away. "I had an ulterior motive when I asked you to dinner, Cole."

"Why am I not surprised?"

"I intend to enter the senate race," Wentworth continued. "I'd like your support."

Nola Ruth's eyes widened, huge chocolate drops in the cream of her face. "But we're Democrats, Quentin."

"People change parties."

"We don't," replied Nola Ruth, "especially when we agree on everything Clayton Duval stands for."

"What about you, Cole? Does Nola Ruth speak for both of you?"

Cole Delacourte smiled. "You've been talking to the wrong people, Quentin. I'm a defense attorney. I specialize in civil rights cases, all of which you know. Who's telling you that you need my support?"

"I'm serious. You've been in these parts for a long time. Before that, you were in Washington. You have influence. I could win if you came over to my side. Hell, you don't even have to become a Republican. All I want is for you to suggest I'm your man."

Nola Ruth looked away.

Cole set down his drink and met the judge's glance without faltering. "I wish you luck, Quentin. I really do. But I'm not *your* man."

Amanda coughed. "I guess we should eat. It's getting late."

Quentin ignored her. "Damn it, Cole—" He

stopped, his gaze riveted to the dance floor, and the willowy, black-haired woman in the red gown that fit like a second skin.

She melted into her partner's arms, angle to curve, breast to bone, cheek to cheek, flame red against tuxedo black. Gracefully, erotically, they moved as one, her right hand extended, captured in his left, his right splayed across the naked base of her spine, her left resting on the back of his neck. Her lips were a whisper from his. It was abundantly clear to all who watched that their level of intimacy extended beyond the dance.

The music rose and fell. Other couples box-stepped around them, their sedate steps a world apart from the intricate, air-light tango of leg and limb displayed by the woman in red and her partner.

Quentin couldn't tear his eyes away. His face burned. *Lizzie Jones. Damn her. Damn her to hell.* His fist clenched, shattering the delicate glass in his hand.

"For God's sake, Quentin." Color flared across Amanda's cheeks. She began mopping up the puddle of alcohol, broken glass and drops of blood.

"Leave it, Amanda," Nola Ruth counseled. "The waiter will take care of it." She lifted her finger, signaling for help.

Immediately, a white-coated server materialized

at her elbow, assessed the damage, cleaned the table and returned with fresh linen and another martini before the music ended.

Wentworth held a napkin under his hand. "Excuse me. I need to take care of this." Instead of walking around the wooden dance floor, he strode through it, deliberately bumping into Lizzie and her partner. "Pardon me," he said, reaching out to grip her arm. "I believe your escort has something that belongs to me."

The man laid a warning hand on the judge's arm. "Mister, you're out of line."

Lizzie Jones's silvery laugh floated across the room. She mocked him. "What might that be, *Your Honor?*"

He shrugged off her defender's restraining arm. "Something for which I paid a great deal."

This time Lizzie's eyes narrowed. Deliberately, defiantly, her hand slid up the judge's chest. She moved closer, close enough so that her long black hair swung across his cheek, hiding their faces. "I belong to no one, Quentin," she whispered in her subtly accented English. "Remember that. Go back to your wife." Taking the lobe of his ear in her mouth, she bit down hard.

He jerked away. Blood poured down his neck, forever staining the white shirt and dinner jacket.

Lizzie leaned against her partner, threw Quentin

a final smoldering glance and swept out of the room.

Looking back, Cole would remember that it seemed as if all the breath and color in the elegant restaurant left with her.

Nola Ruth was completely nonplussed. For the first time in her life she'd encountered a social situation for which her careful upbringing hadn't prepared her. She simply sat and watched while Amanda, white-faced and silent, fumbled with the clasp of her purse, pulling out bills, throwing them on the table.

Cole's voice was low and controlled. "Don't be ridiculous, Amanda. We'll cover the check. See to Quentin. I imagine you have a great deal to talk about."

Without a word, Amanda stood, crossed the room, circled her husband's waist with her arm and led him away.

"Should we follow them?" Nola Ruth asked. Her voice was high and breathless.

"I don't think so," replied Cole. "If the situation were reversed, I wouldn't want anyone else around at the moment."

Nola Ruth shook her head. "There isn't the slightest possibility that you would ever find yourself in Quentin's position."

"No?"

"No."

"You're that sure of me?"

"Absolutely."

"Why?"

She smiled. "You're crazy about me. You have been from the first."

Cole Delacourte studied the olive and cream beauty of his wife's face and acknowledged her truth. "I'm that obvious?"

"You are, and I'm grateful." Nola Ruth shuddered. "I don't think I could bear a scene like the one we just witnessed."

Cole found his wallet, pulled out a hundred-dollar bill. "I've lost my appetite. Let's go home. Serena's bound to have something in the refrigerator."

Nola Ruth gathered her wrap and purse and stood. "I'm sure I can manage something." She hesitated.

"What is it?"

"Did you know about Quentin and Lizzie?"

Cole nodded.

"You never said anything."

"No."

"May I ask why not?"

He looked at her steadily until the blush mounted along her cheekbones. "We all have skeletons, Nola Ruth."

Even though Quentin had consumed enough alcohol to test considerably over the legal limit, he still slid behind the wheel, requiring several attempts to insert the key into the ignition. Amanda didn't protest. In her world, men were drivers, women passengers. Normally, she turned on the air conditioner, even on a cool night, ensuring that she arrived wherever she was going with every hair in place. Tonight she left the air off and the window open, allowing the wind to do its worst. They covered the twenty miles from the restaurant to home in silence.

Tracy was watching television in the den. She turned down the volume and peered into the hall. "You're home early."

Quentin, already halfway up the stairs, didn't answer.

"Your father isn't feeling well," her mother replied. "Go back to what you were doing, honey. We'll be all right." She followed her husband into their bedroom and closed the door.

Quentin rinsed his wounds in the bathroom sink, pulled a towel from the rack and dried his hands, leaving rusty stains on the pale beige terry cloth.

Amanda grimaced. Turning away, she dropped her purse on the bed and sat down in front of the vanity. Staring at her reflection, she carefully removed her jewelry: the pearls she'd inherited from her mother-in-law, the bracelet she'd purchased in Annapolis, the earrings she'd picked out for her birthday that Quentin paid for. Removing her wedding ring, she reached for her lotion and began smoothing it over her palms and the dry skin on the backs of her hands.

Quentin came out of the bathroom, naked except for his shorts. Amanda studied his reflection in the mirror. He was forty-nine years old, a hair under six feet tall, fit and unlined. Except for his steel-colored hair, he looked ten years younger. She hadn't aged nearly as well, another of life's inequities.

She watched while he pulled a fresh shirt and slacks from his closet and began dressing.

"Where are you going?" she asked.

"Out."

"Again?"

He remained silent.

"Answer me, Quentin." His wife's voice was cold. "You're going to her, aren't you?"

Again, no answer.

Amanda left her vanity to stand in front of him. She grabbed his arm. "I won't have this, Quentin. I refuse to be humiliated this way any longer."

His lip curled. He pulled away and mimicked her. "'I won't have this, Quentin.' Who are you to tell me what to do?"

"I'm your wife, in case you've forgotten."

"How unfortunate for you." He buttoned his shirt, stepped into his slacks and zipped them.

"I'll divorce you. You'll be ruined."

Removing clean socks from his drawer, he pulled them on and stepped into his shoes. "You don't have the guts."

Amanda's hands clenched. "Why are you doing this? She's a prostitute. There isn't a drunk or bum with an extra twenty dollars who hasn't had her. For God's sake, you're a superior court judge. If you're caught with her, you're finished. Think of your family, your position. If it was anyone else, anyone but Lizzie Jones, I'd look the other way." Her hands twisted. "In front of the Delacourtes, too. How could you?"

It would be so easy to kill her. He would have, too, if he was someone else, or if there was any chance at all that he wouldn't get caught. He waited, counting the long seconds until the bloodlust had left him. "Shut up," he managed to say at last. "You can't hold a candle to her. She's a real woman, a desirable woman." He gripped her shoulders and turned her toward the mirror. "This is you, Amanda. That miserable, dried-up excuse for a woman with the pinched lips is you. Don't throw the Delacourtes in my face and, while you're at it, take a good look at Nola Ruth, her clothes, her face, her body. Listen to her talk. Watch her move. Then compare yourself. You won't have to ask why I go to Lizzie."

Amanda's lips were pale as chalk. Her eyes were

very bright. "Mark my words, Quentin. You're going to hell, and sooner, not later."

He dropped his arms and laughed cruelly. "My, my, Amanda. If I thought you were actually threatening me, I might have a little respect for you."

She stepped away from him. "Take it any way you like. You and your fancy woman will pay, and that's a fact."

Three

In the purple night of the swampland, the moon was white as bleached bone and the stars so brilliant and numerous they blanketed the sky like a spangled mantle. Still, it was dark, too dark to be driving alone on the dirt road bisecting the wetlands. Quentin Wentworth wasn't concerned about safety or darkness. He knew the twists and turns of the path as well as he knew the lines of Lizzie's body. He'd become intimately familiar with both over the past eight years and even though neither was in his own best interests, he had no intention of abandoning Lizzie or the road that led him to her.

He knew exactly when and where his obsession began. Cybil's Diner was a trucker's pit stop, a dive, not up to his usual style. He no longer remembered why he'd allowed himself to be talked into a card game in the back room. He did remember that he'd lost nearly every hand. He'd never been a gambler. Deciding to cut his losses and quit while he was still sober enough to drive home, he'd stumbled out of the small room into the smoky dimness of the bar. A jazz band played on the makeshift stage. They were good enough for Quentin to cross his arms and lean against the wall, waiting until the song ended. Gradually, his eyes adjusted to the light and he could pick out the couples on the floor.

He told himself he wasn't looking to start anything, but the woman caught his eye immediately. She was young, early twenties at most, and her body moved with the lissome grace of a professional dancer. Her hair was long and straight and very dark. He couldn't see her features in the dim light of the room, but he watched two men cut in to partner her within the same score. His brain had barely registered its intent before he found himself crossing the room, stepping into the squeeze of dancers. He reached for her arm and looked down into her face. She was lovely, ivory-skinned with black eyes and sharp features, clearly of mixed race, mostly white with a hint of Indian or dark blood. Her lips were painted a deep, vivid red. She looked back at him, steadily, without a hint of coyness, knowing exactly what it was he wanted.

The hammering began in his left temple. Heat

speared through his chest and down into his groin. The music began again. He pulled her into his arms. "Who are you?" he asked through her curtain of hair.

She looked at him through lashes thick as feathers. "Don't you recognize me, Judge Wentworth?"

He had to think to breathe. "No."

"I'm Benteen Jones's daughter, Lizzie."

"Lizzie." He tested the name on his tongue. "Lizzie." She smelled like the star jasmine bushes his mother had planted around the porch when he was a boy.

He held her closely, pressing against the blade of her hips, the lines of her legs, the lush roundness of her young breasts. Moving her hair aside he kissed the flesh below her ear and moved down to the spot where her neck and shoulder met. He felt the intake of her breath, the slight stiffening of her back. He turned her head to find her mouth but she resisted.

"For you, I'm expensive," she whispered.

He ran his hand down her body, cupping her buttocks. He was rock hard. "How much?"

"Two hundred."

It could have been two thousand and he would have paid. "Where?"

"This way," she said, keeping hold of his hand. She led him out the door, away from the light to the back of the lot where a dented Ford station wagon sat parked under the trees.

It was the first and only time he paid for the pleasure of Lizzie's body.

That was eight years ago. If he'd been a betting man, he would have laid odds their affair wouldn't last six months. They were polar opposites. He was a superior court judge, well educated, well traveled, highly respected, with family money behind him. She'd barely graduated from high school, never ventured more than fifty miles from Marshy Hope Creek and, by the time she was fourteen years old, she was turning tricks to keep Benteen Jones in liquor and tobacco. And yet, he kept coming back.

To describe a woman like Lizzie by laying out only the facts would be the same as describing *Gone With the Wind* after reading the book jacket. Quentin had never known anyone like her. She laughed easily and often, and she made him laugh, as well. Her compassion was equal to her irreverence, and her lack of inhibition, unusual in a woman, turned him inside out. Her sense of humor showed itself in a thousand different ways and after he'd been with her he felt renewed. He felt young.

In the beginning, the other men didn't bother him. Lizzie was who she was and didn't pretend to be anything more. As long as he could have her when it suited him, he couldn't complain. And it suited him regularly, two or three times a week, without interruption, except for the brief period after she told him about the child.

Quentin hadn't counted on a child and he was furious with what he believed to be her carelessness. She said nothing while he berated her, called her names and swore they were finished. She looked at him calmly, her hands resting on her knees. When he was finished, she turned away from him, picked up a paring knife and continued peeling potatoes. "Don't forget to close the screen door on the way out," she said.

"It's probably not even mine." The minute the words were out he wished them back. Of course the child was his. Lizzie was incapable of lying.

She turned on him, brandishing her knife, her voice deadly calm. "Don't say that. I know who fathered this baby. I'm not asking for anything, but don't you ever say that again."

He left her, storming out to his car, and didn't come back for nearly a month. When he did, they never spoke of her condition, simply continuing as they had before except, now, Quentin paid all her expenses.

The baby, a boy, was black haired and black eyed with the clean, chiseled features of his mother. Quentin avoided him, always visiting Lizzie after he was asleep. They'd gone on that way for years until three weeks ago when Lizzie announced, without explanation, that they were finished.

Quentin threatened, pleaded and offered money. But this time she hadn't wanted money. She wanted what he couldn't, or wouldn't, give: respectability, a wedding ring and a name for her child.

Where once Lizzie was warm and giving, now she was cold, single-minded and stubborn. They could go away, she'd said, somewhere fresh where no one knew them. He told her it wasn't possible. He'd argued his case well, explaining that social status was harder to come by than a wedding band. His career would be forever stalled. Supporting his own family would take most of what he had and he wasn't young anymore. His reasons were valid but dishonest.

The truth, as he saw it, was so much more indefensible. He didn't want to nest with Lizzie, to settle down into the kind of life he knew with Amanda. Lizzie was exotic, alluring, beautiful. He didn't want to wake up with her in the morning, share the newspaper, discuss finances. He certainly couldn't see their families mingling—Benteen Jones, town debaucher, and Gaylord Wentworth the Third, businessman turned politician.

The passion he felt for Lizzie was based on the excitement of forbidden fruit, the clandestine meetings late at night, stolen moments, secrecy, unpredictability, frantic, raw sex performed in silence while her boy slept on the other side of the wall. Respectability would kill the fever. They would settle in. The adventure would end. Normalcy would accentuate their differences. Life would be one long unalterable regret.

Quentin didn't want to go there, not again, not with Lizzie. He stayed away, hoping she'd cool off and reconsider. Three weeks passed and he hadn't seen her, until tonight. Watching her with another man, knowing she'd gone back to her former trade enraged him. He'd behaved badly in front of the Delacourtes. Amanda had been publicly humiliated. She would take her pound of flesh. She always did.

He pulled up to the house he'd paid to have built while Lizzie waited for their child to be born. Hers was the only car parked out front. The house was dark. Quentin hadn't considered what he would do if she wasn't alone. Mindful of the boy, he knocked softly. She didn't answer. Carefully, he turned the knob and stepped inside. A single candle flickered on the coffee table. Lizzie was lying on the couch, smoking a cigarette, one leg bent over the other to form the number four. She still wore the red dress.

Circles of smoke spiraled toward the ceiling. Her eyes were closed.

"Lizzie," he began and stopped.

"I know it's you, Quentin. Go home. We have nothing to say to each other."

"How can you say that after—" he faltered.

Her eyes opened. She challenged him. "After?"

"After all we've been to each other?"

She sat up, flipping her long black hair over her shoulder. "What have we been to each other?"

He searched for words to convince her. "A comfort. We've been a comfort to each other."

She laughed the light, silvery laugh that wound itself around his heart and made him believe all things were possible. How could he live without that laugh?

"We've been nothing to each other, Quentin. You despise your wife and the daughter she's raised in her image. You say you love me and yet you won't name the child we share. What do you want from me? What's to become of me? I have nothing to show for eight years with you." She shook her head. "I'm moving on. It's over. Go home to Amanda."

He stared at her, realizing for the first time that this wasn't a ploy. She was leaving him and she wouldn't be changing her mind. "What about this house? It's mine."

"Take it," she said wearily. "I want nothing of yours."

"And the boy?"

"Bailey's mine. You never wanted him."

"How will you live?"

Her mouth twisted. "Like I've always lived."

"That's no life for a child."

"I'll worry about that."

Thrusting both hands into his pockets, he leaned heavily against the wall. "I can't leave you like this. What can I do?"

She sat up. "What did you come for, Quentin? Is it sex? From now on, if you want sex you'll have to pay just like the rest."

Even now, his body stirred at the thought of sex with Lizzie.

Headlights lit the window and bathed the table and chairs in white light.

Quentin frowned. "What in the hell—? Are you expecting anyone?"

She didn't answer. Rising from the couch, Lizzie pulled back the curtain and looked out the window. "My God, we're in for a scene. Whatever happened to discretion, Quentin? Since when did you start informing your wife that you were visiting your mistress?"

"What are you talking about?" Pulling her away from the window, he took her place, squinting at the glare from the headlights.

"What is Amanda doing here?"

Lizzie's mouth turned up in amusement. "This

is just a wild guess, Quentin, but I think she came for her husband."

He gritted his teeth. "I won't tolerate this."

She taunted him "Are you familiar with the term *paying the piper?*"

"You sound as if you're enjoying this."

"Oh, I am. Believe me, I am." Lizzie dropped the curtain, flipped on the lights and walked to the door. "Do you think she'll knock?"

"I know you're in there," Amanda cried. "Open the door or I'm coming in."

Lizzie threw open the door. "By all means, Mrs. Wentworth. Join our little party, but please lower your voice. My son is asleep."

"Bitch!" Amanda hissed. "Whore!"

Quentin strode to the door and grabbed her arm. "Go home, Amanda. You don't belong here. Think of Tracy and Tess."

"How dare you." Her voice shook. "You've never once thought of them. Do you think no one knows about you and this slut? Do you imagine they believe the boy isn't yours?" She pulled a revolver from her coat pocket. Steadying it with both hands, she aimed at his chest.

He stepped in front of Lizzie. "Amanda, my God!"

Lizzie was still and silent as stone.

Quentin held out his hands. "Easy now, Amanda. You don't want to do this."

"I think I do, Quentin. I really think I do."

He forced himself to speak gently. "You don't mean that, Mandy. Put the gun down. We'll go home. Everything will be all right. Just give me the gun." He held out his hand. "You don't want it to go off. Hand it to me, Mandy, and we'll go home right now."

She shook her head. "It's too late."

"It's not too late. It's never too late." He'd nearly reached her.

Rubbing his eyes, seven-year old Bailey Jones appeared in the hallway. "Mama. I heard yelling."

"Bailey, go back to bed, honey," his mother shouted.

Brandishing her revolver, Amanda whirled toward the sound at the same time Quentin threw himself at her. They fell to the floor, a tangle of writhing limbs.

Lizzie leaped over both of them and grabbed her son, sheltering him with her body. Seconds passed as Quentin struggled with his wife. A single shot rang out. More seconds passed. Blood gushed on to the floor. Lizzie screamed and then there was silence.

Four

Verna Lee sat on the weathered dock beside an old pontoon boat, hugged her knees to her chest and reveled in a day of freedom. The marina, nestled in a flat expanse of marsh grass, was at its most serene at this time of morning, long after the commercial shrimp trawlers had motored to fishing grounds but still too early for the pleasure cruisers. Snowy egrets shared the pilings with brown terns, gulls circled over her head and dragonflies and mosquitoes skimmed across the water's surface. She was conscious of the silence, of gray water and blue sky and green grass, of hot, humid air, the taste of salt on her lips, the black flies biting at her legs and the thick, brackish smell of the bay, teeming with life. Somewhere, close by, was Marshy Hope Creek, its Peninsula Bank, John's Food King, Taft's Hardware—the synthetic world built up along the banks of the Chesapeake. But here and now, there was only silence.

Lizzie was late but Verna Lee wasn't concerned. She would show or she wouldn't. Either way, the day would move along with or without her friend. They'd planned on clamming at Tom's Cove, swimming and then maybe grabbing a bite to eat at Steamers. Bailey loved the ice cream at the Island Creamery and Verna Lee was set to indulge him.

She must have dozed because she woke to Lizzie's breathy voice. "Sorry we're late. Bailey slept in this morning and after the night we had, I didn't have the heart to wake him."

Verna Lee stood and stretched. "No problem. What happened?"

Lizzie raised her eyebrows and nodded at Bailey. "I'd rather not say."

"Suit yourself." She tousled the boy's dark hair. "How're you doing, Bailey?"

He stared at her with expressionless, black eyes.

Verna Lee frowned. "What's the matter, honey? Don't you have anything to say to Auntie Verna Lee?"

Bailey remained silent.

Verna Lee looked at Lizzie. "What's going on?"

Lizzie bit her lip. "Can't we just get started?"

"Sure." She gestured toward the boat. "Hop in."

Lizzie, clad in worn cutoff shorts, a shirt tied in a knot under her breasts and stained deck shoes, jumped into the boat.

Verna Lee took Bailey's hand. "One big leap, Bailey."

Bailey jumped into Lizzie's waiting arms. Verna Lee unwound the line attaching the boat to the dock, hopped onto the deck and started the outboard motor. It revved into life at the first pull and they were off toward the channel. The whisper of a cool breeze blew across the deck.

Keeping one hand on the wheel, careful to dodge the sandbars, Verna Lee pointed out the red-and-white stripes of the lighthouse. Bailey nodded, climbed to the foredeck and lay on his stomach, head over the edge of the boat in an attempt to spot the local fish that had earned this part of the cove the name *an angler's paradise.*

Verna Lee kept her voice low. "Tell me what's happening."

Lizzie narrowed her eyes against the sun. "Quentin came over last night. We had a fight. Bailey woke up. He hasn't said a word since."

"I thought you were through with the judge."

"I am, but he's resisting. He mentioned something about taking back the house."

"Tell the son of a bitch you'll sue him for child support."

"I can't prove anything, Verna Lee."

"You won't have to. The scandal alone would make it difficult for him to live here. He won't want that."

"It won't be easy for me and Bailey, either."

"Is it easy now?"

Lizzie sighed. "No, but there might be a better way."

"What's that?"

"I'm going to ask Quentin to give my daddy's land back."

Verna Lee shook her head and lifted the mop of curls off the back of her neck. "That's a tall order. I think you'd have more luck with the house."

"The house means taxes I can't afford. The land is nothing but undeveloped swamp. Taxes are low. I can sell off a small part for enough to buy a mobile home. That's all we need. I think I can swing it without—" She stopped.

"How will you live?"

Lizzie crossed her ankles, closed her eyes and tilted her face toward the sky. "I'll apply for Aid to Dependent Children. Then I'll go to school."

"What will you study?"

"Nursing. I can start out learning to be a licensed vocational nurse." She shrugged. "After that, if I'm good at it, I could take more classes, maybe even earn a degree."

"What about Bailey?"

"I'll find somebody to watch him while I'm gone." She pushed the hair back off her face. "Maybe I'll ask Drusilla."

Verna Lee didn't say anything.

"You're not buying it, are you?" Lizzie asked.

"It's not that. I'm just wondering if you plan on staying here. Salisbury is the closest community college. That's a long commute. Even if you managed it, what about after you're finished? Where do you plan to work?" The unspoken message was clear.

"This is my home, Verna Lee. I know that certain people don't want me around, but others won't mind." She smiled. "Who I am doesn't bother you."

"We've known each other a long time."

Lizzie considered her friend. "Why doesn't it bother you?"

"I didn't say that it doesn't bother me. I hate that you have to support yourself by selling your body. But I understand why you do it. You've had it rough from the beginning."

"Don't be feeling sorry for me, Verna Lee. I don't want pity."

"I don't pity you. I admire you."

"Really?"

Verna Lee nodded. "The most amazing thing about you is that you don't make excuses. You just take what you're given and keep going. What's not to admire about that?"

"I never thought of it that way."

"I hope you get your land back." Verna Lee spread her arm to encompass the water, land and sky. "Look at all this." Flat marshland covered with coarse grass grew along the shoreline. Haughty cormorants, their long legs rooted in the sand, waited patiently for the leap of flashing silver that signaled lunch was at hand. Egrets, blue heron and an occasional bald eagle sailed across the tranquil sky. Gulls circled the pilings, their sharp eyes intent on a pair of terns arguing over the remains of a mussel. Farther down, pine forests grew right up to the edge of the sand. The harsh soil, rich in salt, deterred all but the fittest. Weak and diseased Virginia pine lay dead on the shore, their white salt-encrusted roots faceup on the banks. The air was alive with the chirping of cicadas, the croaking of frogs and the screams of gulls. Nearly hidden in the shade of an enormous pine, a family of deer waited, silent and motionless.

Quick tears rose in her eyes, momentarily blurring her vision. "Have you ever seen anything more beautiful?"

"It's beautiful," Lizzie replied quietly. "I mean no disrespect, Verna Lee. I know how you feel about this land. But I have Bailey to think of and we need to live." She touched her friend's shoulder. "Besides, it belongs to the Wentworths. I'm not sure Quentin will give it back."

"I have a strong feeling he will."

"Why is that?"

"We wouldn't be having this conversation if you didn't think it was as good as settled. You have an ace up your sleeve. What is it that you aren't telling me?"

Lizzie's smile faded. "There are some things that aren't meant to be told."

A cold chill made its way toward Verna Lee's heart. She fought it back. "If you need anything, Lizzie, you can count on me."

"I know that. It's a comfort to me."

"Maybe some of that Mississippi Mud ice cream from the Island Creamery will get Bailey talking again."

Lizzie glanced at her son. His flamingo-thin legs, mosquito-bitten and brown as dried berries, looked even longer jutting out of last summer's threadbare shorts. His hair badly needed cutting and the way he favored the right side of his mouth when he chewed made her wonder if he should see a dentist. She sighed. Would there ever be a time when she didn't have to worry about money? "I'm sure he'd like that. Thank you for thinking of him, Verna Lee."

Verna Lee nodded and turned away, angry at the

swift and unexpected emotion that closed her throat. People like Lizzie were grateful for the simplest kindness while others were never satisfied. It all boiled down to expectations. If they were low to begin with, every gift was cherished, no matter how small. She couldn't help contrasting Bailey and his mother with the spoiled children, and their parents, she'd wasted nine years of her life attempting to educate.

Verna Lee dropped her beach bag, stepped out of her sandals and turned on the hose to rinse her feet. Drusilla kept an immaculate kitchen and didn't appreciate sand on her floor.

"Is that you, Verna Lee?" her grandmother called out from the back porch.

"It's me, Gran. Can you bring me a clean towel?"

"Give me a minute. I'm folding laundry." A few minutes later Drusilla opened the screen, handing over a warm towel. "Lordy, I thought you'd never get home. Where you been?"

"I took Lizzie and Bailey out on the boat."

"Are you hungry, child? It's way past suppertime."

"No, thanks. I've eaten."

Drusilla sat on the step while her granddaughter towel dried her legs. "How's Lizzie?"

"Well enough, I guess, considering her circumstances." Verna Lee sat down beside Drusilla. "I wish I could do more to help her. She's thinking about going to school to be a nurse."

Drusilla nodded. "That's a good thing."

"I wonder if she'll ever be free of Quentin Wentworth."

Verna Lee twisted the towel into a point and began drying between her toes.

"She'll be free soon enough."

"Why do you say that?"

"You missed all the commotion today."

"Commotion, in Marshy Hope Creek?" Verna Lee laughed. "You're kidding."

"No, missy, I'm not. Miz Wentworth tipped her car over on Highway 39. She was on her way to visit her sister in Mississippi."

"Is she hurt?"

"She's more'n hurt. She's dead."

Verna Lee gasped. "Are you sure?"

"Maurice, from the dry cleaners, was carrying clean shirts back to the judge. He heard it from Camille, Miz Wentworth's housekeeper. Sheriff Grimes and the judge identified her body. Miz Wentworth was burned bad. They knew it was her because of the car. Camille say the car flipped over and went up in flames."

Verna Lee thought for a minute. "Highway 39 is a straight road. Was she drinking?"

Drusilla's eyebrows flew north. "Miz Wentworth? Not on your life. Camille say she and the judge had words over Lizzie, and the missus left late last night. That road is mighty dark at night."

Verna Lee acknowledged that it was. Still, something wasn't right. Lizzie was keeping something to herself, Bailey wasn't talking and the Wentworths had had a fight, serious enough for Amanda Wentworth to take off for Mississippi in the middle of the night.

Amanda Wentworth's funeral was a by-invitation-only event. Russ Hennessey was on the guest list for two reasons only: he was Tess's father and the interlocutory period for his divorce from Tracy Wentworth was still in progress. On paper he was legally married and therefore a member of the family, albeit an unwilling one. Already he regretted accepting the offer of the judge's spare room.

Sliding the knot of his tie into place, he stood in front of the mirror in the guest room dressed in a pale blue shirt and black socks.

Tracy opened the door without knocking and closed it behind her.

Russ raised one eyebrow. "Do you mind? I'm not dressed."

She shrugged. "We're married. Surely you don't think I haven't seen this before?"

"We're soon to be *not* married and that isn't the

point. I'd appreciate some respect for my privacy. What do you want?"

"I know you don't want to sit with the family, but I'm asking you to reconsider."

"Not a chance. I'm here to watch my daughter so you can deal with your family. That's it."

Tracy flushed. "It's my mother's funeral, for God's sake. Would it kill you to be a little bit flexible?"

Russ sighed. "Everyone knows we've split. There is absolutely no point in making it look as if we're one big happy family. You specifically asked that I come, although your reasoning baffles me. Your mother and I weren't close and, personally, I think she'd rest easier if she knew I'd stayed away." He stepped into his pants and zipped them. "I'm sorry you lost your mother, Tracy, but Tess and I are sitting with my brother."

Two pink spots stood out on Tracy's cheeks. "I don't think I can stay in this house without my mother."

Russ tied one shoelace and then the other. "Sure you can."

"You don't know what Daddy's like. He's impossible to please."

"I know exactly what Quentin is like and you'll manage." Picking up his wallet and keys from the nightstand, he shoved them into his pockets. "It's time to go."

"I'm serious, Russ. Tess is five years old. I've got no training. What will I do?"

"Let's see. What could a young, able-bodied woman with a college degree possibly do if she doesn't want to continue living with her parent?" He frowned and tapped his forehead. "Bingo! I know. She could get a job, earn a salary, hire a babysitter and move into a place of her own. What a concept. What an *original* concept."

"You're an asshole."

"Okay. I'll go with that." He checked his watch. "I'm late for a funeral. Do you mind if we table this conversation so that I can make an appearance and go back to my life?"

Head held high, she stormed out of the room. Russ waited until he heard the satisfying slam of a door before starting down the stairs. Lured into the kitchen by the tempting aromas of freshly brewed coffee and cinnamon rolls, he stopped short at the sight of the Wentworths' housekeeper in her usual black dress and white apron. "Camille, what are you doing here? The funeral's about to start."

Camille's smile was a dazzling white triangle in the nut brown of her face. "Miz Wentworth's funeral ain't for black folks. Besides, some people comin' back here after the service expectin' food."

"That's ridiculous. You should be there. You've known her longer than the judge has."

"Yes, sir. I come up with her from Mississippi when she married Judge Wentworth."

Russ filched a cinnamon roll. "Come with me," he said between bites.

She handed him a napkin. "I don't belong there."

"Come anyway."

She shook her head. "It wouldn't look right. No need to get the judge all riled up, especially now that Miz Tracy and little Tess'll be here on their own."

"They'll have Quentin."

Camille pursed her lips. "I hear it'll be a closed casket."

"I heard that, too."

"The judge say she burned to death in that car."

Russ crossed his arms and leaned against the sink. "I guess a closed casket makes sense."

Camille shook her head. "None of it makes sense. Miz Wentworth always told me when she was goin' somewhere overnight so I could pack for her."

"Maybe she packed for herself."

Camille's face was troubled. "Miz Wentworth had two closets, one for clothes she could wear and the other for ones that were too small but she couldn't give away."

"So?"

Camille lifted intelligent dark eyes to his face. "The clothes she took were all too small. She hadn't worn them in years."

Five

Nola Ruth Delacourte's eyes were hidden behind dark glasses. She fingered the pearls around her neck and stared out the car window. Dense pine forests passed unnoticed. Her mind was far away.

"Penny," said her husband with a smile.

She turned. "Excuse me?"

"Penny for your thoughts."

She shrugged. "I was thinking about regrets."

"Funerals always make you pensive."

"Shouldn't they?"

"Life isn't always fair, Nola."

"Why is that?"

"There are no guarantees," he began.

"That's a cliché, Cole, and unworthy of you."

Nola Ruth was in one of her philosophical

moods. Reason would have no role in their conversation. "You know what I mean."

"Actually, I don't. If you're telling me that bad luck is random, I accept that. What I have trouble with is consistent, unpredictable unfairness that tests a person beyond what one should have to bear."

Cole frowned. "Tell me you're not referring to the Wentworths."

"Of course not."

"Then who?"

She shook her head. "I was talking about us, Cole."

Cole debated whether to change the subject and hope her mood lifted, or to press for resolution. They were less than five minutes from the church. He opted for silence.

In the foyer of Grace Episcopal Church, Quentin Wentworth and his daughter, Tracy, greeted their guests. Nola Ruth was not demonstrative. She shook hands with Tracy and Quentin, murmured her condolences and slid into a seat at the back. Nola Ruth was Catholic and even though she denied it, it seemed to Cole that any foray into a Protestant church was, for her, an act of impiety.

The service was mercifully brief. Cole and Quentin grew up together, making Cole's appearance at the funeral mandatory. Their distant professional relationship fell short of friendship. The Delacourtes made a brief appearance at the reception in the church hall and made their escape soon after. Cole turned left onto the highway and headed toward Salisbury.

Fifteen minutes passed before Nola Ruth noticed. "Where are we going?"

"I thought we might have a late lunch at the Pelican. Are you hungry?"

She thought a minute. "I could eat."

"I have an ulterior motive."

"Of course you do."

"We're going to talk about imbalances."

"Oh?"

"Your name for it was consistent, unpredictable unfairness."

She removed her sunglasses, giving him the benefit of her large, dark eyes. "Do you ever forget anything?"

"I forget plenty of things other people tell me, but not you."

"I'm flattered."

"I love you. Always have."

Her face softened. "I know you do. I'm counting on it."

"What have you done, Nola Ruth?"

She bit her lip. "Can it wait until after you've had a drink?"

"Is it that bad?"

She sighed. "Yes, it is."

"I'll wait."

The Pelican, a small restaurant with white table-cloths and tables with spectacular views of the bay, was nearly empty. Cole ordered a martini for himself and a glass of South African sauvignon blanc for Nola Ruth. After settling on crab cakes, salad and corn chowder, they tore off hunks of hot sourdough bread dripping with olive tapenade, ate and sipped their drinks, allowing the sense of calm serenity that alcohol and carbohydrates often brings to seep through them.

Cole wisely refrained from pressuring his wife to reveal whatever was bothering her conscience. He talked of inconsequential matters, the house, their next vacation, her upcoming birthday. Eventually, after they were halfway through their lunch and well into a second round of drinks, his patience was rewarded.

"I have something to tell you," she began.

He waited.

"I withdrew eleven hundred dollars from our checking account."

"You take care of the bills, Nola. I don't monitor how much you spend."

She held up her hand. "There's more. Please hear me out."

"All right."

"On Monday I got a call from Drusilla Washington. I know we haven't spoken of this for years, but you do remember Anton Devereaux?"

Cole's expression didn't change. "I'm not likely to forget."

"Drusilla told me he was arrested for speeding. Apparently, he spent the night in jail. He was driving a late-model Mercedes. I bailed him out. Sheriff Grimes never read him his Miranda rights."

"I have a few questions," Cole said. "But I'm sure you've already anticipated them."

Nola Ruth nodded. "You want to know what he was doing here in the first place."

"The thought crossed my mind."

She played with a forkful of crab. "He was looking for me."

"Undoubtedly."

"He spent ten years in a Mississippi state prison for miscegenation. No one cared that he didn't know I was white."

"It was 1962. His reasons wouldn't have mattered."

"He blames me. He wanted to know why I didn't try to find him."

"Did you tell him?"

"I told him to go away and never come back."

"But you bailed him out of jail."

She nodded. "It was the least I could do."

"He'll have to come back for his court date."

"I don't think so. He lives in France. He's a vintner."

Cole swallowed the last of his martini. "Is that all?"

"People saw us, Cole. We had a very public argument. I was so angry and ashamed. I'm sorry. I shouldn't have tried to help him."

Cole leaned forward and took his wife's hand. "Why did you?"

She looked directly at him. "What happened to him was my fault. I never told him who I was. He was the one who paid with years of his life."

"You paid, too, Nola. You paid dearly. You're still paying."

"So is he," she whispered. "He just doesn't know it."

Cole signaled for the check. "This ends here," he said firmly. "We won't speak of it again."

"There's something else I should tell you."

"I don't need to hear it. You've said enough."

"But, Cole—"

"No more, Nola." He stood. "I'll see what happened to the check and meet you in front."

She stared after him in disbelief. Cole was a firm believer in self-disclosure. This was a side of him she'd never seen.

On his way into the office the following morning, Cole swung by the Marshy Hope Creek Police Station. Sheriff Grimes was sorting through his mail. He looked up briefly. "What can I do for you, Counselor?"

"Nola Ruth tells me you kept a man in jail overnight without reading him his rights."

Silas shook his head. "Not true, if you're referring to one Anton Devereaux. Your wife came by and bailed him out."

"Was he allowed a phone call?"

Sheriff Grimes leaned back in his chair and stroked his chin. "Processing takes up time. Seems to me he declined his call."

Cole sighed. "Silas, unless you police by the book and read a suspect his Miranda rights, the state has no case. You know that. What are you trying to pull?"

"Hell, Cole. We're never gonna see that fella again."

"I'm out eleven hundred dollars."

"Maybe your clientele needs improving." He opened his top drawer, pulled out a toothpick and stuck it into one side of his mouth. "I'd think twice before sending my wife to bail out criminals. Nola Ruth wasn't too happy about it, either, because everybody on Main Street saw her give him a piece of her mind. Then he stepped into her car like he was some movie star and she headed toward the Highway 39 turnoff. I tell you, Cole, you got too much faith in those people. A fella like that is likely to slit Nola's throat and leave her for dead on the side of the road."

"The man violated a speed limit."

"He was driving a Mercedes. Where'd he get enough money for that?"

"He owns a vineyard in France. He makes wine."

Grimes spoke around the toothpick. "I told you he wouldn't be back."

"Two hours, Silas. I want all arrests to be processed and offered a phone call within two hours. I won't tell you again. You're mighty close to collecting your pension. Don't spoil it."

"No, sir. I wouldn't dream of it."

Six

Fifteen years later

It was seven o'clock in the morning and already steamy hot when Dave Yardley unloaded his tripod, his sample kit and his Nikon from the back of a leased Jeep Cherokee. Wiping his forehead with the sleeve of his shirt, he loaded up his backpack, hitched the tripod to his shoulder and crossed the road to hike into a spongy section of marsh that might very well hold up Weber's entire condominium development. The geology report showed a water table that was too high to drain without sinking millions of dollars into construction that wouldn't pay out.

Yardley was a Weber employee but even he couldn't work miracles. The bog was so wet his footprints disappeared within minutes. It didn't look good. Branches, leaves and sludge made walking difficult. He stumbled over what he thought was a tree branch, found his balance and looked down. "What the—" He stooped to examine his find. It was a human fibula, partially decomposed, rising from the swamp like something out of an Alfred Hitchcock movie.

Chloe Richards woke dripping with sweat and the sense that her past year spent in the beach community of La Jolla, California, had been nothing more than a hazy dream. She lay flat on her back, blinking sleepily at the yellow ceiling and white moldings of her summer bedroom, and willed the heat and humidity that was typical of June in Marshy Hope Creek, Maryland, to evaporate.

No such luck. Rolling out of bed, she welcomed the cool wood under the soles of her feet and padded into the bathroom to stand under the tepid spray of the showerhead.

Ten minutes later she hung the towel that would take two days to dry over the edge of the tub, pulled a comb through her wet hair, stepped into a faded pair of shorts and a top with thin straps that revealed more tanned skin than her mother would approve of and made her way downstairs.

Serena, her grandfather's housekeeper, oblivious

to the shimmering heat, was frying chicken-apple sausage and ladling scoops of batter into a crepe pan. Leaning over the black woman's shoulder, Chloe filched a dry edge from the end of a nearly cooked crepe.

Serena slapped her hand away. "You know how I feel about eatin' over the sink, Chloe Richards. Your granddaddy is expectin' you out on the porch."

"Is he up already?"

Serena snorted. "Girl, it's nine o'clock. You're sleepin' the day away."

Chloe sighed. "Give me a break, Serena. For me, it's six o'clock in the morning."

"Mr. Delacourte's been up since five workin' in that garden. I'm countin' on you to stop him before he gets heatstroke."

Chloe nodded, grabbed a forbidden sausage from the platter on the counter and left the kitchen in search of her grandfather. She found him near the front porch, a lean, slightly hunched figure, his head protected by a wide-brimmed straw hat, trimming the gardenias. Staying well inside the shade of the porch canopy, she leaned against the railing and watched him, struck, for the first time, by signs that he was aging. Cole Delacourte was closing in on seventy years old. New lines carved his forehead and the planes of his cheeks. His wrists were bonier, his cheeks thinner. Overall, he appeared frail. She fought off the icy fist that closed over her heart at the thought of losing him and called out, "Morning, Granddad."

Cole Delacourte looked up and smiled. "Good morning, Sleeping Beauty. I was beginning to think I'd starve to death."

"You could have eaten without me."

He pretended indignation. "Not a chance, especially when my granddaughter has come all the way across country to visit me." Cole pulled off his gloves and wiped his forehead. "Come on. Let's eat out back and look at the bay."

They walked arm in arm, the tall, spare old man and the petite, golden girl, through the gracious colonial home that had housed five generations of Delacourtes, out the back door and across a deep, velvety lawn that curved down to the mighty Chesapeake, "the protein factory of the South," her mother had once described it.

Serena had set the table under the canopy of two enormous oak trees. What Chloe would have called pretentious for a Monday-morning breakfast in Southern California, the cloth napkins and white tablecloth, the shining silver and crystal goblets seemed just right here in the shade of her grandfather's house. It was cooler this close to the water. Chloe felt the first stirrings of an appetite. She pulled out a chair and sat down. "So, Granddad, give me the latest gossip."

Cole poured dark, chicory-flavored coffee from the carafe into their cups. "Nothing much has changed around here. Your mama and Russ have their hands full with Gina Marie."

"I guessed as much from Mom's phone calls. Gina's not exactly the typical three-year-old, is she?"

Cole's lips twitched. "Spit it out, Chloe. What are you trying so politely not to say?"

"She's spoiled rotten."

Cole threw back his head and laughed so loudly that Serena, bearing platters of crepes and sausage, heard him from inside the house. "Someone open this door for me," she called out. "I've only got two hands."

"I'll go," Chloe said, moving as quickly as the heat would allow. She crossed the lawn, climbed the back steps and opened the door. "You'll make me fat, Serena." She reached for the crepe platter. "I never eat this much at home."

The black woman raised her eyebrows and gave Chloe's slender legs and concave stomach an appraising look. "You could use a little weight, honey. I doubt you'd tip the scales at a hundred pounds."

Chloe's cheeks flushed a warm apricot. "I'm not very tall," she murmured just as they reached the table.

"Sometimes it's hard to believe you're Gina

Marie's sister," the woman continued. "Now, that one, she's the image of your mama."

Chloe winced. She didn't need reminding that Gina, with her bewitching smile and terrifying temper, was turning out to be more of a Delacourte than Chloe would ever be.

Noticing that her grandfather's eyes were on her face, she recovered quickly and set the plate down in front of him. "These are the most delicious crepes on the planet. I'm having two."

"One will do for me, thank you," said Cole. He nodded at his housekeeper. "We'll take it from here, Serena."

Waiting until she was well inside the house, he cleared his throat. "I don't know if I've ever mentioned it, Chloe, but you look a great deal like my mother did when she was your age. In fact, you resemble the Delacourte side of our family far more than your mother or sister. They're Beauchamps through and through, just like Nola Ruth."

A backwash of affection for this dear man flooded her chest. "It's okay, Granddad. I don't mind that I didn't get Mom's looks." She grinned impishly. "I did get her brains, though. Even Dad admits to that."

Cole wiped his mouth. "Well, now, I think I can take some credit for that. After all, Libba Jane is my daughter."

Chloe laughed. "Be careful, Granddad. I'll tell her you said that."

Cole Delacourte sat for a minute, content to simply look at his granddaughter's vivid face, the Siamese-blue eyes and high-boned cheeks, the small, slightly arched nose and wide sensitive mouth, all framed by that straight swath of floating silvery hair.

When, he wondered, would she discover her power? She was twenty years old, young, but definitely grown. Still, there was an innocence about her that reminded Cole of the women from his own youth. "I hope your mama doesn't mind that you're staying here with me and not at Hennessey House."

Washing down a mouthful of crepe with a swig of coffee so rich and strong she could feel the heat of it all the way to the center of her stomach, Chloe shook her head. "Mom knows I love it here. Besides, there are only two bathrooms at Hennessey House. You have more room and I don't want to put any stress on Russ. It's hard to share your house with someone else's child."

Shocked, Cole stared at her. "Where did you dredge up that absurd idea?"

Chloe shrugged, assuming an offhand insouciance. "Mimi and I had a heart-to-heart the last time I stayed at Dad's."

Cole's mouth tightened with uncharacteristic temper. "Is that so?"

"Yes."

"If I were you, honey, I wouldn't take your stepmother's babblings as the Amy Vanderbilt of familial relationships. Whatever misguided philosophies are practiced in California, remember that this is the South. Nothing is more important to us than family."

She tilted her nose and showed him her profile. "Misguided philosophies and familial relationships," she mimicked. "You sound like a lawyer."

"You don't say."

Chloe frowned, all teasing aside. "I'm guessing that you don't care for Mimi."

"I've never met her and, believe me, I doubt that it's my loss."

"Don't say anything to Mom."

"My lips are sealed."

Chloe leaned over and kissed him. "I'm going now. I love you, Granddad."

"The feeling is mutual. Don't forget your bike."

Chuckling at the four-year-old memory of her need to appear "cool" at the expense of a convenient bike ride into town, Chloe found her bicycle in the shed, swung her leg over the crossbar and headed toward the service road that led to the street.

After the shade of her grandfather's yard, the blast of humidity hit her like a wet blanket. It was three miles into town as the crow flies, a bit longer on the road. Despite the cool promise of the forest, thick with summer foliage and tall trees, hickory, oak, beech, white ash and elm, within two minutes sweat trickled down Chloe's forehead, between her breasts and the insides of her thighs. Gritting her teeth, she tried turning her thoughts to something else, but the brackish, metallic odor of the Chesapeake, the smells of fish and pine and salt and dirt and a billion species of underwater life, assaulted her senses.

Despite her California roots, which Chloe now realized was a brief aberration in her mother's life, a period to be endured until Libba Jane was drawn back to Marshy Hope Creek with its relentless sun, its thick, wet air and its infinite spaces of marsh and woods and dark creek water, all by-products of the mighty Chesapeake, this was home to the Delacourtes. And, whether she liked it or not, Chloe, too, was a Delacourte.

Behind her, the sound of an approaching car interrupted her thoughts. Chloe hugged the side of the narrow road, allowing the driver to pass. Her eyes widened as a late-model silver-gray Porsche, more at home on the expensive beachfront streets of Malibu than here in Marshy Hope Creek, drove past. She caught a glimpse of the New York license plate. She wasn't surprised. Who would own a Porsche in this backwater town? Marshy Hope

Creek's more comfortable citizens thought in terms of Lincoln Town Cars and Cadillacs, gas guzzlers for patriotic Americans who bought only Fords and Chevrolets and who believed in conservation except when it applied to them.

The road veered to the left. Chloe turned the corner, squeezed the hand brake and pulled up abruptly, jumping off in time to avoid a collision with the Porsche, idling in silver splendor by the side of the road. Leaning against the door, black hair falling over his forehead, cigarette dangling from his lips, was a young man with dark hooded eyes and a face so bladed and severe and beautiful it could have graced the cover of a magazine.

"Need a ride?" he asked.

The years rolled back. Chloe drew a long, quivery breath. Bailey Jones hadn't changed much, except for the car and the Rolex and the Gucci shoes.

"It's been a long time, Bailey."

"I guess it has."

"You could have called."

"So could you."

"I needed a number. You had mine."

He drew deeply on the end of his cigarette, dropped the stub and ground it into the dirt. "Do you want a ride or not?"

She looked down at the bike and then back at him. "Nice car, but we wouldn't fit."

"Throw the bike in the bushes. You can come back for it later."

Chloe considered her options. On the one hand was burning curiosity, on the other was her completely understandable desire to show Bailey Jones that spending time in his company was her lowest priority. Curiosity won.

He waited while she stowed the bike out of sight of the road, hiked up the embankment and slid into the soft leather of the passenger's seat.

"So, Bailey," she began. "How have you been?"

He pulled the car out onto the road. "I can't complain. You?"

"Not too bad."

"What brings you back here?"

"This is where I come every summer. My mother lives here. She married Russ. I have a sister."

Bailey nodded. "I heard. Congratulations."

"Thanks. What about you? I thought you'd wiped the dust of Marshy Hope Creek from your shoes forever."

She saw the leap of muscle in his cheek.

"That was the plan. I'm here to sell my land. Weber Incorporated made an offer I can't refuse."

Chloe stared at him. "You can't be serious. Those wetlands are home to thousands of native species." What she left unsaid was huge, important, an impassable, unspoken chasm between them.

His hand was steady on the wheel. "I'm dead serious."

"It's not as if you need the money," she burst out. "I've seen your Web site." She stopped, biting her lip, conscious of her mistake. He was too quick to miss it.

"My Web site has an e-mail address."

"I know."

"So, why didn't you write?"

He had a point. She hadn't contacted him. But she was two years younger and he'd become an overnight celebrity in the art world. She changed the subject. "Don't they have fax machines in New York?"

His black eyebrows drew together. "I'm not following you."

She explained. "If you hate it here so much, why did you come back? People don't have to go places anymore. They have e-mail and faxes."

"I have a few loose ends to tie up before I sign the papers. Besides, I thought I'd look in on Cole. Without him, I'd be in jail."

Mollified at the mention of her grandfather, Chloe tried again. "Bailey, those wetlands are priceless. You can't really mean to sell. Weber builds condominiums."

"So?"

"What about your mother? What would she say if she knew you were thinking of selling?"

"She's dead," he said flatly, "and I'm not *thinking* of selling, Chloe, I'm definitely selling. All that land didn't do my mother any good. She died out there in a miserable little trailer without plumbing or running water. She was blind, in terrible pain and she didn't have enough money to check herself into a hospital, or even pay for a goddamn morphine drip. So don't get sentimental on me, okay?"

Chloe's throat choked up. Poor, pathetic Lizzie Jones, stubbornly loyal to her own sense of morality. "She kept the land for you," she whispered. "She thought it was important."

"And it paid off. It's worth millions. I'm cashing it in."

Chloe stared at him. "What happened to you, Bailey? When did you get to be such a cynic?"

"Why don't we talk about you," he suggested.

"I have a better idea. Why don't you let me out right here, just like you did four years ago, and I'll walk into town on my own."

She expected him to argue. The Bailey Jones she remembered would have argued. But this one didn't. Instead, he jerked the wheel to the right and slammed on the brakes, waiting, while Chloe fumbled with the seat belt clasp, pushed open the door and stood in injured silence while he sped away.

Seven

Sheriff Blake Carlisle leaned back in his chair, as close to the window-mounted air conditioner as possible, and contemplated the clock. Nearly an hour to go before he could reasonably meander down the road to Perks and order his usual ham-and-cheese sandwich with those little-bitty pickles Verna Lee knew he liked.

Meanwhile, he could copy an accident report the insurance company was waiting on and mail it out, or he could head over to Taft's Hardware and pick up a new lock for the cell door. Neither was a pressing concern. He couldn't remember the last time he'd needed to lock the cell and, as for the report, Millie Cooper had backed her 1967 Chevy station wagon into her front window. No one was hurt, her son had fixed the front window, the car wasn't worth repairing and Millie was ninety-four years old, too old to be driving anyway.

Maybe he'd eat early today. He liked visiting with Verna Lee before the lunch rush, when she wasn't too busy to talk. As soon as he heard from his deputy he'd be on his way, shooting the breeze with the locals, checking things out, improving public relations. Blake was big on public relations. He thought of himself as a public servant in the truest sense and he wasn't shy about reminding whoever would listen.

The door opened and a blast of hot air shot into the station, heating it up another ten degrees. Agnes Hobbs stuck her permed, blue-tinted head inside the door. "Blake, if you're not busy, I've got a big ol' box in the trunk of my car that needs to be mailed out at the post office."

"Not a problem, Miz Hobbs." He stood and reached for his hat. "I'll take it over for you. Was there anything else you needed?"

"That'll be all, I guess."

"You just let me know and I'll be there."

Agnes Hobbs slipped her tongue inside her dentures, lifting them off her gums, easing the soreness. Then she dropped them back into place again. "You're a good boy, Blake. I always did like you."

He took her arm and led her back out to her car.

"Thank you kindly, Miz Hobbs. I appreciate that. I was wondering if Ellie Mae knows you took the car this time."

"I didn't tell her, if that's what you mean. Why should I have to tell her when it's my own car I'm driving?"

"Well, the thing is, Miz Hobbs, you don't have a license and Ellie worries about you. She's afraid you'll hurt yourself. You wouldn't want to worry her, now, would you?"

The old woman pursed her lips. "I guess not."

"Why don't you sit right here on this bench in the shade and let me call her for you. That way she'll know you're in good hands."

"I always did like you, Blake," she repeated, patting his hand. "You're a good boy."

"Thank you, ma'am. I'll be right back."

The call was over in a minute, with Ellie Mae instructing him to do whatever was necessary to prevent her mother-in-law from driving until she could get there.

Blake set the phone down in its cradle and sighed. Sometimes he found himself wishing for a real crime now and then to keep from getting rusty.

Ellie Mae Hobbs drove up just as he was leaving the post office with Agnes. Gratefully, he excused himself, answered the mobile call from his deputy, and proceeded with his original plan to lunch at Perks and indulge his fantasies by flirting with Verna Lee Fontaine.

She was talking on the phone and didn't see him, a circumstance that allowed him to look at her for as long as he wanted without embarrassing himself. Blake swallowed. There was no one like Verna Lee. Quite simply, she took the eye in a way that made it seem as if no one else was in the room. Her particular combination of lush, primitive beauty and refined manners was like nothing he'd ever experienced. She was tall, with full breasts and long, lovely, caramel-colored legs, exposed from the knee down through a slit in her skirt. Her hair, wildly curly and secured on top of her head with a chopstick, was the exact tawny-gold of her eyes, and her smile reminded him of those island women on the travel posters beckoning him to places he'd never been. She was a good fifteen years older than him. It didn't bother him a bit. He liked older women especially when they looked liked Verna Lee. He felt safe knowing she didn't take him seriously.

Blake knew she'd been married a long time ago in California. He'd heard the gossip four years back when it came out that she and Libba Jane Delacourte were half sisters through their mother, Nola Ruth. Libba's daddy was Cole Delacourte, descendant of a fine old southern family. Verna Lee didn't know anything about her father, except that he was a black man.

She hung up the phone, saw him standing just inside the door and smiled her aloha smile. "I was just thinking it was time for you to come in."

"Chasing after the criminals here in Marshy Hope Creek gives a man an appetite. You got any of those pickles I like?"

"You bet. What'll it be? The usual?"

"Yes, ma'am." He slid into a table and looked around. Perks was a combination health food store and café. Two deep blue couches sat across from each other with a low chest in between. Small wooden tables and chairs hugged the walls and a glass case as long as the room was filled with herbs and spices all neatly labeled. Candles, colorful crockery, greeting cards, books, beads and checked window coverings gave the place a homey, interesting feel. Blake liked it here. He would have liked anywhere as long as Verna Lee was there, too.

"Bailey Jones is back in town," she began conversationally. "He's thinking about selling his land."

Blake nodded. "I heard. A geologist's holed up at Bonnie's B&B. He's taking a long time to get started."

She set down a tall, sweating glass of herbal iced tea in front of him. "What's holding him up?"

Blake shrugged, trying to ignore the effect of smooth, gold skin against the bright turquoise of her sleeveless blouse. She moved gracefully, efficiently, layering his sandwich, cutting it in two, adding the pickles just the way he liked. He cleared his throat. "Who knows? It's Bailey's land, at least until escrow closes. He's the one calling the shots."

Verna Lee slid the sandwich across the table and sat down across from him. He tried not to look too delighted.

"I'm worried about the wetlands," she said. "I don't think people around here realize what'll happen without them."

Blake sighed. He would never understand her loyalties. As far as he was concerned, there was nothing out there but alligators and mud. Affordable housing, on the other hand, would benefit the Cove. He changed the subject. "I hear Bailey's made something of himself in New York."

"My niece Chloe was really taken with him four years ago when she was here for the first time. She's back for the summer and her mama's worried they'll start something up."

"What's wrong with that?"

Verna Lee looked thoughtful. "I'm not sure. Even though he's had amazing success with his painting, Bailey's had a rough life. He's been on his own for a long time. His mother, Lizzie Jones, wasn't exactly Mother Teresa. I think Libba Jane wants something different for Chloe."

Blake grinned. "You mean she doesn't want history to repeat itself. Seems to me I heard she ran off with an actor when she was about Chloe's age."

"That's ancient history. I'm sure we all have a few skeletons we'd rather not talk about."

"I don't want to talk about skeletons, Verna Lee."

"What do you want to talk about?"

"Sunday. I want to talk about us taking a drive to Chincoteague and ordering up a plate of blue crabs. How about it?"

Verna Lee laughed. "In your dreams."

He finished his sandwich and washed it down with tea. "Well then, since you're turning me down again, I guess I'll be on my way." Settling his hat on his head, he tipped the brim. "I'll see you in church on Sunday."

Blake waited for a minute outside the café, narrowing his eyes against the shimmering heat waving up from the scorching macadam. The sun was at its peak. Shadowed doors and windows looked inky black against the stark white of stucco walls. Two men approached Perks from opposite directions. He recognized Russ Hennessey with his sorry-looking beagle lagging behind. The other man was a stranger, bareheaded, obviously some poor fool who didn't understand the dangers of heatstroke.

Blake nodded at the stranger. "You might want to consider wearing at least a baseball cap in this heat."

Surprisingly, the man stopped. "Are you the sheriff?"

He held out his hand. "Blake Carlisle. What can I do for you?"

Perfunctorily, the stranger shook his hand. "Dave Yardley. I'm one of the geologists hired by Weber Incorporated to inspect a parcel of land north of here belonging to Bailey Jones. We've hit a snag."

Blake waited, conscious that Russ had stopped to hear their conversation.

"What kind of snag?"

"A human body. At least it was. Now it's mostly bones, but it's human all right."

Blake stiffened.

The man continued. "It looks like whoever it was has been there for a while. I thought you might want to know."

Blake pulled out his cell phone and punched in his deputy's number. The connection was immediate. "This is Charlie One to Charlie Two," he said. "Come back in to the station and cover all calls for the next couple of hours. I'm taking a drive out to Highway 39." He waited for an affirmative reply before flipping his phone shut. Noting Dave Yardley's flushed skin and the sweat streaming down his forehead, he spoke. "The police station's at the end of the street. I suggest you get something cool to drink and meet me there in ten minutes. I'll follow you out to the location."

Russ waited until the door to Verna Lee's shop closed behind the geologist. "Well, I'll be damned. What do you think that's all about?"

"I haven't a clue, but I intend to find out. Bailey's sale could take longer than he'd planned." Blake grinned at Russ. "How's business?"

"Not bad. I'm taking a break. Verna Lee's brownies are worth it, but don't tell Libba Jane. She worries about my cholesterol."

"No problem." Blake clapped him on the shoulder. "Say hello for me and get that dog out of the sun."

Russ picked up the dog and walked into the café. His sister-in-law handed the geologist an iced drink and stared pointedly at the dog, forcing her lips into a tight line.

Russ waited until the man left the store. "I know what you're thinking, Verna Lee."

She lost the battle with laughter. "No, you don't. Bring that dog into the kitchen and I'll give her a bowl of water. I can't believe Libba lets you keep that mangy animal."

"She doesn't. I keep her with me at the office." He stroked the dog's head. "Trixie, here, prefers air-conditioning."

"What can I get you?" she asked after settling the beagle with a bowl of cool water.

"A beer, if you've got it."

"How about iced tea or lemonade?"

He sighed. "Lemonade."

"So," she said, sitting down beside him. "How's the fishing business?"

"Same as usual." He frowned. "Did you hear about Bailey Jones?"

"I heard he might be selling his land." Her eyes flashed. "I'm against it, Russ. I can't believe Bailey would do that to his mother's legacy. It's not that he needs the money."

"You don't know that."

"I certainly do. He's going to be a very wealthy young man if he keeps on the way he has. He doesn't need to leave us with acres of pink condominiums. You should be worried, too. There's a delicate web of life here in the Tidewater. Get your wife to explain it to you. We had a huge scare four years ago with all that nuclear waste in the water. What do you think draining the wetlands and bringing in foreign soil will do to the fisheries and oyster beds, not to mention produce, which directly affects me?"

"What is it with the women in your family? You sound just like Libba."

"Damn right."

"It may not come to that any time soon."

"Let's hope it doesn't."

"Well, if what I just heard outside has any truth

to it, Bailey's land will remain untouched awhile longer."

She looked at him. "What did you say?"

"That man who was just in here is one of Weber's geologists. He claims he found a dead body in the swamp. He was telling Blake about it when I walked up. It's probably just some old drifter."

"Maybe," she said slowly.

"Nothing ever came of speculation. Blake'll figure things out and if it's more than he can handle, he'll call in the forensics team from Salisbury." He stood. "Thanks for the lemonade. I'll collect my dog and be on my way."

"Say hello to the girls."

"I'll do that. Maybe I'll send Chloe over with Gina Marie."

"You can keep Gina at home if it's all the same to you."

"You're a cruel woman, Verna Lee, and because I'm a good guy, I won't tell your sister that you're less than enthusiastic about your very own niece."

"I'm enthusiastic about one of them. The other terrifies me."

Eight

Detective Wade Atkins, chief homicide detective of Wicomico County Sheriff's Department, was no stranger to Marshy Hope Creek. He'd spent most of his formative years six miles out of the town limits in a two-room shack set low on a piece of land optimistically called Darby's Cove. The name evoked images of pleasure boats with white sails moored neatly in a harbor, bordered by charming restaurants and shops crowded with tourists. In reality it was a mosquito-infested glade, thick with alligators, toads and catfish all filled with enough radiation from the Pax River to make them inedible. Uncared-for front lawns boasted inoperable vehicles set high on blocks. The view from broken screens led to other faded shacks and mobile homes.

As soon as he was legally able, Wade hitched a

ride on a big rig filled with sweet potatoes and made his way west where a stint in the army and the GI Bill earned him a place at California State University, Long Beach. From there he was accepted at the police academy.

Wade figured he was about as far away from his roots and Marshy Hope Creek as a man could be. Growing up, he and his brothers, the Atkins boys, "river rats" or "white trash," depending on who was doing the describing, weren't big on community service. In fact, you might say they were more of a high-risk factor than anything else. Clem and Howard, the two oldest, spent more nights at the juvenile detention center in Salisbury than they did at home, and it was a known fact that the First Baptist Church took up a collection to buy Mace cans for their elderly, single ladies, just in case they should happen on one or, God forbid, both of the Atkinses' distinctive white-blond heads while walking down the street.

Wade, however, was different, not in appearance but in temperament. Like the others, he was tow-headed with a mass of freckles, so many of them they all ran together, giving his face an attractive tanned look, paired with steely blue eyes, a jutting chin and a wide linebacker's body. But he was missing the mean streak that every male Atkins, from one generation to the next, never failed to inherit.

In fact, Wade managed to clear four years of high school without a single knuckle-bruising scuffle. He was also, according to his teachers, fairly intelligent, with a kind of practical common sense that completely bypassed the rest of his clan. It made some people wonder if Carrie Eileen Atkins had been messing with the postman nine months before Wade was born. But then they looked at old Morris, at the steely blue eyes and that thatch of white hair shared by all his boys, especially Wade, and knew it wasn't so.

Wade didn't subscribe to the notion that he was *born* different. He attributed his path to a mild case of scarlet fever and subsequent bed rest. Carrie Atkins was beside herself trying to keep an active twelve-year-old boy cool and immobile in a house the size of a cracker box. She began by buying comic books. But when it became clear that each ten-cent copy was devoured in twenty minutes, she did what no Atkins had ever done before. She applied for a library card.

At first, Owena Harper, the librarian, was reluctant to allow it. In her experience the folks living on the wrong side of Marshy Hope Creek did not treat books with the proper respect. But when she heard the card was for Wade, she relented. He'd chopped wood for her the last two winters. She paid him fifty cents an hour and he showed up faithfully when he said he would and worked until the job was done. Owena allowed that he deserved a library card, him being sick and all.

That was Wade's introduction to a world outside his own. He read *Tom Sawyer, Robinson Crusoe, Treasure Island, Where the Red Fern Grows, The Yearling, Grimm's Fairy Tales, The Works of Hans Christian Andersen* and many more. For the next six years he was never without a book in hand. Heroes appealed to him. He wanted to be like them.

That was thirty-five years and a lifetime ago, before he'd worked himself up from undercover vice to homicide detective. Now he wore a suit and tie and although his hours weren't regular, the pay was better. He figured he would have lived out his life in Santa Monica, California, quite happily, except that his wife, Susan, died five years before. After that, his workdays were bearable but his free time wasn't. All the old haunts, Diedrich coffee to start the day, a midmorning jog on the boardwalk, dinner at Gladstone's, were miserable without Sarah. So, he came home, not to Darby's Cove or Marshy Hope Creek, but to Salisbury and the Wicomico County Sheriff's Department, both different enough from the white sand beaches of the West to ward off memories.

The call came in at noon, an unusual time for reporting a homicide. Most were called in at night. Sheriff Blake Carlisle from Marshy Hope Creek was requesting a full crime-scene forensics team. Because Wade had high hopes of wrapping this one up in time to go straight home after his shift, he drove his own car.

Soon, he found himself on the back roads of his boyhood, his senses reeling from the brackish smell of the Chesapeake shallows, marsh grass, nesting birds, the contrast of golden sunlight and black shadow, the frustratingly slow pace of a pickup weighted down with tomatoes on a two-lane road. He'd skirted the area countless times, but he'd never been back, not since the death of his mother when he was a teenager.

Highway 39 was a narrow strip of road bisecting miles of marshland and pine forests. A single patrol car with blinking lights and yards of yellow tape signaled the location of the crime scene. Wade pulled the emergency brake, swallowed a goodly portion of his sixteen-ounce water bottle, grabbed his clipboard from the back seat, stepped into his boots, laced them up and hiked out to the tape border. He flashed his badge at the young police officer manning the log, stepped over the tape and, keeping toward the edge, maneuvered his way to the placards, the site of the crime and the officer in charge. "What does it look like?" he asked.

"The coroner's on his way," replied Sheriff Carlisle. "See for yourself."

Wade walked around the site, checking it out from every angle. "Hair and clothing looks good enough for lab samples," he said to the sheriff following close behind. "There's a close-contact entry wound in the head. Who called this in?"

"A geologist from Weber Incorporated."

"Where is he?"

"Back at the bed and breakfast."

Wade jotted down notes on his clipboard. "Get him back here," he said in a clipped voice. Pulling on a pair of latex gloves, he squatted down for a better look at the wound, picked up a fragment of clothing lying next to the body and sealed it in a plastic bag. "This bog is nearly as good as a mummy's tomb. The body's got flesh, hair and a full skull."

Jim Marshall, the coroner, arrived mopping his brow, his bulldog face pulled down by heavy jowls and an extra fifty pounds. "Hot enough for you, Wade?"

"I've seen hotter," Wade replied, unwilling to be distracted. "There's no blood anywhere but on the victim. Whoever this is was shot somewhere else and dumped."

Marshall nodded his head. "Terry Gilmore is on her way. She's our new forensic anthropologist." He looked around. "Has the photographer been here yet?"

Carlisle exchanged a look with Wade. "He's

coming from Salisbury. He could have hitched a ride with you if anybody had thought of it."

Wade laughed. "You don't want to work us too hard, now, do you, Blake?"

"No, sir."

"How old do you think these bones are?" asked Wade.

"It's hard to say." Marshall scribbled something on his own clipboard. "I'll do a field test after the photographer is through and then we'll send everything to the crime lab. It may be that Terry Gilmore can be more specific but, either way, I'll fax you the details as soon as I know."

Wade nodded. "Carlisle," he asked. "Did you get a statement from the geologist?"

Blake handed it over.

Wade skimmed it quickly and handed it back. "How big is your office?" he asked.

"Big enough for one at a time."

"That's too bad because there'll be quite a few of us there until I'm satisfied we haven't missed anything."

"I figured." Blake glanced at his watch. "If we get back in time, I'll have my deputy make a food run. With any luck, Verna Lee might be willing to throw in some of her potato salad with the sandwiches."

"I knew a Verna Lee in high school." Wade

stroked his jaw. "Verna Lee Washington. Pretty black girl with a knock-'em-dead body."

"That would be her, except now she's Verna Lee Fontaine."

Wade frowned at something in the distance. "I wouldn't have figured her for a shopkeeper. She was smarter than the rest of us put together and not afraid to let everybody know it."

"She came back from San Francisco about fifteen years ago and started up her business. It's a health food store, and a little bit of everything else. Verna Lee's a success story."

"Most people don't come back to places like Marshy Hope Creek once they've had a taste of the big city."

Blake shrugged. "Verna Lee and her grandmother, Drusilla, don't have any other family. That's reason enough, I guess."

Wade acknowledged that it was. His attention was diverted by the photographer who had just arrived on the scene. "What took you so long?" he asked bluntly.

"I'm backup for Ken Mitchell. I was in a movie theater."

"Watch where you're stepping," Wade warned him. "We need close-ups of the head wound, a full figure shot, any evidence we find and an orientation photo. Do you know what you're doing?"

The photographer, a young man with a black goatee and hoops in his ears, nodded. "Yes, sir," he said. "This isn't exactly new territory."

"Good." Wade pulled out his dark glasses and settled into his watch-and-wait mode until the forensic anthropologist showed her face.

Fifteen minutes later she was in the field, a tall woman in her forties, dressed in what looked like hospital scrubs and tennis shoes. She pulled on a pair of latex gloves and knelt beside the body. Wade walked over to introduce himself.

"I'll be with you in a minute, Detective," she said tersely.

Wade backed away. He appreciated efficiency when he saw it in action.

Jim Marshall approached him. "We've got a few other cases on the schedule. Is this one a high priority?"

"What have you got?"

"One domestic homicide. Victim was strangled with a necktie." Marshall looked up at the sky. "We've got a three-year-old girl with a head injury and broken limbs. Looks like she was thrown down the stairs."

"Good God." Wade's lips were tight and thin. "Do you ever wonder why we do this?"

"The pension's good."

"I wonder."

"You won't wonder so much when you're my age."

Terry Gilmore had finished her field test. She stripped off her gloves, dropped them into a plastic bag she'd secured to her waist, pulled a pen and small pad from her pocket and began writing furiously.

Wade nodded in her direction. "She looks like she's got it together."

Marshall grunted. "Time will tell. We lose quite a few. Usually our bones are from Indian burial grounds. That's a nightmare of paperwork and waiting."

The woman looked up from her notes and walked over. "We'll grid off the site and cast the skull. There's a good chance I can reconstruct the face. Bone-marrow scrapings tell us quite a bit more. Marks on the pelvis indicate childbirth. It's hard to tell how long these bones have been buried, but my guess is about twelve to fifteen years. I'll have more information for you after I've completed my tests."

Wade was impressed. "Nice work." He waved Carlisle over. "Pull out all your files ten to twenty years old."

"There aren't too many open files here in Marshy Hope Creek."

"I said all of them. After we get the evidence figured out and logged, it'll be just me, you and your deputy. The coroner has bigger fish to fry." He started to walk away, turned back and grinned. "Now's a good time to be thinking about those sandwiches. Tell Verna Lee I'll be stopping by."

"He said what?" Verna Lee's hands were on her hips, a sure sign that a line was being drawn in the sand.

Blake knew something was wrong. He just didn't know what. "He said he'd be stopping by."

"Is that a warning or something?"

Now he was frustrated. "Lord, Verna Lee. How would I know? I thought he was an old schoolmate. You're making it sound as if the guy has some ulterior motive."

"They usually do," she muttered under her breath.

"Can you make up the sandwiches or not?"

She waved her hand. "I can, but you won't get a discount."

"Fair enough."

"You'll have to pick them up. I don't deliver."

"I know that, too," Blake said patiently.

Verna Lee turned her back, fanned her pink cheeks with her hand and began pulling ingredients from the refrigerator. "Give me half an hour." *Wade Atkins.* Who would've thought? There was a time when she'd hoped every one of the Atkins clan would drink too much of that corn liquor old Morris made up with regularity and fall into one of those rarely traveled fingers of the Chesapeake, preferably into the jaws of a hungry alligator. Clem and Howard, and to a lesser degree, Wade, secure in their blond good looks, hazed her unmercifully about her hair, her clothes, her brains, her lack of parents and the pouty fullness of her lips in an era when beautiful meant Christie Brinkley and Cheryl Tiegs.

Time and nine years in a high-school classroom taught her wisdom. The Atkins boys were just as uncomfortable in their skins as she had been in hers. She'd come to terms with their hatefulness a long time ago. The last thing she'd expected was a message from one of them, the least objectionable one, telling her that he would be stopping by.

Her hands shook as she scooped spoonfuls of potato salad into a plastic container. She'd show him. She'd pretend she didn't remember him at all. She'd play it cool, look incredulous, rise above. Nola Ruth Delacourte was her mother and a gene pool meant something after all. She could be just as sophisticated as Libba Jane.

It took her considerably less than thirty minutes to assemble a dozen roast beef and turkey sandwiches. She had plenty of time to twist her curls into place, apply blush to her cheeks and brush mascara on her lashes before the bell on her door jingled, indicating she had a customer. "I'm closed," she sang out from the kitchen.

"Is anyone here? Verna Lee?" an unfamiliar voice called out.

"It's really late," she said, coming through the swinging door, "and—" She stopped in midstride and her mouth dropped. All her resolutions vanished. This wasn't Wade Atkins, or was it? She knew him and yet she didn't. The thin, rangy length of him had filled out, thickening his chest and shoulders. The jutting bones of his face had settled into something very close to handsome. He was still fair, but the white-blond of his teenage years had deepened. His freckles had disappeared into an even brown and his eyes, bluer than ever, twinkled at her. "Good Lord! You've improved."

He chuckled. "You're still beautiful."

Her eyes flashed at the blatant lie. "Since when did you ever think I was beautiful?"

He moved closer.

She retreated until she felt the door against her back.

His voice deepened, a note of intimacy smoothing out the vowels. "Come on, Verna Lee. You're a smart girl. Didn't anyone ever tell you that little boys tease the girls they have a crush on?"

"You and your brothers weren't little boys, and you weren't teasing."

His smile faltered. "I'd prefer not to be lumped in with my brothers."

He was right about that. He hadn't been as cruel as the two older Atkins brothers. But she wasn't about to give him the satisfaction of telling him. Somehow, she knew exactly how to offend him. "Frankly, I couldn't tell the three of you apart."

He blinked and then laughed. "Touché! How about if we start fresh?"

She looked at him, at the attractive golden man he'd become, and her sense of injustice grew. He had no idea what it was like to be the wrong color, the wrong sex, to be judged, before he even opened his mouth, by an accident of birth. "I don't think so."

"C'mon, Verna Lee." That intimate note was in his voice again. "I'll be around here for a while. Why not give a little?"

She crossed her arms protectively. "Why should I?"

"It'll make things a whole lot easier."

"I'm not in a forgiving mood."

"Give it a try," he coaxed. "I've changed."

She pointed to the two large paper bags on the

counter. "Those belong to you. I won't be turning away your business. The bill's attached."

He reached into his pocket and handed her a credit card. "You've got a nice place here."

"I like it."

"The sheriff said you've been here fifteen years. What made you come back?"

She handed him his receipt. "Sign the bottom and don't forget your phone number."

One blond eyebrow lifted. "Are you planning on calling me, Verna Lee, or don't you trust cops?"

"No to the first, and no comment on the second."

"Do you ever take a day for yourself?"

"Sunday. No one comes into town on Sunday."

"How about taking a drive with me to Chincoteague? We could grab a bite to eat at Steamers and catch up on old times."

She stared at him. "Are you serious?"

"Completely."

"Wade, you're amazing! If I haven't made myself absolutely clear that I want nothing to do with you, then you're the least intuitive police detective I've ever met."

He held out the receipt. She took it from him and for an instant their fingers touched. She smelled like his mother's kitchen, cinnamon and apples. "Met a few detectives in your time, Verna Lee?"

She flushed angrily, remembered her resolve and

rallied. "I hope you enjoy the sandwiches. Blake swears by them."

"Thanks. I surely will. See you around, Verna Lee."

Nine

Retired judge Quentin Wentworth, on the way to lunch in his dining room, spotted an errant white thread on the dark blue border of his Persian carpet. His lips thinned. Stooping, he picked up the thread and continued down the stairs.

His daughter and granddaughter were already seated. It was the first time today that he'd seen them. Without even an obligatory greeting the judge launched his complaint. "Tell me, Tracy, where do you find our help?"

His daughter opened her mouth to reply but he cut her off. "I'm curious because their performance has been less than satisfactory. The milk I requested last night never came, my newspaper wasn't delivered to my room and I found this—" he held up the offensive thread "—on the floor in the hall."

Tracy flushed. "Camille hired the new girl. I'll speak to her."

"Why don't *you* oversee the hiring of our help? What else do you have to do besides keep this house running smoothly?"

Tess rolled her eyes. Her grandfather was in good form today. She picked up the pitcher of iced tea and poured herself a glass. "So, Granddaddy, how is everyone in Marshy Hope Creek?"

He directed his piercing gaze at his granddaughter. "If you were home more often, you wouldn't have to ask. Why you would choose New York City for your education when there are perfectly good schools here in the South is beyond me."

Tess was not the least bit cowed. "Why would I want to come home when all you do is insult me?"

"Tess!" Her mother's anguish was obvious.

"Leave the child alone, Tracy. At least she has spunk, which is more than I can say for you." The judge lifted his napkin to his lips. "To answer your question, Teresa, your mother is here and she misses your company. You might have some consideration for her. As for my insulting you, that isn't the case. You're the one female in this family who hasn't disappointed me. I appreciate that. It's your mother I insult, and with good reason. Her life is pointless."

Tess's hands clenched. On principle, she didn't disagree with her grandfather. Her mother's life was a continuous round of shopping and parties, but it didn't give him the right to humiliate her.

Tracy's eyes filled. "I don't know what you want from me. It isn't as though I can read your mind."

"That's hardly the point," replied the judge, dismissing his daughter's comment and returning his attention to Tess. "Have you seen your father?"

"Of course."

"I would have thought you'd be there all the time since you don't like the company here."

Tess's dark eyes met her grandfather's steadily. She knew what he was up to. "Daddy's fine. So is Libba Jane and Gina."

Wentworth smiled smugly. "Do you get along with her?"

Tess frowned and hooked a silky strand of ash-blond hair behind her ear. "Who?"

"His wife, the Delacourte girl."

"She's hardly a girl," Tracy protested. "We're the same age. We went to school together, remember?"

Quentin thought a minute. "She looks younger. Those Delacourte women age well. I remember her mother in her heyday. Boys all over the county would howl after Nola Ruth when Cole first brought her home."

Tracy shivered. "Disgusting."

"Nonsense. You'd give your eyeteeth to have them calling for you."

"Don't be ridiculous."

"Now that I think of it, you always were jealous of Libba Delacourte, even before she married your husband."

Tracy's face, naturally pale, whitened perceptibly. "Russ was not my husband. We were divorced for years before Libba came back to town."

Wentworth cut his chicken-fried steak lengthwise once and then again, forked a large piece, dredged it in gravy and stuffed it into his mouth. "I remember now," he said around a mouthful of steak. "She had him first. The two of them were always together and then she left town with a stranger. He married you on the rebound. He never would have otherwise."

Tess pushed her plate away. Her hands shook. Someone had to defend her mother. "What an awful thing to say."

"Nothing awful about the truth," replied the judge.

"Do you lie in bed at night and think up things that will hurt people, or does it just come naturally?"

"Tess," her mother said again. "Think of how much we owe Granddaddy."

"Funny you should mention it, but I don't think the price he exacts for his benevolence is worth it."

"Please, Tess."

"Don't stop her." Quentin waved his fork. "Go on. Say what you want, but remember, my money pays for your education, your room and board and your car."

"My father pays for half," she said, leaping to Russ's defense, "except for the car," she added.

"Tess," her mother begged. "I can't stand all this conflict. Please, stop."

"That's right, Teresa. Do as your mother says. She doesn't have the gumption of a cotton ball or else she'd tell me what she really thinks and toss my money back in my face."

Gritting her teeth, Tess stood. "I'm going out."

"Where?" Tracy asked.

"Chloe's back. I'm off to see her."

"Oh." Tracy looked defeated. "I thought we'd have the afternoon together to shop and have dinner."

Tess kissed her mother's cheek. Trying on clothes was the last thing she wanted to do when the mercury had already climbed to triple digits before eight o'clock in the morning. "Not today. I already promised Chloe. She could use some help with Gina Marie. Let's forget the shopping and plan on lunch tomorrow."

Tracy tittered. "Russ certainly has his hands full. I can't imagine having a child at his age."

Tess sighed. She tried to remember that her

mother was lonely and jealous. She loved her, of course, just as she loved her grandfather, but sometimes it was difficult to like them. Thank goodness she had another family. "I've heard that children keep you young."

"Well, whatever. Tell him hello for me."

There were only so many battles Tess was willing to take on. The last thing she planned on doing was to bring Tracy's name up to Russ. Her parents hadn't had what anyone would call an amicable divorce. Thankfully, their marriage had been brief, so brief that Tess had no memory of the three of them as a family. In fact, the only traditional family life she'd experienced had been during the last four years when her dad had finally married the love of his life, the one who got away, the acknowledged golden girl of Marshy Hope Creek, Libba Jane.

Tess hadn't been prepared to like her new stepmother. Russ, an architect by trade, came home to take over his family's commercial-fishing fleet after his twin brother died. As far as Tess was concerned, he'd been an absentee father for most of her life. She'd hoped to have him all to herself. But Libba's generous warmth and Chloe's friendship won her over. The thought of seeing Chloe again, sharing confidences in the yellow-and-white bedroom of Cole Delacourte's gracious house, sipping minty iced tea and snacking on Serena's molasses cookies, lifted her spirits.

Turning the air-conditioning to full power, she zipped down the road in the sporty red Mazda coupe her grandfather had given her for her last birthday, toward the town where she was born and raised, slowing down inside the city limits. She noted that not much had changed in the past year, not that it ever did. The graceful columns of city hall, the courthouse and police station stood out starkly white in the blazing sun. Horace's Mercantile and Dry Goods and Clayton Dulaine's Diner, which miraculously hung on despite the success of Verna Lee's shop, were as run-down and fading as ever. Taft's Hardware and Perks faced each other on opposite sides of the street. As usual, the creek was the dividing line of the residential community, the disadvantaged on one side and tall, gracious, white-pillared homes with views of the bay, set back on enormous green lawns on the other. Standing off by itself, just a jaunt down the road, behind a cluster of pine and sand dunes, commanding the most spectacular view of the Chesapeake from its weathered wraparound porch, was Hennessey House, where her father lived with his wife and daughter.

Tess inhaled the soupy, metallic smell of the bay and grinned. She'd never noticed it when she lived here. Natives never did. The scents of marsh and swamp, brine and salt, fish and pine permeated skin, hair, clothes and lungs with a relentless persistence that outlanders couldn't tolerate, a benefit, it turned out, for those who supported population control. The small community on the Maryland side of the bay had maintained a constant population for years. People were born and died at fairly regular intervals. Most were lured away to cities with their promise of high-paying jobs, but a few stayed, or left and then came home, like her father and Libba.

Verna Lee, sweeping off the porch of her shop, waved as she drove by. Tess slowed to a stop, backed up and rolled down her window. "Hi, Verna Lee. How is everything?"

"I can't complain. And yourself?"

"I'm staying at home this summer." She rolled her eyes. "How good can that be?"

Verna Lee nodded sympathetically. She wasn't a fan of either the judge or Tracy Wentworth. "Chloe's back, too. In fact, she should be by right about now. She's bringing Gina Marie."

Tess groaned. "Poor Chloe."

Verna Lee walked over to the car and slapped her hand playfully. "That's my niece you're talking about, and she's not that bad."

"I'm pleading the Fifth. Do you mind if I come inside and wait for Chloe? I was just heading over to see her."

Verna Lee smiled and Tess caught her breath. There were times she looked so much like Libba Jane that it was amazing no one had suspected they were related long before the scandal broke four years ago.

"Please, do. I'd love the company."

Tess was seated on one of the low couches, sipping a soy milk smoothie, when Chloe walked in with the diminutive Gina Marie.

"Tess." Chloe's face lit up. "I was just thinking about you. When did you get in?"

"Last night." She stood to hug Chloe and then stooped to kiss her little sister. "You're huge. When did you get to be so tall?"

"I'm three," said the little girl, holding up three fingers.

"Good for you. I'm having a smoothie. Do you want one?"

Gina shook her head. "I want chocolate milk." She lifted her chin imperiously. "Auntie Verna," she said, losing the "r" in the name. "I want chocolate milk."

"Say please and you'll get some apple juice," replied her aunt from behind the counter. "I don't have chocolate milk."

"Please."

"Coming right up. What would you like, Chloe?"

Chloe sank down beside Tess. "An iced tea would be great. Can you sit down with us?"

"For a while."

"So, what's new with you?" asked Tess when they were all seated and Gina was occupied with her juice and a bowl of crackers.

"I'm finishing school next June," replied Chloe. "I didn't think I'd be able to do it in four years, but it's worked out. I have an internship at the marine institute in San Diego."

"Still environmental studies?"

Chloe nodded. "With an emphasis in marine life."

"Congratulations. We need more people paying attention to marine life."

"What about you, Tess?" asked Verna Lee.

"I'm still prelaw, and I love New York. Hopefully, Columbia will take me when I'm ready for law school."

"Wow." Chloe grinned. "I'm so impressed. Your grandfather must be thrilled."

"He might be, but I'd never know. Positive feedback isn't his strong suit."

"I'm sure he's very proud of you, Tess," said Verna Lee. "Who wouldn't be proud of a granddaughter who's following in his footsteps?"

Chloe sat up. "I guess you haven't been here long enough to hear the latest—Bailey Jones is back in town."

Tess's eyes widened. "You're kidding. Why?"

"He's selling Lizzie's land, but there's been a complication."

"What's that?"

She glanced at Gina and whispered, "A dead body."

"Anyone we know?"

"It's probably been out there for years, some old hermit whose luck ran out," said Verna Lee.

Tess frowned. "If that's the case, why would it matter?"

"It won't matter. As soon as the coroner's report comes through, everyone will know the truth."

Chloe stared at her aunt. "Is something wrong, Verna Lee? You sound upset."

"Auntie Verna's mad," Gina Marie parroted, spilling the remainder of her juice.

"Yes, I am," she snapped, mopping up the table with napkins. "Those wetlands have been here for a thousand years. They're essential to our ecosystem, not to mention our economy. It makes me sick to think Bailey would consider selling them to some condominium developer. I'm ashamed of him. Lizzie will be turning over in her grave."

Chloe flushed and Tess remembered how her stepsister had felt about Bailey Jones four years ago. Not much ruffled Verna Lee's temper, except for the swampland. In that, she was like her half sister, Chloe's mama. Tess searched for a safe topic.

"So, what else is new around here since I've been gone?"

"Nothing at all except this body thing," Verna Lee replied. "There's a homicide team from Salisbury hanging around. You'd think nothing important ever happened here."

"I think I'll have more of this delicious iced tea," replied Chloe diplomatically. "Then I think Gina Marie and I should be heading back home for her nap." She glanced at Tess. "Why don't you come back with me and we'll catch up while Gina sleeps."

"No," Gina piped up. "I don't want to sleep. I want to stay with Auntie Verna."

"Oh, honey." Verna Lee looked alarmed. "I can't watch you today. I'm working. Be a good girl and go home with Chloe and Tess. I'll come and see you later. Your mama invited me for dinner."

Gina's bottom lip stuck out.

Tess had an idea. "Would you like to ride in my car, Gina? We can take a little drive before we go home."

Gina tilted her head, deep in thought. "Can I ride in front?"

Tess looked at Chloe.

"Absolutely," agreed Chloe, hoping that traffic laws here in the Cove were as relaxed as she remembered. "You can ride in front with Tess and I'll sit in back with the stroller."

Gina's eyes brightened. "Okay."

Collectively, the three adults breathed a sigh of relief. A minor disaster had been averted.

Gina Marie fell asleep before they'd traveled a block.

"Thank God," whispered Chloe. "I don't know how my mother does it."

"Me, neither," agreed Tess, grateful for the expensive shock absorbers her grandfather had insisted she buy. "Will she wake up if we carry her inside the house or should we just keep driving?"

"I'm new at this. I have no idea."

"I vote we keep driving."

"Me, too."

"Chloe," Tess said after a minute, "tell me about Bailey."

"There's nothing to tell."

"Have you seen him?"

"He drove me into town the day after I got here. I wasn't thrilled about his plans to turn Lizzie's land over to developers. We argued a little and he dropped me off. That's it. I guess we don't have much to say to each other anymore."

Tess was smart enough to keep silent.

Chloe leaned forward. "Verna Lee sounded really upset."

"I guess so."

"Are you curious about the body?"

"Not really. No one that I can think of has up and disappeared."

"It's probably the remains of some old hermit, just like Verna Lee said."

In the rearview mirror, Tess's eyes, narrow and dark, met Chloe's quizzical ones. "My grandmother's the only person I know who left town and never came back."

"Tess," Chloe was amused. "Your grandmother died in a car accident, years ago, on the way to see her sister. Russ told me. He went to the funeral. The whole town did."

Tess sighed. "You're right." She glanced over at Gina Marie. "She's really kind of cute, isn't she?"

"She's not cute, she's gorgeous. She looks just like my mother, which is why she gets away with behaving the way she does."

"I can't believe Dad tolerates it. He certainly didn't with me."

"People change when they get older," Chloe said.

Ten

Libba Jane Hennessey liberally sprinkled her chicken casserole with Mrs. Dash salt substitute, turned the oven dial to read 350 degrees, set the pan carefully on the middle rack, closed the door and leaned against the counter wondering why she bothered trying to make an impression. She could never compete with Verna Lee when it came to cooking. Not that anyone expected her to. After all, food was Verna Lee's job. Still, Libba was a southerner, company was coming and southern women were supposed to offer up delicious food. Somewhere she'd missed the boat.

Sighing, she opened the refrigerator and rooted through the storage bin. She'd throw together a huge mess of raw vegetables, toss them with olive oil and a vinaigrette, top the whole thing off with cranberries, some almonds and a handful of small red grapes. Voila! A California meal for Chloe.

She heard the *click, clicking* of Gina Marie's Barbie-doll high heels on the wood floorboards. The sound stopped abruptly.

"Mama, I'm hungwy," she called out, mangling her "r." "I need a snack."

Libba continued her vegetable search. "In a minute, sugar."

The child's voice rose. "I need one now."

Libba turned and faced what had become her greatest challenge. Gina Marie Hennessey, dressed in a pink, two-piece bathing suit that wouldn't see another season and sparkly high-heeled shoes from last year's Halloween costume, stared back at her.

"We're eating dinner soon. I don't want to spoil your appetite."

The little girl stuck out her bottom lip. "What is it?"

"Chicken and salad."

"I'm hungwy now." Behind their fringe of lashes, the pansy-brown eyes filled. "I'm starving. I'm starving to my death."

Libba's lips twitched. Between the crocodile tears and the mangled consonants, it was all she could do not to laugh. "We certainly can't have you starving to your death, can we?"

Gina Marie shook her head. "No."

"How about a peach?"

The child tilted her head, considering her options. "Can I have a soda, too?"

"You can have milk."

The rosebud mouth turned down. "I wike soda."
"L's" were a problem, too.

"You know the rules. Milk and juice at home, soda and chocolate milk when we go out." Libba changed the subject. "Chloe and Aunt Verna Lee will be here for dinner." She held out her hand. "Let's clean up the living room."

"No." Gina turned around to walk away, exposing the left cheek of her plump little behind.

Was it worth the scene? No, she decided. She followed her daughter into the toy-strewn living room and groaned.

Lego bricks, dominoes, marbles and Mr. Potato Head parts lay scattered across the ottoman. Two naked, high-heeled Barbie dolls, their legs twisted into Kama Sutra positions, gazed up at her from the Barbie Dream Car. The door of a miniature refrigerator swung on one hinge. Stacked in front on the floor, as if the little fridge had lost its lunch, was an unappealing mass of mini plastic pork chops, eggs, bacon, sandwiches and bread. Real cracker crumbs covered the carpet, and pea-size balls of once-multicolored, now gray, PlayDoh, filled every available niche and crevice. Worst of all, the wall behind the couch was covered with red and green crayon marks. Was it age or selective memory? Libba was sure that Chloe had never tested her like this.

Cora Hennessey, her late mother-in-law, would have turned purple at the sight of her once-immaculate front parlor. Libba glared at her daughter. "What have you done?"

Gina Marie glared back. "Keeping busy."

"What did I tell you about writing on walls?"

The little girl laid her finger against her cheek, her forehead wrinkled in deep thought. "You said not to."

"That's right. You disobeyed me. Do you know what that means?"

Gina Marie pirouetted in her impossible shoes. Dark hair floated around her head. "Time out."

"That's right."

Gina beamed. "But not now."

"Why not?"

"Because Chloe and Aunt Verna Lee are coming."

Libba bit down on the inside of her cheek. Gina was too little to be awful on purpose.

She'd swept the worst of the mess into the toy chest when a voice called out, "Hello, anybody home?"

"Chloe." Libba's face lit up. She hurried to the door. Throwing open the screen, she pulled Chloe into her arms. "Where have you been?"

Chloe laughed and pulled away. "Mom, I left

you two hours ago. After Tess and I brought Gina Marie back, we spent some time catching up. Something smells good. What are you cooking?"

"Chicken casserole and salad."

"Sounds interesting." Her mother's repertoire was limited. A casserole usually meant she'd been experimenting.

"What's that supposed to mean?"

"Mmm, nothing." Chloe had noticed her sister. "Hi, Gina Marie. Did you have a good nap?"

Gina nodded. Her thumb inched its way into her mouth. "I don't like naps."

"Naps are good for you," Chloe improvised. "People grow when they sleep. I could be wrong, but I think you're even taller than you were when I picked you up this morning."

"I'm three," said the little girl, keeping her thumb wedged securely in her mouth. She held up three fingers with her free hand.

Chloe knelt down. "Are you sure? That's pretty old. You can't be that old already."

"Yes, I am." Gina nodded vigorously. The thumb came out. "Auntie Verna Lee's coming."

"That's great." She would have mustered greater enthusiasm if her aunt had done the cooking. She looked around. "Where's Russ?"

"He should be here in a minute. Come into the kitchen and I'll pour you a glass of iced tea."

"No, no, no." Gina stamped her foot. "I want Chloe to stay with me."

"Now, Gina," her mother warned. "Chloe will be spending plenty of time with you later. Right now I'd like to talk with her. Okay?"

Chloe stared at her mother. Was she actually negotiating with her three-year-old? If so, things had certainly changed in seventeen years.

"So," she said when Gina was occupied with her snack and they were seated on the porch facing the water, with two glasses and a pitcher of tea on the table between them. "Do you have air-conditioning yet?"

Libba nodded at the fans spinning at full power from both sides of the porch. "What do you think?"

Chloe groaned. "It's going to be a long summer."

"Tell me about it."

Chloe changed the subject. "You look good, Mom," she said. It was true. No one who didn't already know the dark-eyed woman with her thick, shining hair and long, defined legs would guess her age correctly. Elizabeth Jane Hennessey was forty-one years old. She looked thirty except for the tiny lines around her eyes. "Tell me what's going on with your job. Granddad said you'd give me the dirty details."

Libba smiled her wide, generous smile, the smile she'd inherited from Nola Ruth, shared with her half sister, Verna Lee, and passed down to Chloe and

Gina Marie, the smile that had, on one occasion or another, reduced half the men of Marshy Hope Creek to incoherent babblers. "I have no dirty details. I'm just so glad to have you home for the summer."

A voice called out from behind them. "Hello, hello. I require a glass of something cold and a hug from my wife and kids, in that order."

Chloe laughed and stood to greet her stepfather, a tall, lean man with red-brown hair, a chiseled nose and the crystal-blue eyes of a waterman. His arms closed around her tightly. "How are you, sweetheart? Long time no see."

"I'm healthy, happy to see you're looking good, and really hot. It takes a while to adjust to this weather all over again. How are you?" She pulled away but kept her hands on his arms.

"I'm the same as you, especially the hot part." He grinned at his wife. "Any chance of that cold drink?"

Libba stood. "One iced tea, coming right up."

Gina Marie held up her sticky fingers. "Look, Daddy. I'm having peanut butter."

"I can see that. Are you finished?"

She nodded. Russ swooped down, lifted her out of her chair and, wincing, swung her around several times before settling her on his lap. Gina was his miracle child, conceived after everyone told him it would never happen.

Libba set the tea in front of him. He kissed her briefly on the lips and downed his tea in a single long swallow. "I stopped in for a sandwich at Perks today."

Chloe brightened. "How is Verna Lee?"

"Chipper as usual. She said she might be a little late and not to wait for her." Russ snapped his fingers. "I ran into Blake Carlisle. Apparently, there's some controversy over that piece of land Bailey Jones inherited."

"What kind of controversy?" asked Chloe.

Gina squirmed in Russ's arms. "Put me down, Daddy. It's hot."

"Say please."

"Please."

Russ set the little girl on her feet and waited until she left the porch for the cooler rooms of the main house.

Libba repeated Chloe's question. "What kind of controversy?"

"The geologist found a decomposed body. Blake called in a forensics team. If it turns out to be a homicide, the sale could be held up for as long as it takes."

"How could that be?" Libba asked. "No one's missing."

"The person may not be from this side of the Cove. Maybe someone dumped the body."

Chloe frowned. "Bailey said—" She stopped.

Her mother was staring at her. "Finish your sentence, Chloe."

"He said he hadn't sold anything yet."

"So? I'm not following your reasoning."

"Why are people snooping around his land if it hasn't even sold yet?" Chloe swallowed. "I mean, I don't think it's a good idea to sell the wetlands to a developer."

"I imagine there are quite a few people who share that sentiment," Russ agreed. "Verna Lee seemed pretty upset, too. She said the place was a wildlife sanctuary and ought to be left alone." He grinned. "I guess tree hugging runs in the family, but you can't blame Bailey. That kind of money is a tremendous incentive."

"Bailey doesn't need money," protested Chloe. "He's twenty-two years old and already he's an incredible artist. His paintings sell for thousands of dollars."

Libba spoke. "I didn't know you and Bailey kept in touch."

Chloe felt the red stain creep into her cheeks. "We don't. I ran into him on my way into town this morning. That's when he told me he was selling his land but that he hadn't signed the papers yet because he had a few things to take care of first."

Russ chuckled. "I hope that doesn't mean he had to get rid of a dead body."

"Russ!"

"Take it easy, Libba Jane," he soothed her. "Chloe knows I didn't mean anything. Bailey's trial was a long time ago. He was proven innocent, remember? I was one of his strongest supporters."

"It's true, Mom," Chloe agreed. "Don't be upset."

"We went through a lot," her mother reminded her. "It was one of the most difficult periods of your life, and mine."

"I'm only twenty," Chloe teased her. "I have plenty of time to remedy that."

Libba's laugh was forced. "Oh, all right. I'm done preaching. Sorry to be so sensitive. Would anyone like something more to drink?"

"Hello, hello." Verna Lee's voice sang out from the front door. "Ready or not, I'm coming in."

"We're back here on the porch," Libba called back.

"Auntie Verna, Auntie Verna," Gina Marie screamed. The sound of her small feet pounded on the bare wood.

"My goodness, what a welcome." Verna Lee scooped the little girl onto her hip, walked through the house to the back porch and handed Libba a covered dish. "Just a little something I made this morning. You can't keep food more than one day."

Libba lifted the lid and groaned. "Key lime pie. Five hundred calories a slice."

Verna Lee laughed. "And worth every one." She sat in the empty chair and settled Gina on her lap. "How have you been, sweet pea?" she murmured.

Gina held up three fingers. "I'm this many."

"I know. You've been this many for six months." She manipulated the little hand to show three fingers and half the pinkie. "You're really this many, three and a half."

Gina's eyes rounded. She held up her hand. "Look. Look. I'm three and a half."

Chloe rolled her eyes. Everyone else clapped and exclaimed. Gina slid off her aunt's lap and left the room beaming at her new discovery.

Verna Lee looked around. "Y'all look serious. What's going on?"

"We were talking about the body found on Bailey's land."

"Oh, that." Verna Lee began fanning herself. "One of these years you'll break down and buy yourselves an air conditioner."

"Amen," said Chloe.

"Libba Jane and I are traditionalists," said Russ.

"Speak for yourself," replied his wife. She looked at her sister. "What do you think, Verna Lee?"

"About what?"

"The body."

Verna Lee sighed. "I imagine it's probably someone who was passing through. Who else could it be?"

"You were here fifteen years ago. Can you remember anything?"

"Nothing important." Her forehead wrinkled. "I'm worried about the wetlands. Libba, do you think the sale will really go through? Isn't that protected land?"

"The air station is protected and parts of the Chesapeake itself. Other than that, private land can be sold."

"What about loopholes?"

"I don't know of any."

"You work for the Environmental Protection Agency. Surely you can come up with something."

"Give me a break, Verna Lee. I didn't know Bailey was selling his land until Russ came in a few minutes ago. You're computer literate. Do some checking on your own." She glanced at her daughter. "You, too, Chloe. Meanwhile, can you give me a hand with dinner?"

Russ perked up. "What are we having?"

"Chicken casserole, and don't you complain."

His eyes twinkled. "I never complain. Don't give your daughter the wrong idea."

Chloe followed her mother into the kitchen and automatically began pulling silverware from the sideboard. "Is everything okay, Mom? Russ was only teasing and I haven't heard from Bailey in years."

"It isn't that. I guess I'm getting goose bumps at the idea of a body out there in the swamp right beside my running path."

"Does it bother you that Bailey's back?"

Libba pulled her casserole out of the oven. For a minute she didn't answer. Chloe watched her turn off the heat, wipe up a drop of spilled sauce and rinse the blade of her knife. Finally, she leaned against the counter, arms crossed against her chest, dark eyes wide and serious. "Four years ago you were fascinated with Bailey Jones and it scared me to death. I'm afraid you'll feel that way again."

"Would that be so terrible?"

Libba bit her bottom lip. "We don't really know who Bailey is. His mother—"

"Was a prostitute," Verna Lee finished for her. She'd come into the kitchen during the end of their conversation. "She was a good mother, Libba."

"Was she? Would a good mother ask her son to help her die?"

"There are circumstances you don't understand. Your life was different. You can't imagine not having medication and health insurance and painkillers. Not everybody is as fortunate."

Chloe shuddered. The temperature in the muggy

kitchen suddenly dropped. "You can't judge a person by his parents, Mom. Look at Dad."

"Excuse me. Eric Richards may have personality flaws, but compared to Lizzie Jones, he's *Redbook's* parent of the year."

"I didn't realize you disliked Bailey so much."

Libba sighed. "I don't dislike him, honey, but I don't want my daughter involved with him, either."

"I'm twenty years old, Mom."

"She has a point, Libba," said Verna Lee.

"Yes, she does." Libba smiled and changed the subject. "Shall we take bets on whether Russ will take more than one bite of this creation?"

"Why didn't you make something he likes?"

"I'm trying to add to our menu. We can't eat meat and potatoes every day."

Chloe's lips twitched. "I see your problem."

Libba Jane looked pointedly at her sister. "The truth is, he probably ate a sandwich at Perks and browbeat Verna Lee into loading on the mayonnaise."

"Actually, my mayonnaise is low fat, but don't you tell a soul or I'll be out of business." She frowned. "There is something I wanted to ask you about. Do you remember Wade Atkins?"

Libba thought a minute. "The name's familiar."

"He's a homicide detective assigned to the body found on Bailey's land."

The diversion proved a useful one. Libba was

distracted, leaving Chloe free to think about Bailey Jones. She pretended to listen. Occasionally, she threw out a noncommittal response, but her mind was far away, back to that summer four years ago when a truck, so rusty and banged up it no longer had a discernible color, left her choking on its dust.

When the truck came back for her, Chloe remembered being afraid, until she saw the driver. At eighteen, Bailey Jones already had the kind of dark archangel beauty that graced the canvases of Goya paintings. She'd fallen instantly and hard, asking nothing more than to share his silent spaces. From that moment on, the last emotion Bailey would inspire in her was fear, not even when he told her how he'd held the pillow over his mother's face and pressed the life from her body.

Eleven

Wade Atkins closed the file on his makeshift desk, leaned back in his chair and visualized waterfalls, ice cubes, mountaintops, ski slopes, anything and everything cool. His shirt stuck to his back and every muscle ached with the strain of opening up an investigation in weather so hot and wet the pavement on Main Street was showing the footprints of anyone who weighed over eighty pounds. What in the hell was the matter with the air conditioner? How did people expect a person to do anything about crime when he was sweating four gallons a minute?

This morning he'd walked into the police station at six o'clock to find a fax from the coroner's office. According to forensics, the human remains discovered on the Jones' property was a fifteen-year-old homicide. Six o'clock was eleven hours ago and he was still flipping through old files with no respite in sight. Wade knew where he wanted this day to end up, but he didn't know exactly how he would go about getting there. Still, there was something to be said for spontaneity. A good many things turned up when a person visited the unexpected.

Blake Carlisle wandered in from the back room. "I'm calling it a night, Wade. Can I get you anything?"

"Not a thing, Sheriff. I'll see you in the morning."

Carlisle glanced at the label on one of the files. He picked it up. "You won't find anything in here. Cole Delacourte is a straight shooter even if he did spend his life defending criminals. Don't waste your time."

Wade nodded. "I was just curious about a few things."

"What things?"

Wade experienced a flicker of annoyance. Sometimes it was better to work alone. "Did you know his wife?"

"Nola Ruth?"

"Yes. Nola Ruth Delacourte." Wade experimented with the name on his tongue.

Blake Carlisle grinned, looking younger than his thirty years. "Mrs. Delacourte and my grandmother would have been the same age, but they didn't run in the same circles. There's something you might have missed given you hightailed it out of here years ago."

"What's that?"

"Nola Ruth Delacourte was Verna Lee's natural mother. The news broke about four years ago."

Wade stared at him. "Holy shit. You're not serious?"

Carlisle nodded. "You'd think it would've been a scandal they couldn't live down, but those Delacourtes acted like it was the most normal situation in the world. Eventually, everybody just accepted it."

"Who's Verna Lee's father?"

"I doubt even Verna Lee knows that." Carlisle replaced the folder. "I'm gone. Don't work too hard."

"I never do."

Wade stared at the file in front of him. Was there anyone still alive who had run in Nola Ruth's circles, anyone besides her family? And what was her relationship to the black man who'd jumped bail fifteen years ago? Cole Delacourte was a civil rights attorney. Maybe that was the connection. He had a hunch it wasn't. After more than twenty years on the job, he'd learned to listen to his hunches. It was time to do some legwork.

"Hi there."

Wade hadn't heard the door open. He looked up and saw the tawny-haired woman standing uncertainly in the entrance. Pleasure surged through him. He stood. "Hello, Verna Lee."

"I thought you might like another sandwich." She held out her peace offering.

"Thanks. I skipped lunch. Will you come in and sit for a spell?"

She smiled her incredible smile, the one that showed her strong, white teeth and a hint of gum. Stepping inside, she allowed the door to close behind her. He watched while she trailed her finger across the top of his desk, stopping at the edge. "I guess it wouldn't hurt to stay for a minute."

He pulled a chair from behind the deputy's desk and motioned for her to sit down. "Coffee?"

She shook her head, sat down and crossed her legs, exposing the long length of her calf and a good eight inches of golden thigh. Wade swallowed and lowered himself into his own chair. "What can I do for you?"

Her eyes widened. "I didn't come for anything in particular. This is purely a social call."

Wade didn't pretend to have the inside track on the workings of a woman's mind, but he was a good ol' southern boy who'd spent more than his share of harvest nights hunting down raccoons that were nearly as unpredictable. He wanted to believe her, but he wasn't born yesterday. He smiled blandly. "Well, isn't that nice. How's your grandmother?"

She waved her hand. "Granny's fine, still going strong."

"Have you given any thought to my dinner invitation, Verna Lee?"

He watched the blush color her cheeks. "I brought you a sandwich, Wade. That's it."

"Fair enough," he said agreeably. Leaning back in his chair, he clasped his hands behind his head and waited. He could pass the time as well as anyone. "How's business?"

"Fine. You know how summer is. People eat less and drink more."

"Uh-huh."

"How is your investigation going?" she asked after a minute.

"My investigation?"

"You know, your murder investigation?"

Something clicked in his mind, the hazy glow of well-being giving way to steely alertness. He rocked forward so that all four legs of his chair rested on the floor. "It's going well, thank you, although I don't believe we've narrowed down the cause of death to murder."

"So, nothing new to report?"

"Such as?"

"I don't know. I just assumed—"

He prodded her. "You assumed—?"

"Well, I'm not sure, really," she fumbled. "I guess I thought you would know how long the body was there or how it happened. You know, some real statistics."

He laced his fingers together and leaned forward. "You wouldn't have any information for me, would you, Verna Lee?"

"Me?" She shook her head. "Of course not."

"If you did, you'd tell me?"

"Yes. I would."

"We're a long way from knowing anything at all. These things take time."

"I guess so." She sounded doubtful.

His voice gentled. "This whole town must have turned upside down when folks found out who your mama was."

She looked startled. "I don't remember mentioning anything about that."

"This is a small town, Verna Lee."

"I guess it is." She stood. "I'll let you get back to work."

He reached into his pocket. "How much do I owe you for the sandwich?"

"It's on the house."

"Thanks. I'll make it up to you."

He waited, puzzled, for a full minute after she'd left, breathing in the subtle lingering scent of peaches. Then he sat down at his desk, pulled out a steno pad, scribbled a few quick notes, replaced it in his bottom desk drawer and walked out into the thick, humid summer dusk.

Wade followed the road for a few miles along the creek. At the fork, he turned down a carriage path of twisted weeds and low-hanging trees he never could remember the names of. The path opened to a view captured on many an artist's postcard. At the end of a driveway of hard-packed earth, set back on a lush green lawn, bordered by ancient oaks, sat a glorious colonial mansion complete with deep porches, wide pillars and a thousand sparkling windowpanes, all reflected by the back-lit sky and the mighty Chesapeake, an ocean of liquid copper set aflame by the melting sun.

Wade, inured to the beauty of his home state by a lifetime of priceless landscapes, caught his breath. Yes, sir, it was one hell of a view, and the best part was that no one held the mortgage. It was completely paid for by dead Delacourtes long buried in the family plot. Cole Delacourte was definitely one of the haves of Marshy Hope Creek.

Setting the hand brake, he walked up the front steps, rang the doorbell and waited.

A black woman with ageless skin answered. She smiled when she saw Wade. "How can I help you?"

"I'm looking for Mr. Delacourte. Is he at home?"

"Who shall I say is calling?"

He flashed his badge. "Detective Wade Atkins, Wicomico County Police Department."

"I'll check for you." She didn't ask him inside. He bit back a smile. The humor of his position wasn't lost on him. He wasn't a guest, therefore he wasn't invited into the parlor, but he wasn't a servant, either. What, he wondered, would be the appropriate setting for an officer of the law? He didn't have long to wait. Within minutes, the woman led him through the long hallway out to the back porch.

Cole Delacourte sat on a patio chair facing the bay. "Good evening, Wade. It's been a long time. Can I offer you anything?"

"Nothing, thanks." Wade took a seat beside the old man. "Excuse me, sir, but have we met?"

"I helped out your brother Clem now and again. You were too little to remember."

Was it his imagination, or was there tension stiffening the man's shoulders?

"What brings you out here?" Delacourte asked.

"I guess you heard about the body that turned up on Bailey Jones's land."

Cole frowned. "Actually, I hadn't heard. I don't go into town much when it's this hot."

Wade nodded. "I understand your granddaughter is staying with you for the summer."

Cole's forehead cleared. "Yes, she is."

"Do you know about her relationship with the Jones boy?"

"They were friends. His name hasn't come up in a long time. Why do you ask?"

The detective leaned back in the comfortable patio chair. "Can you fill me in on the situation with his mother and the land she left him?"

"You must have the report. My memory isn't what it was."

"I'm not talking about the arrest and trial. I want to know about Lizzie Jones. Who was she close to? Who's the boy's father?"

"Lizzie was—" Cole paused "—unusual. She liked men. They liked her. Why ask me?"

"I've been looking through police files. You helped her out a number of times. There's the matter of the wetlands. They belonged to the Wentworths. Then, all of a sudden, about fifteen years ago, they changed hands. Why is that, I wonder."

"How should I know? I didn't help with that transaction. You should ask Quentin."

Wade grinned. "I intend to, but I'm fairly sure not much happens around here that you don't know about."

"I'm flattered," Cole said dryly, "but you're barking up the wrong tree. I know that land originally belonged to Benteen Jones. How Wentworth got his hands on it, I can only imagine."

"Don't like him, do you?"

Cole's lips tightened. "Not particularly."

"Care to tell me why?"

"It's ancient history, and it has no bearing on our conversation. Wentworth may not be my choice of company on a long plane ride, but he operates by the book. He was a superior court judge, for heaven's sake."

"We both know that doesn't necessarily follow."

"What exactly are you implying?"

Wade was saved the trouble of a reply by the opening of the French doors leading to the house. A slender, dark-haired woman stepped out onto the porch carrying a glass of lemonade. He recognized her immediately. Libba Hennessey had turned out to be one good-looking woman.

"Daddy, I didn't know you had company." Her soft, delta-flavored voice was very like Verna Lee's.

Wade stood. "Good evening, ma'am. I'm Detective Wade Atkins."

"I thought so. Verna Lee told me about you." Kissing her father on the forehead, she dropped into an empty chair and groaned. "I'm exhausted. I can only stay for a minute, but the lure of pure calm was too tempting to pass by." She smiled at Wade. "What's going on?"

"I came to ask a few questions. Maybe you can help us out."

"Ask away. I'll help if I can."

Wade found himself staring at her, comparing her to Verna Lee. She was lighter skinned, but her eyes were darker, huge brown orbs against the creamy canvas of her face. She was long-legged, too, and full-breasted, but her bones were finer, her features sharper. Her ancestry was obviously French, not African, more refined, less exotic. Libba's hair was the color of expensive French roast, thick and fine and straight, nothing at all like the tangled mop of tawny curls that was Verna Lee's trademark. Still, the resemblance between the two was striking. He'd noticed the smile immediately.

She said something and he wasn't listening.

"I beg your pardon?"

"I said, any news on the mysterious body?"

Cole frowned. "You know about that, too?"

Libba laughed. "Who doesn't? What else is there to talk about?"

Wade looked out across the bay, pretending interest in a pair of coots sitting on the water. "I'm still trying to fit the pieces together. Like I said, I have a few questions." He smiled. "But maybe I'm asking the wrong ones." He could see the fine line between her eyes. Wade prided himself on knowing people. She was curious, nothing more. "Tell me about Ms. Fontaine and your mother."

"Verna Lee is more like Mama than I am, isn't that right, Daddy?"

"I'm hardly an expert on Verna Lee."

Libba laughed, scooped an ice cube from her glass and, unselfconsciously, rubbed it under her chin, down her throat and between her breasts. "You know what I mean. Verna Lee is seductive in the same way Mama was. It didn't matter what my mother wore or how she twisted up her hair. She had a sultry, mysterious flair, and her voice, well, it was sugary and dangerous and lazy all mixed into one." She warmed to her subject. "When Mama walked into a room, she was the only woman there. It's the same with Verna Lee. They're like Delilah from the Bible, every man's fantasy."

Cole stared at her. "What a shame you never considered writing as a career."

"I wish I'd met your mother," said Wade.

"There wasn't a man who didn't appreciate her, but she certainly had her standards. She was very particular about who I brought home."

"How is that different from any mother?" Cole asked mildly.

"Given her past, she could have been more understanding."

Wade pretended ignorance. "Her past?"

Cole sighed. "Libba's referring to the years before her mother married me. She met a man in New Orleans. They married, but Nola's father used his influence to have the marriage annulled. He didn't know she was pregnant with Verna Lee." He cleared his throat. "Even if he had…the times were difficult."

"I can imagine," Wade said dryly. "What happened to him?"

"Who?"

"Verna Lee's father."

"I'm not sure. Nola Ruth never heard from him again."

Not by the flicker of an eyelash did Wade reveal anything other than perfunctory interest in the conversation. Casually, he assessed the older man sitting across from him, noting the lean, aristocratic cant of his bones, the thick, white hair, the faded blue eyes, the gently lined skin. Cole Delacourte was a principled man. No hint of scandal had ever been attached to his name. What must it have been like for him when his wife's secret was revealed? And why didn't he know what Wade knew; fifteen years ago Magnolia Ruth Delacourte had hustled herself into town to post bail for a certain Anton Devereaux who'd been arrested for refusing to sign a speeding ticket. He never showed up at the subsequent hearing and Nola Ruth forfeited her money.

How could an important white civil rights attorney not know that his wife had bailed out a black man from the county jail?

Or, maybe he did know and just wasn't saying.

Twelve

Chloe Richards ducked into the cereal aisle at John's Food King, hoping no one she knew, even remotely, would associate her with the screaming child blocking the candy and comic-book section. Nothing in her entire babysitting experience, which was negligible at best, had prepared her for Gina Marie. At this very moment, her baby sister was sprawled out in front of the Reese's Pieces and Milky Way bins, holding her breath and pounding her small fists on the floor. With any luck she would pass out and Chloe would be able to haul her out without suffering a black eye from the flailing fists. It would be too much to hope that the distraught three-year-old wouldn't be recognized.

An amused voice spoke up behind her. "I think you lost something."

Chloe braced herself and turned around. Bailey Jones, carrying a six-pack of Budweiser, looking cool and expensive in a buttery linen shirt with the sleeves rolled up and jeans so soft and faded they were nearly white, laughed down at her.

"Don't start," she muttered. "You have no idea how awful this is for me. I can't handle her. No sane person would do this, not even for her own mother."

"Quitter," he taunted, the lights dancing in his black eyes.

Her eyes narrowed. "I suppose you think you could do better."

"I know I could."

"Twenty bucks says you can't."

"Shame on you, Chloe Richards. You know I can't turn down a challenge."

She folded her arms across her chest. "Go for it. You have five minutes."

"What do I get if I win?"

"I told you. Twenty bucks."

"No offense, Chloe, but I don't need money."

She shrugged. "That's all I've got that you could possibly want."

He stared at her, an odd expression on his face. "How about meeting me tonight at the water hole behind Hadley's peach grove?"

"What time?"

"Ten o'clock."

Gina's sobs hadn't subsided. "What if you can't do it? What do I get?"

"I'll babysit for an afternoon while you go swimming at the club."

A smile played at the corner of her lips. "You're on."

He handed her the six-pack and disappeared **around** the corner.

Within seconds Gina Marie was silent. Chloe waited. Surely she was only catching her breath and would start up again as soon as the novelty of Bailey Jones passed. The silence continued. Curious, Chloe peeked around the corner. Gina, her eyes twice their normal size, was sitting upright with her thumb wedged tightly in her mouth. She stared at Bailey, watching as he tore open a package of Reese's Pieces. Tentatively, she held out her hand while he crouched down and shook several pieces of candy into her palm.

Chloe was furious. She marched down the aisle to stand before them. "What do you think you're doing?"

Bailey grinned. "You said I couldn't get her to be quiet. She's quiet. You lose."

"You weren't supposed to use candy. I could have given her candy myself. That's the reason she's crying. I told her she couldn't have it."

"You didn't tell me I couldn't use it," he said reasonably.

"Well, now I'm telling you and you lose."

"Too late. She's already eaten it."

Chloe looked at her little sister. Gina's mouth and the palms of her hands were stained chocolate-orange. "She's not supposed to have candy."

"Why not?"

"It isn't good for her. My mom doesn't like her to have candy."

Bailey stood. "Libba Jane needs to come down to earth."

Chloe dug her fists into her hips. "What does that mean?"

"She can't expect you to step in and take over without some tricks of your own. You're not a mother. This is new for you. You won't be able to do things the way she'd do them."

Chloe eyed him suspiciously. "When did you get to be so smart?"

He emptied the rest of the bag into Gina Marie's sticky hands. "There's nothing to it. Give 'em what they want, I always say."

Her voice cooled. "Really? Does your philosophy apply to anything else?"

"Whenever it works." He smiled at Gina Marie. "C'mon, kid. I'll give you and your big sister a ride home."

Obediently, Gina scrambled to her feet.

Chloe shook her head. "No, thanks. We'll walk."

"I don't want to walk," said Gina Marie.

Bailey ignored her and spoke to Chloe. "It's too hot to walk and I'm going your way."

"You don't know where I'm going."

"Let me guess." He frowned, pretending to think. "The way I see it is you have two choices, your mother's house or your granddad's. Either way, I can handle it. Besides, Gina Marie might like riding in my car."

"You don't have a back seat."

"She can sit on your lap."

Chloe shook her head. "It's against the law. She needs a car seat."

"This is Marshy Hope Creek, Chloe, not Los Angeles. Who's gonna see us? The sheriff's caught up in figuring out who the hell showed up dead on my mother's land. He's not gonna care if a little girl doesn't have a car seat."

"That isn't the point. It's dangerous."

"I'll drive slow."

"I don't want to drive slow," piped up Gina. "My daddy drives fast."

Bailey glanced at the little girl. "She sounds like Tweety Bird."

"She's three years old," Chloe replied. "She'll grow into her *R*s.'"

"C'mon, Chloe," Bailey coaxed. "Live dangerously."

"I don't think so." She returned Bailey's Budweiser and reached for Gina's hand. "Let's go home."

The corners of Gina Marie's mouth trembled. "I don't want to walk home. It's too hot. I want a drink of water."

"We'll have lemonade at home," Chloe promised. "Mommy will be home. We'll see Mommy and have lemonade. You'll like that."

"No." Gina's voice cracked, a sign Chloe was learning to recognize. "I'm telling Mama you made me walk. I don't like you."

"She doesn't have her *L*s, either," Bailey observed.

Chloe snapped. "That does it." She swooped down on Gina Marie, picked her up and carried her, arms and legs flailing, out of the store.

Bailey threw a ten-dollar bill on the counter and caught up with Chloe. "Stop this," he said when they were safely outside. "You're turning this into something it isn't." Gina Marie was screaming in earnest. "You can't carry her all the way home the way she's behaving. You'll kill each other. Get in the car and I'll take you wherever you want to go. I'm sorry I ever started this."

She stared at him, pride warring with the idea of a quick, convenient ride back to her mother's house. Her resolve wavered. Then Gina's elbow caught her squarely in the mouth. Without another word she dumped her sister unceremoniously in his arms. "Gina, you're a spoiled brat and, right now, I don't like you, either." She nodded at Bailey. "Let's go."

Within three minutes of pulling out on to the road leading to Hennessey House, Gina was asleep in her arms. "Thank God," Chloe said fervently.

Bailey grinned, keeping his voice low. "Poor kid. She's tuckered out. She isn't much more than a baby. Have a little patience."

"You try taking care of her all day."

"I doubt if I'd fare any better than you. She wants her mother. Why are you on baby duty anyway?"

"My mother's working today. She thinks I should get to know Gina."

"Give it a try. You're reasonably intelligent. It shouldn't take long to figure it out."

She looked out the window, no longer interested in arguing. On both sides of the road, the bay, massive, serene, light-struck, golden in the lingering rays of the afternoon sun, tea-colored in the shadows, rolled out before them. Fingers of water lapped the grassy, tree-lined shore. An occasional late-season duck or osprey flew overhead, bound for the cleaner, cooler climate of Maine. The wetlands squirmed with life. Thick as soup, the air brackish, fecund, stinking slightly of decay, permeating hair, skin and clothes, seeped through the sealed windows. Gradually, she felt herself relax.

Her mood was interrupted by a groan from Bailey.

"What's the matter?"

Cursing, he pulled to the side of the road and waited.

Chloe glanced over her shoulder. An unmarked car with a flashing red light parked behind them. She watched as a tall, blond man in civilian clothes approached the car, motioning for Bailey to roll down the window.

"Bailey Jones?"

"Yeah?"

He held up his badge. "I've left three messages for you to call me, one I taped to your door. You've ignored all of them," He glanced inside the car. "There's a car-seat law for kids in the state of Maryland."

"Write me a ticket."

"Step outside the car, please."

"Jesus Christ. What's your problem?"

Wade remained polite. "Step outside the car," he repeated.

White-lipped, Bailey climbed out and spread-eagled himself against the side of the Porsche.

Wade kept his voice low. "Listen up, smart-ass. Try out all the attitude you want on your own, but when you've got a lady and a kid with you, you better think twice. You're this close—" he held his thumb and forefinger an inch apart "—to having your car impounded, not to mention the embarrassment of having your passengers watch while I cuff you and then drive you away in the back of my car. It so happens that today is your lucky day, mostly because I'm not a traffic cop and I've got other things on my mind, like the bones on that land you're in such a hurry to sell. Now, the way I see it is you have two choices—you can make a U-turn right now on this road, drop off the lady and the little girl and we can meet somewhere and have a conversation or you can ride back to the station with me. Either way, we're gonna talk."

Slowly, Bailey straightened. "Do you know where I'm staying?"

"I do."

"I'll be there in twenty minutes."

Wade nodded and walked away.

Bailey took a minute to settle his nerves before making his way back to his car.

"What happened?" asked Chloe.

"He wants to talk to me about the body on my land."

"That's it? That's why he pulled you over?"

"It appears so."

"That doesn't make sense. How did he know where to find you? He must have been following us."

He shrugged.

"What's going on, Bailey?"

"Drop it. Okay?"

The tension inside the car was thick with unsaid words. Conversation, such as it was, dwindled to the merest monosyllable. Even Gina, who'd awakened, sensed the mood and burrowed down in Chloe's arms, unusually silent. Bailey dropped them off in front of Hennessey House with a casual "See you around," and sped off.

Chloe watched him drive away. Bailey was an enigma, as disturbing and volatile as he'd always been. She wouldn't bother with him. She would call Tess. Maybe she could be talked into a movie. If not, there was always Verna Lee, sexy, dramatic-looking, sensible, independent Verna Lee, who had escaped the drama of a husband and children.

Wade was leaning against his car waiting when Bailey pulled in to the driveway of the Busby house.

"I had to drop Chloe off at her mother's."

"Chloe?"

"Libba Hennessey's daughter."

Libba Jane. Nola Ruth's daughter, Verna Lee's half sister. Wade filed the information in the think-about-it-later part of his brain. "Nice house," he commented as he followed Bailey inside. The temperature was an arctic seventy-two degrees.

"It still belongs to the Busbys. I'm renting it for

the summer." Bailey flung himself on the couch. "What do you want with me anyway? I heard those bones are fifteen years old. I'm twenty-two, which makes me all of seven when that body was dumped on my mother's land."

"Rumor gets around fast in a small town. Who said anything about the body being dumped?"

Bailey shrugged. "It was a not-so wild guess."

Wade pulled a straight-backed chair from around the dining-room table and sat down. "Tell me about your mama."

Bailey reddened. "I thought that subject was old news."

"Tell me about the land you inherited from her."

"What are you getting at?"

"That land belonged to Judge Quentin Wentworth. Fifteen years ago it was deeded to your mama. How do you suppose that happened?"

"I don't know anything about that."

"Think about it. I've got time."

"The land belonged to my granddaddy, Benteen Jones. He lost it in a poker game. Maybe Quentin had an attack of conscience."

Wade shook his head. "That doesn't sound much like Wentworth."

"You know him?"

"You might say that." He changed the subject. "I

mean no disrespect, son, but was Quentin Wentworth having an affair with your mother?"

"How the hell should I know?" Bailey flung back angrily. "I was a little kid, for Christ's sake."

Wade stared at him for what seemed like longer than the minute it actually was. "Fair enough," he said at last. He pulled out his card. "If you think of anything, let me know."

"Keep your card. I won't use it."

Wade laid the card on the coffee table. "Stranger things have happened."

Thirteen

His mind on autopilot, Wade Atkins navigated the road leading to the small two-bedroom house he'd occupied for most of the last five years. The single lot, sandy, strewn with pines and bordered by a small finger of the Chesapeake, appealed to him the minute he first saw it. He'd built the house himself, board by board, shingle by shingle, down to the maple cabinets in the kitchen, the skylights in the bedrooms and the distressed-wood floors on all three levels. The rear foundation sat securely on a slab of concrete, while the front deck balanced on stilts directly above the water.

His view was spectacular. As the sun set, the bay awoke. After dishes were washed and the trash dumped, he would pull two beers from the back of the refrigerator and sit out on his deck, pleasantly buzzed, reeking of insect repellent, watching fire-flies flicker around the gas lamps, dancing toward the light and back again until, eventually, they succumbed to their addiction and baked in the deadly glow. When night settled over the bay, frogs croaked in the marshes, water moccasins slithered through the tepid, tea-colored water and crickets sounded as loud as foghorns across the Atlantic.

As far as Wade was concerned, this was his own slice of heaven. Other people needed vacations to Florida, Europe, Hawaii, the Grand Canyon. Not Wade. Give him a hot grill, eight ounces of fresh shad, some steamed crabs, a hunk of sourdough bread, a cold beer, a good book and his own back-yard. A man couldn't ask for more, except maybe a good woman to share it with. He didn't regret that Susan and he never had children. If they'd come, they both would have welcomed them, but he was just as glad they hadn't. Children muddied the wa-ters, complicated the equation, upset the applecart, so to speak. He said the words out loud, enjoying the way the clichés rolled off his tongue. Whichever way he looked at it, the responsibility was more than he wanted to handle.

Inside the house, Wade flipped on the air-conditioning, threw the files he'd brought home on the coffee table and shrugged into a well-worn T-shirt and faded-denim cutoffs. Then he popped the top off a bottle of light ale, walked into a pair of flip-flops and carried the files, a box of crackers and a brick of cheese out to the deck where he sank into a low beach chair.

Relishing the slide of cool liquid down his throat, he closed his eyes and savored the moment. A faint breeze fluttered across the water. Soon the sun would set. Life was good. It was better than good. It was interesting.

Before his slight doze became a bona fide nap, he roused himself, gnawed a hunk of cheese off the brick, swallowed a few crackers and washed them down with beer. Reaching for a file, he settled down to concentrate, looking for something, anything, that would give him a lead.

An hour later, the light was nearly gone and it was closing in on nine o'clock. He debated whether to finish looking through one last folder or call it a night. The name on the folder caught his eye and curiosity won. He picked it up and began to read.

He grinned. Apparently Verna Lee Fontaine was a rabble-rouser. She'd picketed every new developer within forty miles, handed out pamphlets, made speeches, even chained herself to trees and ended up spending a night in jail. Wade grinned. That was her California influence. Children in Appalachia couldn't read, ended up with rickets for lack of milk and had six kids by the time they were twenty-two, while residents of the Golden State were lying down in front of bulldozers to save a tree. He sifted through the news clippings. Nothing new here.

Skimming quickly, at first he didn't see the note buried in the middle of the third paragraph. But when he did, it was as if everything else faded into the background. Quickly, he read the fifteen-year-old report once through completely, and then again, slowly. What did it mean? Verna Lee was a teacher. She had a degree from UC Berkeley. Fifteen years ago she'd come home. The question was, *why?* Why was a graduate of a top-ten university serving coffee in Marshy Hope Creek?

The following morning Wade poured an extra scoop of coffee into his French press. He hadn't slept well and he needed the jolt of caffeine. He debated between trying to sweet-talk Verna Lee into spending time with him so he could get some answers, or he could visit her in an official capacity. For some reason, both avenues bothered him.

Verna Lee was a strong-minded woman and she wasn't stupid. She wouldn't take to a man who withheld the facts. Why that would weigh with him at all was still a nebulous thought, without form or definition, in his brain. He'd stop in at Perks and test the waters, order up some of those famous lemon muffins Carlisle was always talking about.

The drive to town was uneventful. Wade followed a tomato truck stuffed so full that the juice pouring out of the overflow vents was like a hose bathing the streets. Eventually, he passed on the shoulder, taking the detour to Marshy Hope Creek and Perks Coffeehouse.

Verna Lee, busy blending cappuccinos, had her back to the door. He studied her for a minute, trying to imagine her in a classroom, dressed in conservative clothes, her wild hair restrained. He couldn't do it. She was colorful and flamboyant and no one would ever call her tactful, not the typical blueprint for a teacher. Was that why she'd given it up, or was there another reason, one she didn't relish owning up to?

She turned and caught him staring at her. "Hey," she said. "You're here early."

He smiled engagingly. "I came in for some of your lemon muffins."

"I'll be with you in a minute." She turned back to the cappuccino machine.

Wade sat down on one of the couches, looking around to see if he recognized anybody. He didn't. The price of progress.

Eventually, the shop emptied out. Verna Lee poured a cup of coffee and set it in front of him.

"Start on this and I'll heat up your muffin. I haven't had breakfast yet. Do you mind if I join you?"

"Nothing would please me more."

He sipped the steaming coffee, waiting patiently until she was seated beside him. Biting into the moist lemon muffin lifted his spirits. "Where did you learn to bake the way you do?"

"I've had some interesting jobs in my life," she replied. "Once, when I lived in San Francisco, I assisted a pastry chef. I loved it. I always knew I wanted to do something that had to do with cooking."

She'd opened the door. Wade decided to step over the threshold. "Tell me about it."

"There's nothing much to tell," she hedged. "I tried it and didn't like it, so I came home."

"Is that where you went to college?"

She looked at him, her tawny eyebrows lifted. "How do you know I went to college?"

"You talk like a college girl. I heard there are some mighty fine colleges in California. My guess is you went to one of them."

"I graduated from UC Berkeley."

"In what?"

"Art history."

"That doesn't sound much like cooking to me."

"I guess not."

"What made you change your direction?"

She sat completely still without answering.

"I'd really like to know, Verna Lee," he said gently.

The bell on the door jingled, a sign that she had a customer.

He shrugged. "Saved by the bell."

She surprised him. "You know, Wade, maybe I will take you up on that dinner invitation. I sure hope you can cook, because I have no intention of doing so, and the kind of restaurant food I like isn't possible on a public servant's salary."

He grinned. "You're on. How about tomorrow night at seven, my house?"

"Where do you live?"

"About thirty miles from here. I have a house on the bay."

"That's a long way to go for dinner."

"I'll make it worth your while."

She appeared to be considering her options. Finally she nodded. "All right. I'll be there."

"You're serious."

"I am."

"Somehow, I thought this would be harder."

She shrugged. "I guess it's your lucky day."

He stood, walked to the door and then turned back. "When's the last time you saw Bailey Jones?"

She frowned. "A few days ago, I guess. I don't remember."

"Did you see him at any time yesterday?"

She thought for a minute and shook her head. "Definitely not yesterday. Why?"

"No reason. I'll see you tomorrow."

Wade drove down the main highway and took the narrow surface road for another three miles. He turned the air conditioner to full blast, allowing the refreshing flow to bathe his face one last time before turning off the engine. Regretfully, he left the car to climb the steps of the largest, most ostentatious home ever built on the right side of the small waterway that had given Marshy Hope Creek its name, and rang the bell.

A pale blond woman dressed in a slim-fitting sheath and matching sandals answered the door. Beside her stood Bailey Jones. Wade's mind logged in several possibilities even as he schooled his expression into one of polite disinterest.

Tracy's hand flew to her throat. "May I help you?" she stammered.

Wade held up his badge. "I have a few questions for Judge Wentworth."

She waved her hand, dismissing the young man beside her. "Bailey was just leaving."

Wade noted the tensing of Bailey's jaw and the thin white line around his lips. "Morning, Mr. Jones," he said softly.

Bailey nodded.

"Don't let me chase you away."

"Like the lady said, I was just leaving." Without a backward look, he was down the stairs heading toward the silver Porsche parked in the shade.

Wade turned back to Tracy. She looked cool and composed once again. His brain acknowledged that she was attractive, but for reasons he couldn't explain, she didn't appeal to him. Not that a girl from a place like this would have accepted so much as a tissue to blow her nose from the likes of him. Girls like Tracy Wentworth set their sights on boys from families who lived on the right side of the creek, and sometimes even they weren't good enough. "If the judge is home, I'd like to speak with him."

"Is something wrong?"

"I'd like to speak with him, please."

"Oh." She attempted a laugh. "He's popular this morning. I'll tell him you're here."

Once again, Wade found himself relegated to the entry. This one had a bench seat, but he decided against it. He took advantage of his wait by peering through an open door into the living room. Above the fireplace hung a life-size portrait of the judge in his heyday. "Tight-looking son of a bitch," muttered Wade under his breath. He heard footsteps in the hall and moved back to the entry.

Two bright spots of color stained Tracy's cheeks. "Judge Wentworth will see you now."

Wade wondered what it would take to get her to call the judge "daddy." He followed her down a long hall past several sterile, impeccably kept rooms. Tracy stopped at the double doors and knocked. Without waiting for an answer, she waved him inside, closing them behind him.

Quentin Wentworth sat in a chair of burgundy leather behind an enormous mahogany desk, the top so empty and champagne polished Wade could see his own reflection plain as day. Surrounding the judge were the tools of his profession, glass-enclosed shelves with gold-embossed, leather-covered books, degrees from Vanderbilt and Duke, an expensive laptop computer, an inkwell and a heavy, personally engraved fountain pen. Two high-backed chairs faced the desk.

He neither stood nor offered his hand. "You're an Atkins, all right. Don't try to deny it."

"It hadn't occurred to me." Wade sat down without waiting for an invitation.

Color flared along the judge's cheekbones. "To what do I owe the honor of this visit?"

"I passed Bailey Jones on the way out."

The judge's color deepened. "So?"

"I was told you don't run in the same circles."

"Please. Don't insult me."

"Mind if I ask what he was doing here?"

"Not at all, as long as you tell me why it's of significance."

Wade rested his leg across his knee. "I'm conducting an investigation. At this point it's all fact finding." He looked pointedly at the judge.

Wentworth sighed. "He wanted legal advice."

"Why would he come to you?"

"I was a lawyer, Detective, a damn good one."

"So was Cole Delacourte. If memory serves me right, he was the one who got Bailey acquitted the first time."

"This isn't a criminal matter. He wanted to know if he had to return the escrow deposit to the buyers."

"What was your answer?"

Wentworth frowned. "That isn't your concern. Surely you didn't come here this morning to ask about Bailey Jones."

"No," agreed Wade. "I came to ask you about the late Mrs. Wentworth."

The judge's face lost some of its color. "What on earth—? Amanda has been dead fifteen years. Of what interest could she possibly be to you?"

"Well, it's like this, Quentin." He relished using the judge's given name. He had a hunch it riled him. "I was thinking what a coincidence it is that Mrs. Wentworth happened to lose her life in the very same year and on the very same road as the body that was found on Bailey's property."

"I'm sure a great many people lost their lives that year in the state of Maryland."

"You're right about that, but not on the same road. In fact, I can't think of a single other person who died on Highway 39 that year."

"My wife had an unfortunate car accident on the way to visit her sister. Her funeral was well attended. She's buried, per her request, in her family's plot in Laurel, Mississippi. I'm sure her sister will be happy to give you a tour if you're so inclined."

"As a matter of fact, I might be so inclined, Quentin. I'd sure appreciate it if you'd give me directions."

"I'll be happy to do so."

Wade waited.

Wentworth's eyebrows rose. "You want it now, this minute?"

Wade smiled blandly. "If you don't mind."

Thin-lipped, the judge pulled a pad of paper from his top drawer and took the splendid, monogrammed pen in his fingers to scribble down an address and phone number. He tore off the sheet of paper and pushed it across the desk toward Wade. "I hope this concludes our visit," he said.

"There is one more thing."

"Yes?"

"Exactly what was the official cause of Mrs. Wentworth's death?"

"Her vehicle rolled over the embankment. The car ignited. Silas Grimes, our sheriff at the time, found her."

Wade stroked his chin. "No autopsy?"

"There was a pathology report on what was left of her."

"Whatever happened to old Silas?"

"I believe he retired somewhere in Florida. He was certainly of an age. In case you're wondering, I don't keep track of ex-police officers."

"Of course not." Wade stood and pocketed the piece of paper. "Thanks for your time. I'll see myself out."

Deep in thought, Wade drove back to town trying to piece together the fragments of his recent conversation. So far, he didn't have much. There was nothing shady about Amanda Wentworth's death. Still, her husband's reaction was interesting. Reactions meant something when it came to cracking a case. Reaching into his pocket, he felt the edge of the paper the judge had given him. He had every intention of following up.

Drusilla Washington, wearing a wide-brimmed straw hat, knelt in the dirt, tugging weeds from around her purple string bean plants. She dropped them into her apron pocket. Verna Lee stood over her looking anxious. "God, it's hot. Take a break, Gran. You've been at this all morning. It's time for lunch. I'll make you a sandwich and a glass of iced tea."

"In a minute. I'm near done." The old woman wiped her forehead with the back of her hand, leaving a smear of dirt. "You go on in and start fixin' the food. I'll be there in a minute."

Verna Lee bit her lip. "There's something I want to talk to you about. It's important."

"Everythin's important to the young," Drusilla muttered. "Hurry, hurry, hurry. Slow down, girl. What's the hurry?"

"You've got to eat."

Drusilla looked up. The brim of her hat shaded her face, hiding the deeply wrinkled skin, the red-veined eyes. "I don't get hungry much anymore, Verna Lee. Don't go to no trouble."

Verna Lee sighed. "All right, Gran. Come inside when you're ready. I'll wait."

Washing her hands at the kitchen sink, she wondered how her grandmother made ends meet. In her younger years Drusilla had been midwife to the sharecropper families in the Cove. Cash poor, they'd paid her in goods, chickens, eggs, an occasional round of cheese, fresh vegetables, a cured ham, loaves of bread, whatever surplus they could spare from their own families. But age had changed all that. She could no longer move quickly and, on occasion, her mind wandered back to people and places Verna Lee didn't recognize.

The old woman's small house had been Verna Lee's home for as long as she could remember. She'd never asked her grandmother how she'd actually acquired it and Drusilla never offered an explanation.

Years ago Verna Lee learned that Drusilla was not a blood relation. She'd delivered Nola Ruth Delacourte's half-black baby girl and ended up taking her home. In retrospect, she realized that life with Drusilla wasn't all that bad. It was just that she'd wanted so much more. She'd left home to attend college in California and learned, all too quickly, what *more* meant and hightailed it back to her roots. Even that hadn't turned into the safe haven she'd imagined. For years the events surrounding her return to Marshy Hope Creek simmered in the back of her mind. She'd nearly suppressed them, and now this.

Behind her the door opened. "I'm done for today," Drusilla said. "What did you bring me?"

"I made those chicken-salad sandwiches you like. You know, the ones with cream cheese and raisin-walnut bread. I even cut off the crusts."

"That's wasteful, Verna Lee," her grandmother

gently chided her. "Ain't nothin' wrong with crust. Was a time when I would've been grateful for bread crusts."

"That time's over, Gran. Go wash up while I set the table."

Seated across from each other at the small dinette Drusilla had picked up at a yard sale, Verna Lee brought up the subject foremost on her mind. "I was thinking about when I first came back here from San Francisco."

Drusilla nodded. "About five years ago, wasn't it?"

Verna Lee was used to her grandmother's lapses. "More like fifteen years ago, Gran."

Drusilla's forehead creased in thought. "Time sure does fly by when a body gets old."

Verna Lee continued. "I tried to get a teaching job, remember?"

"I remember."

"Something happened in California, Gran. Do you remember what I told you about that?"

Drusilla thought. "No," she said at last.

Verna Lee tried another approach. "What about Lizzie Jones? You remember her, don't you, Gran?"

Drusilla was looking at her as if she'd lost her mind. "What's got into you, child? How could you think I'd be forgettin' Lizzie?"

"She was in love with Judge Wentworth."

Drusilla nodded. "I remember when her boy was born. She was so proud."

"Something happened to her, Gran. It was about the time Amanda Wentworth died." Verna Lee leaned forward. "Do you know anything about that?"

Drusilla's eyes clouded over. "My memory's not so good anymore."

"Think, Gran. Think hard."

"Camille told me something about the girl."

"What girl?"

"Tracy's girl."

"This isn't about Tracy, Gran. It's about Lizzie and Mrs. Wentworth. Did Lizzie ever say anything about them?"

Drusilla picked apart her sandwich, scraped off the cream cheese and licked her fingers. "This is good. You always were a good cook."

Verna Lee gave up. She hadn't really expected Drusilla to answer, but she had to try. She poured her grandmother another glass of iced tea and began clearing the table. "I'll do these dishes and run along when I'm finished. Promise me you won't do any more work outside today, or at least until the sun goes down."

"You worry too much."

"Just say yes, Gran."

"Yes," parroted the old woman.

After leaving Drusilla's house, Verna Lee didn't go directly home. Inside her car, she aimed the air-conditioning vents at her face, turned left on the main road and headed toward the highway. Cold air dried her eyes and her lips and straightened the tiny whorls of hair around her face. She fumbled for the water bottle she always kept in her glove compartment, twisted off the cap and drank deeply, grimacing. The water was warm, metallic tasting.

She was closing in on Cole Delacourte's big white house. Verna Lee liked Cole. He was a fair man, a decent man. Who else would marry a woman with the kind of past his wife had brought with her? Nola Ruth hadn't hidden it from him. She'd confessed right after he'd proposed. Nothing dishonest about Nola Ruth.

Verna Lee's mouth twisted. Nothing except the small matter of keeping her own daughter in the dark for thirty years and then, even after said daughter knew the truth, pretending she didn't exist. Anything to protect Libba Jane, the planned child, the golden girl, the fortunate and inevitable union of two, wealthy, blue-blooded southern families.

Whenever Verna Lee thought about her half sister, her resentment eased. There must have been a strain of Gypsy blood somewhere in the Delacourte/Beauchamp lineage, because Libba Jane was her own person. At the age of twenty she'd thumbed her nose at her parents and run off with Chloe's father, an actor bound for Hollywood. It took her seventeen years to swallow her pride and come home and that was only because her mother had suffered a debilitating stroke.

At the end of her life, Nola Ruth wanted both of her children around her. Libba Jane gained a sister and Verna Lee found a family. There had been a few glitches but, for the most part, the blending had been a smooth one. Libba's warm acceptance set the stage for Verna Lee's forgiveness. The children helped, too. Verna Lee adored her nieces and, after seventeen years in California, Libba Jane needed a confidante who'd seen more of the world than Marshy Hope Creek, Maryland.

By and large, Verna Lee was happy. There were few things she would change about her life. Why, then, was she dredging up a past no one alive could possibly know about?

Fourteen

The sheriff wasn't in. Wade nodded at the deputy, sat down at his desk in Carlisle's office and tried once again to contact Amanda Wentworth's sister, the one she was planning to visit when her car drove off the road and ended her life. He was beginning to think that the woman had gone away somewhere. She was either out of town or she was screening her calls. He ran his hand through his thatch of white-blond hair and shook his head. "Get a grip, Wade," he said to himself. "Just because the woman hasn't called you back doesn't mean she's avoiding you."

She answered on the fifth ring. He wasn't prepared for a real person. "Mrs. Dixon?"

There was the slightest hesitation. "Who's calling, please?"

"Sheriff Wade Atkins from Marshy Hope Creek, Maryland."

"What can I do for you, Sheriff?"

"I'd like to ask you a few questions, if you have a minute."

"I'm seventy-four years old, Sheriff. I have more than a minute. What else would I be doing?"

"I'm hoping you'll give me some information regarding your late sister."

"Why?"

"Some questions have come up about her accident."

"I'll try."

"I understand Mrs. Wentworth was on her way to see you when she died. Is that true?"

"As far as I know. Amanda frequently told me she was coming home, but the fact is, she rarely did."

"Why is that, Mrs. Dixon?"

"I suspect it's because Quentin didn't like it when she asserted her independence. Driving all the way down here to see me didn't suit him. She was at his beck and call."

"I take it you and the judge aren't on the best of terms."

"We aren't on any terms. We don't speak. We never cared for each other."

"Would you mind telling me why?"

"Quentin liked to be in control. I wouldn't submit. That's reason enough."

"Did your sister ever tell you how she felt about her marriage?"

Violet Dixon snorted. "Of course she did, but that won't do you any good. Women complain about their husbands all the time. You won't get anywhere with that one. Quentin Wentworth was a nasty son of a bitch. He probably still is but, thankfully, I no longer have to put up with him."

"Did you come for the funeral, Mrs. Dixon?"

"I certainly did."

"At any time, did you actually see your sister's body after she died?"

"The casket was closed. It was what she wanted. I doubt if anyone would have stopped me if I'd asked to see her. Under the circumstances, I saw no need."

"Thank you, Mrs. Dixon. I appreciate your time."

"Sheriff?"

Wade waited.

"If you find anything untoward, please let me know."

"I'll do that."

He stared at the phone for a long minute. There weren't too many women who used the words *untoward* and *son of a bitch* in the same conversation. If Amanda Wentworth was anything like her sister, the sparks must have flown quite often in the Wentworth mansion. Sparks, however, were a long way from murder.

Wade scribbled a few notes, closed the folder and replaced the file. There was value in knowing when to quit beating a dead horse.

Verna Lee sat on the dock, slapping the blackflies away from her ankles. She squinted at the letters blurring together on the page attached to her clipboard. Lord, she couldn't need reading glasses already. Rubbing her eyes, she lifted her focus from the fine print of her order form and stared out at the bay.

Fingers of light, sharp-edged as a photograph, poked through the cloud cover slowly bringing color to the earth, mud green to the marshes, slate blue to the bay. A single trawler, already on its way to fisheries near Smith Island, marred the pristine perfection of the landscape. Overhead, egrets and a lone seagull circled below the horizon line.

There was only one other person she knew who appreciated the velvety silence of early morning here on the dock, the gentle slapping of the tide against the hulls of fishing boats, pelicans lined up on pilings waiting patiently for their breakfasts, the camaraderie of watermen shaking out their nets, untying their lines, double-checking their bait tanks and fuel supplies, the jolt of caffeine from chicory-rich coffee heating her insides and the gentle roll of the deck under her feet. Where was Libba Jane anyway? This was her running path. Nothing less than a major emergency would make her change her routine.

She tilted her face toward the sun and closed her eyes. Then she felt a tug on one of her curls. A soft, southern drawl broke the silence. "Hey there, Verna Lee. What are you doing out here at this time of the morning?"

Verna Lee smiled. "I was hoping to run into you."

"I have a telephone."

Verna Lee raised her amber-gold eyes to her sister's dark ones. "We've got to do something about the wetlands. All of this—" she waved her arm to encompass the dock, the boats, the horizon "—will be gone."

Libba sighed. "You're anticipating again. The sale is on hold until this investigation is over."

"That means we have some time. Why isn't the EPA involved?"

Libba hesitated. "I don't think the sale of a few hundred acres of privately owned wetlands is seen as destruction of an ecosystem."

"You know better than that, and you know it's not just a few hundred acres. For the last ten years developers have bought up thousands of acres. Where will it stop?"

Libba sat down beside Verna Lee. "I don't know."

Verna Lee studied her sister's profile, the small straight nose, the long eyelashes, the sun-gold skin and the straight coffee-dark hair caught up in a ponytail. "Have you lost heart for all this?" she asked.

Libba looked at her. "Not at all. But I choose my battles. If I want to succeed with the big ones, I have to let the small ones go. Condominiums aren't dangerous, Verna Lee. Nuclear waste, pesticides and PCBs are. I save my energy for those." She laid her hand on Verna Lee's arm. "This isn't California. We don't have celebrities who will take up our causes. What made you come back here anyway?"

Verna Lee shrugged. "I wasn't happy. My marriage broke up. My grandmother needed me. I guess I'm a small-town girl at heart."

"I accept that. You've made a success of your business, but what about your personal life? You're an attractive woman. Don't you want to grow old with someone?"

"Not particularly."

"I don't believe you. What about sex?"

"What about it?"

"Don't you miss it?"

Verna Lee freed her arm. "What makes you think I don't have sex?"

"Because I know every single man in this town and each and every one is terrified of you."

Verna Lee was about to open her mouth and tell her sister that single men weren't the only ones in town looking for sex without commitment, when she thought better of it. Libba Jane was an educated woman, a contemporary woman, two generations removed from her mother's New Orleans ancestors but, because of Nola Ruth, she'd been raised in their traditions, Catholic, superstitious, guilt-ridden, confident that punishment followed too much good fortune. Quite simply, Libba was naive when it came to men and Verna Lee had no good reason to burst her bubble. She changed the subject. "Wade Atkins invited me for dinner."

"Are you interested?"

"I'm not sure yet. His brothers were awful to me when we were kids. Maybe I'm out to get even."

"I heard that he told Bailey Jones not to leave town. What do you think that means?"

"I have no idea."

"Bailey can't possibly be a suspect."

"The body is fifteen years old. Bailey is twenty-two."

Libba looked puzzled. "How did you know that?"

Verna Lee wet her lips. "I must have heard it somewhere."

* * *

Tess Hennessey picked up her straw and stirred the melting ice cubes in her lemonade. She was having lunch with her mother at the Lamplighter Restaurant and, although Tracy had been talking without a break for the last five minutes, Tess had no idea where the conversation was going. She sighed. These lunches, with just the two of them, were always too long. How sad, she reflected, to feel so bored and impatient with your own mother. Maybe it was because they had nothing in common. Tracy didn't work, travel made her nervous and some time ago, she'd decided that volunteering was a waste of time. Her life was caught up in Marshy Hope Creek's limited social circle and, therefore, she could only discuss topics in which Tess hadn't the slightest interest.

"So," her mother finished, "what do you think?"

"About what?"

"You haven't heard a single word I've said."

"That isn't true," protested Tess. "But—" she leaned forward clasping her hands together "—have you ever thought that maybe you're wasting your life?"

Tracy's delicate skin flushed an angry red. "Thank you very much for your wonderful opinion of me. You and your grandfather certainly know how to destroy a person's confidence."

"I didn't mean it that way," Tess began, and then stopped, realizing that she really did.

"Apology accepted."

"I didn't mean to apologize exactly."

"Wonderful." Tracy's voice dripped with sarcasm.

Tess searched for the right words. "You're still young and you're really smart. I think you could do much better. You can't possibly be happy doing what you do all day."

Tracy's laughter was bitter. "What has happiness got to do with anything?"

"Haven't you ever wanted a career?"

"No," her mother snapped. "I wasn't raised to have a career. I was supposed to get married, have children and support my husband's career. That's all I know."

Tess studied her mother's pale gray eyes, regular features and smooth blond hair. With a little work, and if she got rid of that sour expression on her face, she'd actually be quite pretty. "If that's so, why didn't you?"

Tracy tapped her manicured nails on the table-top. "Why didn't I what?"

"Why didn't you get married again? There are lots of men who would be thrilled to have someone like you."

"Name one."

Tess sighed. "Mama, I don't live here anymore.

How would I know anyone's name? I'm speaking in generalities. I bet you don't even date."

"Your granddad would make my life miserable if someone showed up at the house asking for me."

"Move out."

"With what?"

"Don't you have any money of your own?"

"Your granddaddy gives me an allowance."

"You're forty. How can you take an allowance from your father?"

Tracy looked surprised. "How else would I live?"

"You could get a job."

"Oh, please. What would you have me do, earn minimum wage frying burgers?"

"What about a receptionist position or maybe even real estate? People can make a nice living in real estate."

"Tess, this is Marshy Hope Creek. People here have lived in their homes since the Flood."

"I know there's something you can do. Why not open your own business?"

Her mother stared at her. "What on earth are you talking about? What kind of business do you see me starting up? I can't do anything."

"You like to read," Tess suggested. "Why not open a bookstore and invite writers to give readings."

"Why would authors want to come to Marshy Hope Creek?"

"Because you're selling their books. We aren't all that far from Annapolis and D.C. I know they would come."

"Where would I get the money?"

"You can borrow against your inheritance. Granddad will give you the money. I know he will."

"No, he won't, because I'm not asking him. You're not to discuss this with him at all."

Tess sighed, admitting defeat. "Have it your way. Live and die right here in this town and never try anything new."

"I'm not you," her mother said softly. "I don't think of my life as so terrible."

"I didn't say it was terrible. It's just that you don't seem happy." Across the table, brown eyes met gray. "What was your mother like?"

Tracy's face softened. "You don't remember your grandmother at all, do you?"

Tess shook her head. "Not really. Sometimes I think I do, but maybe it's because of what you've told me."

"Things were different when she was alive," Tracy began. "Your granddad wasn't as obvious."

"It must have been awful for him to lose her like that."

"They argued," her mother said unexpectedly, "all the time. She didn't let him get away with anything, especially when it came to me. Sometimes I think she would have left him but for me. It was hard for a woman to leave her husband in those days." She shivered. "After she died, I wasn't worth much for a long time. You were five and probably don't remember, but your dad and I were already divorced. He came back to attend the funeral and ended up staying to take care of you. After that, we moved in with Granddad." Again she laughed her brittle laugh. "That was the biggest mistake of my life. I should have gone back to court for more alimony and kept my own house."

"You should have done something to prepare you for making a living on your own," Tess corrected her.

Tracy's thin eyebrows drew together. "I already told you, I wasn't raised to work."

"Times change," Tess said flatly. "Women work, especially when they're not married."

"Tell that to Libba Jane," Tracy said pointedly. "The first chance she got, she quit to stay home."

"That's not fair. She had Gina Marie. Then she went back to her job."

"My goodness, Tess. You certainly are touchy when it comes to that woman. You'd think you were her daughter and not mine."

Tess sighed. "Wouldn't you rather I had a good relationship with my stepmother?"

"A little loyalty wouldn't be out of place, either."

"She didn't take anything from you, Mama. Why do you have to be so jealous of her?"

Tracy's back stiffened. "I am *not* jealous of Libba Delacourte. The very idea." She fanned her face with her hand. "Is it me or is there something wrong with the air-conditioning in here?"

Tess changed the subject. "I could use a nap. Let's skip dessert and go home. Chloe and I are going out tonight and I don't want to fall asleep on her."

"By all means, cut lunch short with your mother so you don't inconvenience Chloe Delacourte."

Tess frowned at her mother. Had Tracy always been like this, or was she getting worse with age? "Her last name is *Richards,* Mama, not Delacourte. You keep forgetting that."

"On the contrary. I never forget anything."

Verna Lee paid careful attention to her appearance, standing in front of the mirror and craning her neck to check the panty lines beneath her white capri pants. She'd decided against wearing a thong. They were just about the most torturous things invented, right next to high heels, and she'd heard, on one of those talk shows her grandmother listened to, that nine out of ten men preferred seeing the lines of a woman's panties under her clothing. Tonight, she would oblige. Wade was going to see panty lines and plenty of skin. The pants hit just below the knee, a very sexy length for someone with long, brown legs. Her top was cropped, cut in at the shoulders and red. Verna Lee liked red. It suited her, as did the messy, butterscotch ringlets that spilled down her back. She sprayed Dolce & Gabbana Light Blue on her pulse points, slid into a pair of white sandals and grabbed her purse.

Ready as she would ever be, she let herself out the front door, locked it behind her and made her way to her car. Now, if only she could control the nerves twisting her stomach, maybe she could make it through the night. "It's only Wade," she told herself. "You have nothing to worry about."

She'd driven past the turnoff to Wade Atkins's house on her way to Chincoteague Island many times, but she'd never actually seen it. The back of the house faced the road. Curious, she climbed the steps and rang the bell.

"Come on in," he called out. "Door's open."

Admiring the gleaming wood floors and custom windows, she followed the sound of his voice and the smell of burning charcoal to what was really the front of the house. Stepping out on to the deck, she looked around and gasped with pleasure at the low-hanging trees, the still water and the sea grass growing along the edges of the marsh. "This is gorgeous. You have an incredible view."

He handed her a chilled glass of white wine. "Thank you. It suits me."

"It would suit anyone. How long have you lived here?"

"About five years. It's small, but it's paid for and, like you said, you can't beat the view." His glance moved up from her legs, lingering on her lips. "You look very nice."

"Thanks." She sipped her wine, working to hold back a laugh.

He wasn't fooled. "Go on. Tell me. I can take it."

She nodded at his ragged cutoffs and T-shirt. "Is this your typical entertaining attire or did you dress up for me?"

Wade held out his arms. "This is me, entertaining or otherwise." He thought a minute. "Come to think of it, I can't remember if I've ever invited a woman home before. Most likely not."

"Why not?"

"Until I met you, no one appealed to me enough to disturb my privacy." He waved his arm to encompass the air, the marsh and the water surrounding them. "It's pretty spectacular here. I love the seclusion."

She looked at him steadily, the wine loosening her inhibitions. "Why me, Wade?"

"I've always had a serious crush on you, even when I was a kid."

"You don't know me."

"No," he said, surprising her. "I don't." He topped off her wineglass from the bottle on the small table. "I'm hoping to change that. Have a seat." He patted the back of a canvas-slung chair.

Verna Lee sat. She watched him tilt the bottle of beer so the liquid flowed down his throat. "How?"

He swallowed and sat beside her. "By asking the right questions. Is that okay?"

She noticed that his accent wasn't so pronounced. "That depends on why you're asking the questions."

He leaned back and smiled. "What if I said my interest was strictly personal?"

"I'm not sure I'd believe you. Honesty will get you a whole lot further than flattery."

"Help me out, Verna Lee." He was no longer smiling. "I'd like to know you better, but you're like a stick of dynamite, ready to explode no matter which way you're lit. Questions between two people starting out are normal, even if one of us is a police detective. I'm curious about your life after you left Marshy Hope Creek. Nothing's set in stone. Tell me to stop if you're not comfortable."

"What do you want to know?"

"What inspired you to be a teacher?"

Verna Lee relaxed. This was all right. She could handle his questions. "I like children. I communicate well. It's an important job."

"Why aren't you teaching anymore?"

She shrugged. "I lost interest, I guess."

He looked at her, the steely blue eyes cool and assessing. "You never considered teaching here in your home state?"

"No." She met his gaze without blinking. "Why are you looking at me like that?"

"Like what?"

"As if I'm a science experiment and you're about to dissect."

"No reason, Verna Lee," he said, his accent thick and southern again. "No reason at all." He changed the subject. "I imagine you were shocked to learn who your mother was."

She studied her wineglass for a minute before speaking. "Drusilla told me about Nola Ruth a long time ago. By the time everyone else found out, it was old news for me."

"Why didn't *you* tell anyone?"

"Who was I gonna tell, Wade? The woman gave me up for adoption. By keeping silent she made her preferences clear."

"I know a few people who would take advantage of the information you had."

Verna Lee shrugged. "Possibly. What good would that have done?"

"Payback, maybe."

"I didn't want to be paid back. I just wanted to know who my family was."

"What about your father?"

"Never met him."

"Did you look for him?"

"No."

"Why not?"

"I didn't know his name. Nola Ruth and I worked our way to a relationship, such as it was. I had a feeling my questions wouldn't have been appreciated."

"What about now? She's been dead for a few years. You have no obligation to protect the dead."

Again, she shrugged, a simple lifting of her honey-colored shoulder. "There doesn't seem to be a point. He probably has a family. I'd be an intrusion, a half-white daughter he had no idea he had."

"Or, he might love the idea of having someone like you in the family."

She smiled. "It's a risk I'd rather not take."

"What have you got to lose?"

"It might not be a fairy tale ending, Wade. It's possible that I'd face a hurtful rejection. I don't need that."

"Okay. Fair enough." He lifted his beer bottle to check the liquid level. "If someone else had information on him, would you want to know?"

She hesitated. "Maybe, if he's dead."

"And if he's not?"

"Never mind."

"Okay." Wade stood, picked up the tongs and rearranged the charcoal.

Verna Lee waited a full thirty seconds. "You're kidding, aren't you?"

"Kidding?"

"You aren't really going to end this conversation just like that."

"Like what?"

"For pete's sake, Wade. Give me a break."

"You said you didn't want to know."

"I changed my mind."

He picked up the wine bottle and poured her another glass. "Okay. Here it is. Fifteen years ago, one Anton Devereaux, a black man traveling through town, was arrested for refusing to sign a speeding ticket. Nola Ruth Delacourte bailed him out of jail. He skipped out before the trial and Mrs. Delacourte lost her money. Apparently, Cole never knew."

Verna Lee stared at him. The name was familiar. Where had she heard it before? Suddenly it came to her. The man with the Mercedes. *The black man Nola Ruth was arguing with on the steps of the police station.* "Are you saying that my father is Anton Devereaux?"

"Possibly."

"What does it mean?"

"I was hoping you'd know. You were back in town by then."

She cradled the wineglass in her hand. It was a

long time ago. She needed time to think. "I have no idea," she said after a minute. "Nola Ruth wasn't into full disclosure. I never even spoke to her until just before she died. It makes sense that she wouldn't tell me my father was here." She looked at Wade. "Pardon me if I don't get emotional over someone I never knew." She set her glass on the table and folded her hands in her lap. "Now, tell me the truth. Why did you really invite me here?"

"I told you. I've had the hots for you since we were kids."

"You hid it well."

He laughed, set down his glass and rose from his chair. "Don't go away."

Verna Lee closed her eyes. She was flushed and warm from the alcohol and the attention. A Frank Sinatra tune floated across the deck.

Wade stood in front of her. "May I have this dance?"

She smiled, nodded and held out her hand. He pulled her into his arms, his palm settling low, on the small of her back. Finding her rhythm, he guided her smoothly, effortlessly, around the deck.

Verna Lee sighed and slid her arms around his neck. She'd had little to eat that day and the wine was blurring her senses. Resting her head on Wade's shoulder, she hummed the melody, giving herself up to the hot humid night, the red glow of ash-tipped coals, the whine of a mosquito and the deep, warbling hoot of an owl on the hunt.

Later, much later, long after the music stopped and the cicadas took up their song, the spangled sky continued to spin and the thrumming of her body escalated to a level she recognized from so long ago it seemed like another lifetime, she lifted her head and opened her mouth to his kiss, welcoming the inevitable. After all, when a man tells a woman he's interested, that he's been interested from the very beginning, it puts everything into a new perspective.

Fifteen

Chloe sat on the floor in front of the long mirror in her yellow bedroom applying smoky-blue shadow to the crease in her eyelid. Carefully, she tapped the angled brush against her skin and then used her pinkie finger to blend in the color with the softer shade just below it. Eye makeup was all she used. Her sun-dark skin, inherited from her maternal grandmother, was good enough without foundation and the no-lipstick look accented her startling blue eyes, her best feature, especially when she lined them with navy pencil.

Hanging out tonight at Cybil's Diner was Tess's idea. She said the local band was good, and a few old friends who had come home this summer would be there. Chloe was going because of Tess and the band. As far as Chloe was concerned, she had no old

friends in Marshy Hope Creek, with the exception
of Bailey Jones, and look how that had turned out.
Her brief few months at the local high school wasn't
a memory she wanted to dredge up with regularity.

She checked her watch. It was already
nine o'clock. Her grandfather had probably fallen
asleep in front of the television again. He was an
early riser. By eight he would nod off in his recliner
and then, not too long after, climb the stairs to his
room. By the time Chloe tiptoed in, he'd be a few
hours short of greeting another day. It must be age,
she reflected, that made people hop out of bed before first light. She couldn't imagine having the op-
tion of sleeping in and choosing to wake up early.

One of the advantages to living with her grandfather was his calm assumption that she was sensible and her safety wasn't his concern. He patted her
cheek and told her to have a good time without the
usual litany of admonitions her mother never failed
to ply her with. Libba Jane was a born worrier: look
both ways before crossing the street, wash your
hands, call me no matter what time it is, don't touch
anything in public restrooms, drink lots of water,
never accept rides from strangers, call me no matter what time it is, brush your teeth, take your vita-
mins, eat fiber, always keep five dollars in cash with
you, call me no matter what time it is. The list was
exhausting. The funny thing was, Chloe had never

given anyone cause for serious worry. All in all, she was a fairly easy kid. There had been a year or two, during her actress stage, when she'd tested her mother, but other than that it had been smooth sailing. Gina Marie was another story. She would definitely give them all a run for their money. Chloe only hoped that her mother, now that she was older, was up to the challenge.

She heard a soft knock, followed by her grandfather's familiar voice outside her door. "I'll say good night, Chloe. Have fun. Remember, you only live once."

She laughed. "Come in, Granddad. I'm decent."

He opened the door. "My goodness, don't you look nice."

Chloe fluttered her lashes. "Why, thank you, sir."

Cole bent over to kiss her cheek. "Turn off the porch light when you come in tonight, and say hello to Tess for me."

"I will. Good night, Granddad. Don't worry. I'll be careful."

The lines radiating from his fine blue eyes deepened with his smile. "I never doubted it, sugar. Good night."

He closed the door, his footsteps light on the floorboards leading to his bedroom. He was getting old. No one lived forever. What would she do without him? It wouldn't be the same as when her grandmother died. It had been different with Nola Ruth. Chloe never knew her grandmother before the debilitating stroke left her crippled and slow to speak. They'd come to Marshy Hope Creek expecting her to die. But Granddad was different. He was the heart of their family, the connection, the glue that kept all of them, Libba Jane, Chloe, Gina Marie and Russ, together.

Chloe said as much to Tess when she stopped by to pick her up.

Her stepsister sighed. "You're so dramatic, Chloe. Why on earth do you think something will happen to your grandfather? He's in good health, isn't he?"

"I guess so."

"Then stop worrying. First of all, it won't do him any good and secondly, there's no reason for it. Has anybody ever told you that you're a worry-wart like your mother?"

Chloe's mouth dropped. "I'm not."

"Yes, you are. Now quit thinking the worst and start enjoying the evening. You hardly ever get out." She tossed her head, turned the radio to the local country-music station and pressed the power button to roll down the windows. "Don't you just love summer nights, even if our choice of music is limited to country and soul?"

Chloe laughed. She closed her eyes and breathed

deeply. Warm air, thick and wet, rich with the decay odor of the marsh, slapped her cheeks and tangled the fine silky threads of her hair. Ahead, the white lines of the twisted two-lane road divided the marshland in two. A full moon illuminated the wetlands and sandbars, nesting grounds for cranes, sea turtles, crocodiles, loons and coots. The night was heavy with heat and growth and the sounds and smells of burgeoning life. Chloe could feel it on her skin like the tingle of a mild electric shock. Outside, sounds erupted from the undergrowth, hooting owls, chirping crickets, croaking frogs and, occasionally, the angry growl of a cat or the hiss of a water moccasin. "Yes," she murmured, closing her eyes to better absorb the sensations of sound and touch. "I do love summer nights."

A Willie Nelson tune poured from the speakers, the brilliant, evocative words of country music's greatest balladeer easing over them. Tess turned up the radio. Chloe leaned back against the headrest. If only she could hold on to the present, to this very minute and this feeling, to keep it and remember, to take it out and savor it when her mood changed. If she knew for sure that she could bring it up again, on demand, then it wouldn't be so hard to accept the rest of it, the bleak hours and days when nothing seemed to go quite right.

Twenty minutes later, Tess pulled in to the parking lot of Cybil's Diner, formerly a truck stop known to locals throughout Frenchman's Cove, Marshy Hope Creek, Salisbury and a select few long-distance truckers who bothered to break away from the interstate highway and drive the back roads bordering the bay. Through fat years and lean, the bar managed to stay in business, recently earning the label *trendy* in youthful circles.

Chloe wrinkled her nose at the stench and haze of tobacco that clouded the air. Either the manager was unaware of the no-smoking law, or he was deliberately ignoring it. Small hurricane candles on the tables and inside the sagging booths barely illuminated the shadowy darkness. A pool table dominated the center of the room, and beneath her feet Chloe could feel the distinct crunch of peanut shells. A television, its sound muted, tuned to reruns of *The Simpsons,* hung above the bar where the hard drinkers sat swilling, in various stages of inebriation. Garth Brooks blared from the jukebox. Two long-haired men in boots and cowboy hats were setting up near the stage. Most of the booths and tables were filled. Seated in the far corner, in the largest booth, was a group of vaguely familiar faces. Chloe followed Tess through the warren of tables.

Skylar Taft scooted toward the center, making room for them. "Hey, Tess, Chloe. Sit down. You sure took your time."

"We've only been here ten minutes," a blond boy protested. His face was familiar but Chloe couldn't remember his name.

Skylar shrugged, flipped the ends of her dark hair over her pale shoulders and stared hard at Chloe. "You remember everybody, don't you?"

"Not really," Chloe confessed. "It's been a long time."

As expected, Skylar made the introductions. Not much changed in Marshy Hope Creek, reflected Chloe. The queen bee still ruled. Casey Dulaine was the redhead, leaner and less freckled now that four years had passed. Scott Owens was the boy who spoke up. Chloe still didn't remember him. Buzz Evans was recognizable. He and Skylar had been an item all through high school. Joni Marcoux was a pleasant surprise. Still athletic-looking, the curly-haired brunette had befriended Chloe on that awful first day of high school four years ago.

Chloe smiled a genuine smile. Gratefully, she slid into the booth. "Hi, Joni, what's going on with you?"

"I'm at school in Seattle, studying forestry. What about you?"

"Marine ecosystems at UC San Diego."

Skylar interrupted them. "So, Chloe, how come you're slumming this summer?"

She frowned. "What does that mean?"

Skyler's eyebrows lifted. "Don't you live in California?"

"Yes."

"If I had a choice between San Diego and Marshy Hope Creek, I sure wouldn't be here."

"My mother lives here. She married Tess's dad. Both of us come here in the summer."

"How is that working out?" asked Skylar. "I mean, isn't it weird that your mother is married to Tess's dad?"

Chloe looked at Tess. She wasn't saying anything. "I'm not sure what you mean by weird."

Skylar sipped her drink, something pink with an umbrella in it. "It just seems strange, that's all. You're Libba Jane's daughter. Tess is Russ's daughter. Libba and Russ are married and now there's Gina Marie. That makes you and Tess stepsisters and at the same time, Gina's half sisters. How do you keep it all straight? Isn't it sort of incestuous?"

Why wasn't Tess saying anything? Come to think of it, she'd never said anything around Skylar. Why were they even here? Chloe drew a deep breath and leveled the full focus of her cool blue gaze on Skylar. "I don't have trouble keeping it straight and neither does Tess. What I'm wondering is, why it's any of your business?"

Beside her, Joni choked and pressed her napkin

to her lips. Tess looked miserable and Scott Owens laughed.

Chloe smiled sweetly and stood. "Excuse me. I have to find a bathroom. If the waitress comes while I'm gone, I'll have the shelled shrimp and a beer. If they ask for an ID, order a Coke."

It was inky black in the narrow hallway. Chloe pushed open the door to the ladies' room. Thankfully, it was the one-stall kind. She locked the door and leaned against the sink, castigating herself for allowing Tess to talk her into coming. She'd never liked Skylar Taft and her circle of genuflecting disciples and she resented Tess for telling her they'd changed. Her stepsister turned into someone Chloe didn't care to know whenever she was around the steel magnolias. There was no way of getting out of this evening until Tess was ready to leave. Once again she'd blown it by not driving. Granddad would have loaned her his car if she'd asked.

She stared into the mirror, wiped a dark smudge from under one eye, washed and dried her hands and smoothed her hair. Immediately she felt better. She looked good tonight, exotic and unusual in a lime green top with spaghetti straps that emphasized her tan, and tight white jeans. Her confidence restored, she opened the door into blinding darkness.

The door of the men's room opened at the same time. Someone stepped out. She waited for him to pass. When he didn't, she assumed the initiative and moved into the hall, only to feel a firm grip on her arm.

"Let go of me," she said tersely. "Let go or I'll scream."

"Keep your claws in, Chloe. It's only me," said a familiar voice.

"Bailey?"

"In the flesh. What are you doing in a place like this?"

Chloe's eyes began to adjust to the lack of light. "I came with Tess and I wish I hadn't. What about you?"

"Hell, these are my old digs." He grinned and she saw the white of his teeth. "This is the real Bailey Jones. All those other places, Manhattan, London, Paris, they mean nothing. This is it, the real me, Bailey Jones right here in Cybil's Diner." He slurred his words.

She drew back. "You're drunk."

"So is everybody else. You can't hold that against me. That's the point of coming here."

"It is not. I can't believe this. What's happened to you?"

"Don't be such a prude, Chloe. At least I'm of age. That's more than you can say about that little group you're sitting with."

Her mouth dropped. "You knew I was here all the time. You came after me."

He leaned back against the wall as if he needed the support. "It worked, didn't it?"

"Why do you have to be like this, Bailey? Why didn't you just come up and ask to join us?"

"Are you kidding?"

"You're afraid of them, aren't you?" Her lips tightened contemptuously. "You're afraid of those snobby kids who haven't done half of what you have."

"I'm not afraid of anything, Chloe, not anymore. You, of all people, should know that." He no longer sounded drunk.

"Prove it."

He moved closer, looking down at her. The irises of his eyes were so black they merged with the pupils, twin dark orbs filling the centers. "You won't let it be, will you?" he said softly. "You've got to take a stand, make a scene, expose their bigotry so they can't squirm out of it."

"Why not? They deserve it."

He reached out and tucked a wing of hair behind her ear. Her breath caught. She couldn't remember when Bailey had voluntarily touched her.

"Chloe, Chloe." His voice was amused, warm, filled with concern. "Why won't you ever learn? They'll hate you for it. Your family lives here. Your mother, your sister. Are you really that selfish?"

She jerked away, from him, from the rush of

emotion, the revealing, vulnerable tears, and stumbled down the hall toward the bar. How dare he? How dare he pretend to care and then crush her with a single humiliating word? Why did he continue to have this power over her? He was right. She never learned.

He followed. "Let's dance," he said, gripping her arm once again.

She pulled away. "I don't want to dance and, if I did, it wouldn't be with you."

He laughed and pulled her into his arms, fitting his body against hers. The band, such as it was, crooned "Love Me Tender." "You don't mean that."

"Yes, I do. I hate you. I've always hated you."

"Shut up, Chloe," he muttered. "Shut up and dance with me. You smell good. You always smell the same, do you know that, like those bushes that grow outside your granddad's front porch."

"Honeysuckle." She could barely get the word out. Her face was pressed against his shoulder.

"No, the other one. You know, those little white flowers that die the minute you pick 'em."

"Gardenias."

"That's it. Gardenias. You're like one of those gardenias, small and perfect and sweet-smelling." His arms tightened around her.

Her heart hurt. She had questions, a million questions, but she couldn't manage a single one.

* * *

Libba removed her tennis shoes on the porch. Dropping them by the front door, she opened it and stepped into her living room. It was dark. She checked her watch. Nine o'clock. Was everyone in bed already?

She walked down the hall to the large back room they'd converted into a den. Russ sat on the couch with Gina Marie nestled in his arms. Both were sound asleep. On the television screen, *Finding Nemo* played to an unconscious audience.

Libba tiptoed across the room and turned off the power. Then she turned back to her husband and kissed his forehead. He stirred and opened his eyes.

"What time is it?" he asked.

Libba held her finger against her lips. "Shh. It's just after nine," she whispered. "You're wiped out. Put Gina to bed. I'll take a shower and join you in a few minutes."

Russ yawned. "I almost forgot. Your daddy called. He said for you to check in with him the minute you got home."

Libba groaned. "I forgot. I was supposed to stop in and see him on the way. So much happened today that it slipped my mind. I'll call him now." She looked back at her husband. He seemed to be drifting off again and she wasn't in the least bit tired. "Go to bed, Russ. I'm still kind of wired from the day. I think I'll drive over and talk to Daddy in person."

Russ's eyes opened. "It's kind of late, isn't it?"

It was late, but it was mid-summer and the last lingering rays of sunlight hadn't yet disappeared into the bay. "Maybe he'll still be up."

"Be careful."

"I will."

Slipping into a pair of sandals, she grabbed her purse and left the house. Rolling both windows down in the car, she backed out of the driveway, increased her speed and let the wind cool her cheeks and lift the hair off her shoulders.

Her father's house was dark as pitch except for the porch light. Maybe Chloe was still awake. Parking the car, Libba climbed the stairs, rolled back the azalea pot, found the spare key and unlocked the door. She flicked on the hall light. Her father's bedroom was upstairs at the back of the house, not too far from Chloe's. The light wouldn't disturb them.

Libba climbed the stairs quietly. Chloe's door was open and obviously empty. She frowned. Where was she? She debated whether to go home, wake her father or wait for her daughter. Just then the door to her father's bedroom opened. Cole Delacourte, wearing striped pajama bottoms and a T-shirt, stepped out into the hall. He saw Libba and rubbed his eyes.

"Libba Jane, is that you?"

"Hi, Daddy."

"What on earth are you doing here at this hour?"

She bit her lip. "It's only nine-thirty."

"Is something wrong?"

She shook her head. "No, I'm sorry for coming so late, but I just got home and you said you wanted to see me. I thought I'd spend a little time with Chloe if you'd already gone to bed."

"Chloe's out with Tess. I woke up and couldn't get back to sleep. I thought I'd have some of Serena's peach cobbler and a glass of milk. Care to keep me company?"

Libba smiled. "The thought of peach cobbler makes me drool."

Together, they walked into the kitchen. Without having to think, Libba opened the cupboard to the right of the refrigerator and found two bowls. The ice-cream scoop was in the dishwasher and the spoons in the flatware drawer.

Serena's cobbler, delicately browned and thick with peaches, sat in a covered glass bowl in the refrigerator. "Do you want yours warmed and topped with ice cream?"

"Always."

Within minutes, they were digging into heaping bowls of the rich dessert. It wasn't until they couldn't eat anymore that Libba remembered why she'd come. "What did you want to talk to me about?"

Cole swallowed his last bite and pushed his bowl away. "It's about the investigation. A few interesting things have come up."

"Such as?"

"Did your mother ever tell you about Verna Lee's father?"

Libba frowned. "Nothing specific."

"She never told you his name or where he was from?" Cole prodded.

"What is this about, Daddy?"

"His name was Anton Devereaux. His father had a dry-goods store somewhere in Virginia. According to Nola Ruth, he disappeared. After your grandfather chased them down and forced the annulment, she never heard from him again."

"That's right. What about it?"

Cole sighed. "I'm not sure. Apparently her version wasn't entirely accurate. Fifteen years ago, a man by the name of Anton Devereaux came to town and was arrested for a speeding ticket."

"A speeding ticket?" Libba's eyebrows rose. "How can that be?"

"He refused to sign the ticket. I don't know the details. The point is he was taken to jail and bailed out by your mother."

"Good Lord."

"My sentiments exactly. He jumped bail and never showed up for the arraignment."

"When did you find out about this?"

"Your mother told me right after we attended Amanda Wentworth's funeral."

"What does that mean?" Libba wondered aloud.

He leaned forward. "I'm not sure, but I have a hunch. Let's say Anton Devereaux did come to town. Maybe he threatened to expose your mother's secret. Think how terrified she must have felt."

"Yet she bailed him out."

"Maybe that's why. It's possible he blackmailed her. Lord knows he had no reason to protect her."

"Why didn't she tell you? You knew all about him. She had nothing to hide from you."

He shrugged. "I have no idea. It's a bit late to ask."

Libba swallowed. "What are you thinking about, Daddy?"

"That body on Bailey's land."

Libba's hand moved to her throat. "You can't mean—"

"I don't know."

"That's ridiculous. Mama isn't a murderer. You lived with her for forty years. You'd know if she was capable of something like that."

"You never know that, honey. Desperation changes people."

"Someone would have had to help her. Mama wasn't that big. How could she murder someone and transport the body all the way out there. It isn't possible."

"Probably not," Cole agreed. "I'm a foolish old man with an overactive imagination. It's just strange, the timing and all. Nola Ruth wouldn't hurt anybody. It nearly killed her to spank you."

"I don't remember that she ever did, except once when I ran out into the street."

Cole nodded. "I don't remember who cried more, you or your mama. I wasn't around much then, was I?"

Libba smiled. "You're making up for it."

His smile was forced. "Forget all about this, honey. It's absurd. Talking it through made me see that. Leave the dishes. Serena will get them in the morning."

Libba walked around the table and wrapped her arms around her father's neck. "It doesn't help to worry about this, Daddy. Mama's gone."

"I'm thinking about Verna Lee. I wonder if your mother said anything to her. It sure would make me feel better if I knew she'd been in contact with her father sometime during the last fifteen years."

Libba kissed the part of his head where his hair had started to thin. "If it'll make you feel better, I'll ask her."

"Can you do that, Libba Jane? Would you feel comfortable?"

His look of relief stiffened her resolve. "Of course," she lied. "I'll make a point of getting her alone. We'll get to the bottom of this and put it behind us."

"You're forgetting something," he said gently.

"What's that?"

"She might tell you that she's never been in contact with him, or worse, that all communication stopped fifteen years ago."

"Maybe so, but that doesn't mean it has anything to do with Mama."

Cole smiled. "You're a smart girl, Libba Jane, and a loyal one. Your mama would have been proud of you."

Sixteen

Chloe stood very still and stared at the brown column of Bailey's throat, the part that was level with her eyes. All around her couples, locked together on the dance floor, swayed to the beat of the country band. A wealth of emotions passed through her, the foremost of which was confusion, followed by embarrassment. Bailey was obviously drunk and, she rationalized, not in any condition to be reasonable. She spoke into his ear. "Give me your keys. I'll drive you home."

"Let's get out of here," he muttered, pulling her off the floor.

Too relieved to protest, Chloe stumbled after him, out the door and across the dirt lot to where the cars of the diner's customers were haphazardly parked. Bailey's silver Porsche stood out among the Dodges and Chevys like a newly minted dime on a stack of vintage pennies.

He was pulling her at quite a clip. A stitch began in her side. "Where are we going?" she gasped.

"Right here." He pushed her against his car and lifted her chin so that she looked directly at him. "We need to talk."

She swallowed. "Okay."

"I'm tired of arguing with you."

Deliberately she widened her eyes. "Were we arguing?"

"We're always arguing, ever since we met up again. That's not the way I want it to be with us."

"Us?"

He shook her slightly. "Come on, Chloe. Stop playing games."

Gently she broke his grip by pushing against him with her arms. "I'm not playing games. Except for a few brief encounters, we haven't spoken in four years. What do you mean by *us?*"

"We used to be friends."

She raised one skeptical eyebrow. "Friends keep in touch."

He swore and turned away so that only his profile was visible. At every angle, Bailey Jones was beautiful.

"So, what are you saying? You don't want to have anything to do with me?"

"I didn't say that."

He looked at her and grinned. Once again, she felt that crazy drop in her stomach, the tingling, sharp-edged awakening of her nerves that only Bailey could bring.

"Maybe you don't know that most girls would die to be in your position."

"My position?"

"Out here, with me."

The edges of her temper curled. "Do you have any idea how arrogant you sound?"

"When we were kids you hung around me like a fly on a honeycomb."

"Maybe so," she admitted, "but that was a long time ago."

He pulled a pack of cigarettes and a book of matches from his back pocket, struck the match and bent his head to inhale. "So," he said, blowing out a stream of smoke, "what do we do now?"

Chloe shivered and rubbed her arms. The temperature had to be somewhere in the nineties but she was cold. "What do you want from me, Bailey?"

He looked bewildered, as if it was the last question he expected her to ask. "What is it?" she demanded. "Sex? Do you want to sleep with me?"

"God, no! I can't believe you said that." He shook his head and looked up at the sky. "If that's what you think, you really are naive. It isn't that at all."

"I'm sure there's a compliment in there some-how, but I'm not hearing it. So, what is it?"

"I don't know," he said slowly. "I hadn't really thought about it."

She looked at her watch. "I'll give you three min-utes to think. After that, I'm going back inside and we'll forget we ever had this conversation."

The beat of the music inside the diner matched the ticking of the second hand on her watch and the thumping of her heart. One minute passed, then two. She'd pushed him too far, but she wasn't sorry.

Bailey cleared his throat. "How about this? How about if we start talking again, just friends, and see where it goes."

She looked at him, a steady look out of slanted blue eyes. "That might work."

"Can I drive you home?"

"How do you know I'm ready to go home?"

He laughed. "That wasn't hard to figure out. The look on your face when you saw Skylar Taft was plain enough for anyone with half a brain to figure out."

"I shouldn't leave Tess."

"Why not? She's a big girl. If she wants to hang out with Skylar and company, that's her problem. Why inflict it on you?"

Since that had been her exact train of thought, Chloe couldn't take him to task for insulting her stepsister. "I'll go back and tell her I'm leaving."

"Who are you gonna say you're leaving with?" The headlights of a departing car caught her in their glare. There was no mistaking the set of her jaw and the sudden involuntary clenching of her fists. Chloe Richards was a fighter.

"Claiming you were my friend was never my problem, Bailey. I don't need approval, not from anyone, but especially not from that group inside."

He watched the door of the diner close behind her. "Go for it, Chloe," he said out loud.

"Where have you been?" asked Tess. "I looked for you. I was ready to call your house."

"I wasn't worried," said Skylar. "It's not the first time Chloe has disappeared from a party. She's got a mind of her own."

"I'm going home with Bailey."

Casey Dulaine's mouth dropped. "As in *his* home or yours?"

Chloe ignored Tess's shocked expression. "Not that it's anybody's business, but we're going back to my granddad's." She glanced at each one of them, Skylar, Buzz, Scott, Casey, Joni Marcoux and, finally, Tess. "We have some catching up to do and this isn't the place." She threw twenty dollars down on the table. "Enjoy the shrimp."

Tess caught up with her before she reached the door. "Are you crazy?" she hissed. "What's going on?"

"I told you. Bailey and I have some catching up to do. He's taking me home."

"Just like that?" Tess demanded. "Do you have any idea what this looks like?"

Chloe's eyes narrowed. "Why the third degree? You're not my mother."

"You'll be the topic of conversation for the rest of the night."

"I don't care." Chloe sighed. "Tess, this isn't high school. I never have to see any one of those people again if I don't want to."

Two red spots appeared on Tess's cheeks. "What about me? How can you be so selfish?"

"Excuse me?"

"Think about the position you're putting me in. I either have to talk about you or defend you. If I go along with them, I'll feel guilty and if I tell them where to get off, I won't have a friend left around here."

Chloe laughed. "Poor Tess. I give you permission to tell them I'm a slut. I won't hold it against you. Will that make it easier?"

"Why is everything a joke with you?"

"Why are those people so important to you?" Chloe countered. "You're living in New York. You want to be a lawyer. Who cares what they think?"

"All right, Chloe." Tess's voice was cold. "Have it your way."

Chloe watched her walk away. Shrugging, she stepped out into the sultry night air and headed toward the red glow that was the tip of Bailey's cigarette.

"All set?" he asked.

She nodded and held out her hand for his keys. "Let's go. I'm driving."

He handed them to her without protest and slid into the seat beside her. Above their heads, a panel in the roof opened automatically. "So, you faced down the dragons."

Chloe looked up and saw stars. "I did."

"Any casualties?"

"None that I know of."

"Where shall we go?" he asked.

She backed out of the parking lot. "Home. Serena made peach cobbler. We can fill our stomachs and talk on the porch."

"I have a better idea. Come to my house."

She kept her eyes on the road. "Do you have a house?"

"In a manner of speaking. I'm renting the Busby house while they're up north visiting their daughter."

"I didn't know you were friends."

He grinned. "I made them an offer they couldn't refuse."

Chloe shook her head. "We're going to my house. Next time, maybe, we'll do yours."

"Don't you trust me, Chloe?"

"I'm surprised you trust *me*," she countered. "According to you, I'm the one hanging around you like a fly on a honeycomb."

This time he laughed, a low rich chuckle that made her glad she was sitting down. "Okay, sweetheart, we'll go to your house. I only hope everybody's asleep. If not, you'll be facing down a few more dragons tonight."

"Maybe." She leaned back against the headrest and smiled into the wind. "But this time I won't face them alone."

Libba Jane was digging through her purse for her keys when Chloe walked into the kitchen with Bailey. Her eyes widened with that strained look Chloe had memorized from the more difficult moments in her life.

"Why, Bailey, how lovely to see you again," her mother lied.

"Thank you, Miz Hennessey."

Chloe's mouth twitched. No matter what the circumstance, her mother always defaulted to the Beauchamp manners. "We came home for cobbler and ice cream."

"Granddad said you'd gone out with Tess."

"I did, but I met Bailey and we decided to come home."

"You didn't leave Tess?"

"Actually, I did, but she wasn't alone."

"Who—"

Chloe lifted her hand to end the conversation. "Trust me, Mom. It's better this way." She looked pointedly at the keys in Libba's hand. "Were you leaving?"

"Yes. I stopped by to have a word with Granddad."

"Keeping late hours at work, Miz Hennessey?" Bailey drawled.

"No. I came from home. Everyone was asleep and I was restless."

Chloe frowned. Her mother was babbling. "Well, like I said, don't let us keep you."

"Oh. Right. I'll say good night. Don't stay up too late."

"We'll be fine. Stop worrying."

"You're right. Bye, Bailey. I'll see you tomorrow, Chloe."

"Good night, Miz Hennessey."

Minutes later, they heard the sound of a car pulling away.

Bailey chuckled. "In the future, remind me that you're a match for any dragon, Chloe Richards."

She reached for two bowls in the cupboard. "That's my mother you're talking about."

"Now that I think about it, you're a lot like your

grandma, Nola Ruth. Your mama's a pussycat compared to the two of you."

Heaping two bowls full of cobbler, she set them in the microwave and pushed the power button. "How well did you know my grandmother?"

He sat down at the table. "I knew her by reputation only."

Chloe scooped vanilla ice cream from the carton onto the warmed dessert and handed Bailey his. "I wish I'd known her before her stroke."

Bailey dug into his cobbler. "This is great."

"She was hard on me when I first came here," Chloe continued, "but that didn't last long."

"She had quite a temper."

"I heard that, too."

"Heard it. Hell, I saw it. It isn't something I'd forget. I must have been about seven, walking home from town. She comes speeding down the road in that big car of hers when suddenly she pulls over and the passenger door opens. Out steps this tall, well-dressed black guy. Miz Delacourte gets out on her side and starts shouting, moves in real close to him and pokes his chest. Then he gets mad right back and grabs her wrist. She yells and he lets her go, turns around and walks right past me as if I don't exist. Then she gets back in the car and drives away."

Chloe stared at him, her cobbler forgotten. "You're kidding."

"No. I'm not. That's the way it was."

"I wonder what it means."

Bailey was making a serious dent in his dessert.

"Did you notice anything unusual about him?"

"The whole situation was unusual." He thought a minute. "The guy wasn't from around here. His accent was different."

"I can't imagine why my grandmother would be arguing with a black man, unless he was Verna Lee's father."

"That's a leap."

"No, it isn't. Think about it. My grandmother was Verna Lee's mother. Verna Lee is black. It all fits. He came to town looking for his daughter. Maybe my grandmother didn't want anyone to know. The whole thing came out only four years ago. Maybe the body found on your land is the same man you saw with my grandmother."

"That's a long shot, Chloe. I don't think Nola Ruth was the murdering kind. She wasn't big enough for one thing. You aren't trying to say that your granddad did it for her, are you? Because if you are, I'd consider you a candidate for the loony bin."

"No. I didn't really know my grandmother very well, but there's no way Granddad would kill anyone."

"No way."

She leaned forward, the bright hair falling over her cheeks. "Aren't you even a little bit curious?"

"About what?"

"About the body on your land?"

Bailey didn't answer for a long minute. When he did, his words sent a warning shiver down Chloe's spine.

"No good comes from dredging up secrets of the past."

Seventeen

The blaring of the alarm jarred Verna Lee from a sound sleep. Bleary-eyed, she rolled over and glanced at the clock. It couldn't be five already. She felt as if she'd been unconscious no more than ten minutes. Pulling the covers over her shoulders, she turned, reaching out to tuck the pillow under her cheek when the palm of her hand hit the hard plane of a man's chest, taut muscle, wiry hair, a ladder of rib bones and heat, heat beneath her hand, leaping to her chest, flowing through her body, penetrating deep into the center of her belly.

Instantly, she was awake. Blue eyes looked down at her, moving over her face. A hand cupped her breast. She closed her eyes. Did she want this? Good Lord, what a question. She smiled. Yes, she wanted it, never more than now, at this moment, with this man.

What was so satisfying about rough hands on her skin, warm lips on the slide of her throat, the slope of her breast, about the long, delicious wait for her mind to relax, readying her body to open and stretch and welcome the sharing of an act of intimacy so tender, so complete, so primal, so familiar and instinctive that, since the dawn of man, it remained unchanged?

Later, much later, the smell of rich chicory floated down the hall. Through the fog clouding her brain, it registered that someone was making coffee. Footsteps sounded on the floor. She felt the sudden depression of the mattress. The coffee smell was stronger. A half smile lifted the corners of her mouth.

Wade's breath tickled her ear. "Good morning, Sleeping Beauty."

She opened her eyes. "Are you talking to me?"

"I am. In two minutes you'll have some home-brewed New Orleans coffee, the twenty-dollar-a-pound variety."

"It sure smells good. To what do I owe this unusual honor?"

"You said to wake you at seven, but I was hoping you'd reconsider."

She smiled her sensational smile. "What did you have in mind?"

He traced her spine with his finger. "Sleeping

late. Breakfast in bed. Another round similar to the one we had earlier."

She sat up, clutching the sheet to her breasts, her curls wild around her face. "You're certainly tempting, but I have a business to run and you have a murder to solve."

He leaned over, his breath toothpaste clean, and kissed her mouth. "I'm disappointed, but there's always tonight."

A tiny vee appeared between Verna Lee's eyebrows. "This was fun, Wade, but it was strictly impulse for both of us. We're not a thing. We don't know each other."

"You're one straightforward woman, Verna Lee. Those are supposed to be my lines."

She shrugged one honey-gold shoulder. "I didn't think you'd say them."

"Or maybe you wanted to say them first."

She flushed. "Maybe. Or maybe it's because I'm a realist. This isn't Baltimore. There are people who would object to our seeing each other."

"You can't live your life that way."

"It's worked so far."

"I like you, Verna Lee. I've always liked you. You're different."

"You like things that are different."

"Is there something wrong with that?"

"Yes," she said. "I think there is. It would be all

right if you liked something that happened to be different. But it isn't all right if you chase after what's different just because it is."

Wade Atkins had learned a few things in his forty-five years, and one of them was patience. He looked at her, a half smile playing on his lips. "Are you willing to share my shower, or do you want to go first?"

She liked Wade Atkins. She liked him more than she thought she would. But Verna Lee had experienced enough of life to know that it was the differences between people that drove them apart. And Wade and she were different, an understatement if she'd ever heard one. She swung her legs over the side of the bed. "I'll go first."

Two hours later she was mixing up her homemade chicken salad with fresh sprigs of rosemary, a herb that grew wild in the marshy wetlands outside of town. Humming to herself, she added to her roasted chicken equal parts regular and low-fat mayonnaise, a culinary secret that would brand her a heretic here in Marshy Hope Creek.

"Anybody here?" a voice sang out.

"I'll be with you in a minute, Libba Jane," she called from the back of the café. "Help yourself to coffee, or anything else you want."

"I want chocolate milk," Gina said, looking hopefully at her mother.

"I don't have any chocolate milk, baby," Verna Lee called out. "Chocolate inhibits the absorption of calcium. If you want chocolate, just have it."

Libba frowned. She'd grown to appreciate Verna Lee, but sometimes her preoccupation with all things healthy rankled. "I guess everything doesn't have to be good for you."

"Like I said, if you want chocolate, have a Hershey's Kiss. There's a jar by the register."

"Can I have milk?" asked Gina.

"I'll get it," Libba said hastily. She poured a glass of milk, set it on the counter, found two silver, foil-wrapped Hershey's Kisses and settled the little girl into a chair. "Here," she said, handing her the chocolate and pushing the milk, complete with straw, toward her. "Will you sit here quietly while I talk to Aunt Verna Lee?"

Gina nodded and began the arduous task of pulling the foil from the candy.

Verna Lee laughed. "I thought you were opposed to sugar?"

"I've adjusted," replied Libba. She walked to the back of the café and leaned over the counter. "Can I help you with anything?"

"I'm nearly finished. Why don't you pour us some iced tea. I tried a new recipe. It's been slow this morning. Maybe it's too hot for coffee. I sure hope it picks up by lunch."

Libba returned with two glasses of clear, green-tinted liquid. Positioning herself on a tall stool, she sipped tentatively. Immediately, her forehead cleared. "This is delicious. It's sweet and yet tart at the same time. What did you put in it?"

"Lemongrass and dissolved sugar water." Verna Lee's golden eyes rested on her sister's face and narrowed skeptically. "What's going on, Libba Jane? Don't tell me nothing, because I can see it. You always were an open book."

Libba flushed. "Is that so terrible?"

"Not at all." She leaned forward. "Now, what gives?"

Libba Jane considered her options and decided on the truth. "Did you ever consider looking for your father?"

Verna Lee stared at her. "What makes you think I didn't?"

"Did you?"

"I considered it."

"And?"

Verna Lee sighed. "I decided against it."

"Why?"

"You're certainly full of questions today. Do you mind telling me why this subject suddenly interests you?"

Libba turned her glass around and around on the counter, leaving conjoined circles on the gleaming wood. "Wade mentioned something to my daddy the other night that shook him pretty badly."

Verna Lee said nothing.

"He told me that a man named Anton Devereaux was arrested for speeding fifteen years ago." She swallowed. "Apparently, Mama bailed him out of jail."

"Wade told me the same thing," Verna Lee admitted. "But why should that concern your daddy after all this time?"

"Anton Devereaux is your father, Verna Lee."

"I've *never* heard from my father, Libba Jane. I never even knew who he was. Neither of my parents wanted me in their lives, and you still haven't answered my question. Why should something our mother did fifteen years ago bother Cole Delacourte now?"

"Daddy thinks it may have something to do with the body found on Bailey's land."

"I beg your pardon?"

Libba bit her lip and looked back at her daughter. "Are you okay over there, Gina Marie?" She was blowing milk bubbles with her straw. "Do you want to come here and sit with Mommy?"

Gina shook her head. Reluctantly, Libba turned back to matters at hand. "I know it sounds silly, but—" She frowned. "Do you think Daddy's mind could be going just a little bit? He's getting older."

"There's nobody more lucid than your daddy," Verna Lee said flatly. "Can we just cut to the chase?"

"He thinks the body could be your father's."

Verna Lee's mouth dropped. For a minute no one spoke. Finally, Verna Lee broke the tension-fraught silence. "He can't be serious."

Libba shrugged. "We talked it through and he agreed it was probably impossible."

"But enough of a possibility that he had you come over here and ask me if I'd had contact with my father in the last fifteen years."

"He said he would feel a lot better if you had."

Verna Lee shook her head. "It doesn't make sense. Is he suggesting that Nola Ruth had something to do with it?"

"He's not suggesting, Verna Lee. He's a lawyer. He's trained in tangents and possibilities."

"And motives?"

"Yes," Libba replied faintly.

"The motive being that Anton was going to expose her."

Libba looked down at her glass.

"All she'd have to do is deny it, unless he knew about me." She laughed bitterly. "I'm not sure which is worse, that he knew he had a daughter and wanted to use her for blackmail, or that Nola Ruth did away with him."

"You know which is worse," her sister said quietly.

"We don't know anything about him." Verna Lee was thinking out loud. "We do know that she was capable of deception and keeping secrets."

Libba looked at her steadily. "We're all capable of those. Lying isn't murder."

Verna Lee sighed. "You're right. Besides, she wasn't big enough to do it all by herself. I doubt if she would have trusted anyone to help her. The ramifications are enormous."

"Well." Libba Jane looked relieved. "I guess that settles things."

Verna Lee nodded. "We'll have to wait and see what Wade turns up. Sorry I wasn't more help."

Draining the last of her tea, Libba stood. "Like I said, the idea was a silly one. Don't give it another thought. I'm not myself lately." Libba laughed. "I don't know how you do it, but I always feel better after our visits."

"It's the lemongrass," Verna Lee replied, collecting their glasses and setting them in the sink. "I swear by it."

"I promised Gina I'd take her swimming. Would you like to join us?"

"Not today, but if you're game on Sunday, I'd be glad to." She wet a napkin and crossed the café to wipe Gina Marie's mouth and hands. "You're a mess."

Gina nodded.

Verna Lee kissed the top of her head and laughed. "Have fun swimming."

She stood in the doorway and watched Libba buckle her daughter into her car seat, waving as they drove away. Closing the door against the suffocating heat, she poured herself another glass of tea and sat down on the low couch.

Her head swam with questions. She had a great deal to think about.

Eighteen

Wade picked up the phone on his desk and punched in the number code for Sheriff Blake Carlisle's mobile line. "Any news on your meeting with Tracy Wentworth?" he asked when Blake answered.

"Nothing that means anything. No one seems to know how or why Quentin deeded the land back to Lizzie Jones. I do know Tracy's mighty opposed to the condominium development. She'll be at the town meeting tonight."

"Is it being held at the usual place?"

"First Methodist Church, at seven o'clock. Looks like they're expecting a crowd even though it's last minute."

"Can you meet me over there? I know we've both been at this since dawn, but I'd sure appreciate it."

"I'll be there." Wade ended the call and checked his watch. He had enough time to grab a quick bite before heading over to the church.

Less than five minutes later Wade was staring at the Closed sign posted in the window of Perks. Reluctantly, he crossed the street to the diner and ordered a bowl of chili put together with enough grease and peppers to give him the runs for a week. He ate half of it, left a tip and made his way over to the church hall.

The time and location of town meetings hadn't changed. As far back as Wade could remember, they were held in the Methodist Hall. Mostly, the residents of Marshy Hope Creek were Baptists and Methodists, with enough Presbyterians, Fundamentalists and Catholics sprinkled in to make it interesting, but there was an underlying assumption that the Methodists were the most worthy of the bunch. Down by the mill, in Darby's Cove, on the wrong side of Marshy Hope Creek, where Wade and his brothers were raised, everyone knew that the only real distinction between Methodists and Baptists was that the former could read. Given that people preferred dealing with their own kind, those considered the most capable were generally the ones in charge, hence the Methodists hosted the meetings.

The room was filled to capacity, with all five town council members in attendance facing the au-

dience. Wade was surprised. He didn't think the
condominium development on the Jones land would
inspire strong feelings in anyone other than the few
environmentalists in the group. He knew the Delacourtes and the Hennesseys were among the affluent few who could afford to be concerned with such
things. But life was full of surprises.

Blake Carlisle walked over to stand beside him.
He pointed to the thin blond woman seated front and
center, in the row reserved for speakers.

"I would never have pinned Tracy Wentworth
for an activist," Blake said. "Other than hosting the
annual Ladies' Aid Society garden party, I can't re-
call a time when she was involved in politics. Heck,
I don't know when she last voted in a local election.
I know because I'm usually the one stuck manning
the polls when volunteers are short." He stroked his
jaw. "I wonder why she's here."

"I suppose we'll find out." On the other side of
the room Wade recognized Bailey Jones seated beside the same slim, bright-haired girl he'd had with
him in the car the other day. He nodded in their direction. "Delacourte's granddaughter is with the
Jones boy again. What do you think it means?"

"Could be anything. They're probably just
friends."

Wade glanced over the crowd. The Hennesseys
weren't in attendance. Neither was Cole Delacourte.

There were a hundred good reasons for staying home on a weeknight, including resting up after a full day's work and sitting around the dinner table catching up with the family.

Verna Lee appeared at the south entrance. Framed by the door, she stood for a minute, as if undecided about where to go.

Wade waited, willing her to look at him, knowing that the gauntlet would be worse for her than for him if she took up his challenge and met him halfway. The millennium had come and gone but Marshy Hope Creek was still a small town. He understood her position. She'd made it plain enough. There was no point in antagonizing her customers for something that might be as fleeting as snow in October. He knew the instant she saw him. Their eyes connected. He lifted his hand briefly. The corners of her mouth turned up, acknowledging his salute. She sat down in an empty chair at the end of the first row.

Disappointed, Wade positioned himself in back next to the exit and waited for the show to begin. A representative from Weber Incorporated was scheduled to speak first.

The man presented his case well. The lure of high-paying construction jobs was strong. There was no practical reason to hold up development. The seller was willing to sell. The buyer needed an investment before year-end. After he took his seat a murmur of agreement swelled through the crowd. They liked him.

Fred Baxter, a local, spoke next. He reminded them of the radiation scare in the water a few years back, of fishing blackouts and fertilizer pollution that leaked into the Susquehanna from farms up north. He spoke of the price of progress and the disappearance of a way of life and of how the wetlands around Marshy Hope Creek was home to thousands of species of animal life.

Heads nodded, and again the crowd buzzed with conversation. They liked him, too. Sides were being drawn. Wade hid a smile. Personally, a plethora of condominiums complete with Starbucks and Laundromats and strip malls wasn't his idea of progress, but people had to live somewhere and he wasn't rabidly opposed to local development so long as it didn't infringe on his privacy. Besides, new faces meant new ideas, a loosening of inhibitions, more revenue for businesses, higher taxes, all positives as far as he was concerned.

He was beginning to think his presence was nothing more than a waste of time, when Verna Lee approached the podium. In a low, hesitant voice she spoke into the microphone, quieting the whispering crowd, stopping him in his tracks. He watched her, his eyes glued to the striking, caramel-skinned figure, and waited.

Verna Lee had presence. Her unruly curls were pulled away from her face in an elegant twist at the back of her head. Her navy skirt was simple, skimming her curves, hiding her knees, and her white blouse with its cap sleeves was high-necked, the material opaque. She wore flat sandals and no jewelry. She looked, thought Wade, like a schoolteacher, and then he remembered why that was. She spoke firmly and clearly now, gathering momentum, her voice commanding attention without being the least bit loud or intrusive.

"You all know me," she began, looking around the room, making eye contact with each member of the town council, picking out individuals in the audience. "I came back to the Cove because I wanted to live and work in a place where I knew my neighbors, a place where if I forget to lock my door or if I leave my wallet on top of my car, it's an inconvenience because I have to go back for it, not a disaster because its been stolen." She smiled. "We don't have traffic jams here in the Cove. We have a single traffic light. Children play baseball in the streets. We have one grocery store, one hardware store, a post office where no one waits in line. That's paradise, ladies and gentlemen." She looked up from her notes. "You've all been to Salisbury and Annapolis.

You know what traffic is. Weber Incorporated tells us we'll have jobs, but what about the jobs we'll lose? What will happen to the fishermen and crabbers when our population grows to the point where our waters are polluted? What will happen to local businesses when a Wal-Mart moves in next door? Do we really want that? Do we need a population explosion here in Marshy Hope Creek? Isn't there a better use for the land than condominiums? Lizzie Jones didn't have many friends, but I counted myself one of them. She loved that land. We weren't very kind to her in life. Let's honor her memory by saving her land. Thank you." There was a spattering of applause and she sat down.

Wade stared at her as if seeing her for the first time. Where in the hell did all that come from? She hadn't mentioned one word of her feelings about the marshland the entire night they'd spent together.

Out of the corner of his eye, he saw Bailey Jones brush away Chloe Richards's restraining hand and rise from his seat. Wade settled back against the wall, arms crossed. This should be good. It was the boy's land, after all.

Bailey stood before them, ignoring the five council members, his eyes on the audience, a leanly muscled young man, not much more than medium height, with the kind of bone structure that graced men's clothing advertisements in the Sunday newspaper. Wade remembered that Lizzie, his mother, was good-looking, but nothing like Bailey. The man who fathered him was a mystery she had taken to her grave.

"Good evening," he said easily, as if he spoke to packed town-hall meetings every day, as if he'd never been on trial for the murder of his mother, as if he'd walked among them tall and proud all the days of his life. "You all know me, too, and with all due respect to Miss Fontaine, it doesn't really matter what anyone thinks is the best use for my wetlands." He spoke without notes, fueled by the heat of his own anger. "The operative word here is *my*. The land is mine. It was willed to me by my mother to do with as I please. How many of you would sit by and let someone tell you that you couldn't sell your house or paint your front porch or put in a pool because it might hurt someone else's interests? My guess is, not too many." Heads nodded. The boy had a point. There was a states' rights mentality that still existed down here below the Mason-Dixon and Bailey's appeal was hitting home. "If I can't sell my own land," he continued, "be careful, because someday somebody'll tell you that you can't sell yours, either."

Wade didn't stay for the vote. It would be in the paper tomorrow and he wanted to catch up with Verna Lee who had slipped out the side door. She had some explaining to do.

He caught up with her just before she climbed into her car. "Whoa there," he said. "You're off in a hurry."

She shrugged. "I said what I had to say."

"But you're not staying around for the vote."

"No," she said woodenly. "What's the point?"

A muscle leaped along the clean-shaven line of his jaw. "It seems to me that if you were bothered enough to stand up and speak, you'd want to know how it turned out."

"No, Wade. It's me we're talking about, not you. *You* might want to stay and find out, but I don't." Her voice was level and very calm, as if she were attempting to explain something to a hysterical child. "Like I said, my staying won't change the way they vote. I'll find out tomorrow morning and that'll be soon enough."

"What does this have to do with you, Verna Lee?"

"Pardon me?"

"The whole time we were together you never let on you were going to this town meeting. Did you plan that little speech you gave? How did this meeting come about in the first place? More to the point, why did I find out about it late this afternoon from Blake Carlisle?"

"I don't know which question to answer first."

"Any one will do."

"Why should I have said anything to you? What's this all about?"

"Fifteen years ago, at the same time a life was taken and dumped in the swamp, Quentin Wentworth deeded that same swamp back to Lizzie Jones. I'm wondering if you know anything about that, given your *special* friendship with her."

"Of course not."

"I don't believe you."

She wet her lips. "My friendship with Lizzie is none of your business."

The silence stretched out, long and uncomfortable, between them. "It took a lot of words to say that, Verna Lee," he said evenly. "I'm giving you a chance to tell me the truth."

"You think mighty highly of yourself, don't you?" she taunted him.

"Actually, it's an acquired confidence. I don't come by it naturally."

She sighed. "My fighting for the wetlands has nothing to do with Lizzie. If you knew me at all, you'd know that I meant every word I said in there. I like things the way they are. It's beautiful here and unspoiled. We don't have crowds or pollution or crime. Life is balanced, like nature."

"So speaks the woman who left it all for San Francisco."

"People change, Wade. Sometimes we don't

know how much we appreciate something until we no longer have it."

"Why don't I believe you?"

"You're a police officer. You're naturally suspicious."

"And you're a college graduate with a degree from a top-ten university." He stepped toward her. "What happened in California, Verna Lee? Why did you come back?"

Her eyes narrowed. "That folksy charm is just an act, isn't it? You aren't interested in me. All you care about is solving your murder."

"Listen, lady, I'm forty-five years old. Believe me, getting it up three times in one night requires interest."

She changed her tactics. Her voice softened. "Wade. Please. This isn't important."

He steeled himself against her appeal. Something wasn't right and until he figured it out, he couldn't afford to get any more involved with her than he already was. "I'll see you around, Verna Lee." Without looking back, he walked toward the lighted building determined to find out what had happened out there in San Francisco that had sent Verna Lee Fontaine running back home with her tail between her legs fifteen years ago.

Nineteen

Wade almost walked into the sheriff, who was positioned against a tree trunk just outside the back entrance of the church hall. He shook his head. "Call me a fool, Blake, but the number fifteen keeps coming back to me." He ticked the events off on his fingers. "Our murder took place fifteen years ago. Quentin Wentworth deeded Lizzie's land back to her fifteen years ago. Verna Lee came back to the Cove fifteen years ago and Amanda Wentworth was killed in a car accident fifteen years ago."

The door to the hall opened. Wade blinked. Blake held his finger to his lips and pulled him into the shadows, camouflaging them both.

A square of light blinded Wade for a minute, but when he could see again, he recognized Tracy Wentworth.

She'd nearly reached her car when the door opened again. Bailey Jones, his black shirt and slacks rendering him nearly invisible in the darkness, caught up with her. Wade could barely make out their voices.

Tracy was furious. "It doesn't matter what happens in there. You can't prove anything."

"I won't have to. It'll prove itself."

She turned on him. "Why do you care anyway? Your mother got plenty out of all this. You'll make millions because of it."

"Not if I can't sell the land."

Her voice shook. "How much is it worth to you?"

He laughed, a soft triumphant sound. "You don't have enough."

"How do you know?"

"Because there isn't enough money in the whole world."

"I knew it. You aren't interested in profit. All you want is revenge."

"Maybe," Bailey conceded.

"What else could it be?"

"Maybe I just want to see justice served."

"What do you want from me?" Tracy demanded.

His voice changed. "This isn't about you. You're nothing to me. Just stay out of it. Stop fighting his battles and you won't get hurt."

Once again the door opened. This time it was

Chloe Richards who stood framed in the light. "Bailey? Is that you?"

"Give me a minute, Chloe."

"Who are you talking to?" She squinted into the darkness and then stepped outside, closing the door behind her.

Wade watched her run toward Bailey. She stopped abruptly when she saw Tracy. "Oh," she said. "Hello."

"I suppose you've told her everything," Tracy said bitterly, "along with her mother and my ex-husband."

Chloe remained silent.

"That isn't your concern," replied Bailey. "Go on home and it'll be all right."

"No, it won't." Tracy fumbled for her keys. "It isn't exactly a picnic now, but when it all comes out, there won't be anything left for Tess and me."

"Tess is going to be a lawyer," said Chloe. "She'll be fine."

Tracy's laugh held a note of hysteria. "We'll see how far she gets trying to support herself."

"She has a father."

"Her father is otherwise occupied with his new family."

"That's not true," Chloe protested. "My mother works hard. She has a lot less than she used to have because of what Russ gives you."

"I certainly hope Tess sticks up for me the way you do your mother, even if it isn't true," Tracy snapped.

Bailey stepped between them. "Easy, Chloe. She's on the edge. You can't hold her to what she's saying."

"That's right. Protect her," Tracy hissed. "What is it about the Delacourte women that men just fall at their feet even at the expense of their own families?"

Wade, completely caught up in the drama playing out before him, barely registered that the church double doors had opened and a steady stream of people poured out of the building, deep in conversation.

Cursing the timing, he watched Tracy climb into her car and drive out of the parking lot. Bailey and Chloe had disappeared, merging with the flow of bodies melting into the darkness.

Within minutes the parking lot had emptied. Wade whistled softly. "That was one interesting conversation."

Blake shrugged. "If I'm thinking what you're thinking, how in hell do we handle this case now? We're gonna need proof."

Wade's expression was deliberately blank. "Proof is for prosecutors. All we need is a confession. I think it's past time for me to pay another visit to Judge Wentworth."

* * *

Tracy Wentworth smelled the acrid scent of cigar smoke and knew her father was still awake. Normally, she would have slipped off her shoes and tiptoed up the back stairs. Once she was safely locked in her room, he rarely interrupted her. Tonight, she didn't feel like hiding. Throwing caution to the winds, she opened the door to his study and coughed, waving away the smoke with her hands. "We'll never get the smell out of the wallpaper. Why don't you smoke outside? It's certainly warm enough to sit on the porch."

He leaned back in his leather chair. "It's my house. I can do as I please."

"It's my house, too," she asserted bravely.

He snorted. "You're forgetting who pays the bills."

"It was Mama's house and you've obviously forgotten that I'm your only child."

"Now, *that's* something I never forget. Biggest disappointment of my life."

Tracy flushed. "Don't you ever get tired of being so despicable?"

Judge Wentworth removed the cigar from his lips and stared at his daughter. "My, my, you're in a temper tonight. I guess it didn't go well at the church."

"That depends on your perspective."

"What does that mean?"

"Bailey Jones is an articulate speaker, maybe because he's a chip off the old block."

"Don't be crude."

She laughed bitterly. "Crude? What a joke. You've got the patent on crude."

Wentworth sighed. "Just tell me what happened."

"We'll have John Deere tractors razing the whole area by the end of the week."

The judge's face looked grim in the lamplight.

"What difference does it make now anyway?" she asked. "It's closing the barn door after the horse has already escaped."

"We'll come about. You'll see."

"There's no *we*, Daddy. This is your baby." She lifted her hands to her forehead and rubbed her temples. "You deserve everything you get."

"I don't like your tone, daughter," Wentworth said coldly. "I've worked very hard for what I have. I wish you'd appreciate that. God knows I've done enough for you. Everything you have, even Tess—"

She lifted her head, eyes narrowed, mouth tight with rage. "Don't you dare say anything about Tess."

"I only meant—"

A voice cut through their argument. "Why are you yelling at each other?"

Like a movie reel set in slow motion, the judge and his daughter turned toward the sound.

Tess stood in the doorway in cotton pajama bottoms, her shoulders bare and brown beneath the spaghetti-strapped tank top.

Tracy moistened her lips. "Nothing, honey. You're in bed early. Do you feel poorly?"

"I had a headache. What are y'all excited about?"

Wentworth stubbed out his cigar, watching the smoke rise and curl around his nose. "Nothing that concerns you, Tess, honey."

Tess frowned. "Does this have something to do with Bailey's land?"

"Your mother was at the town meeting," the judge explained. "Neither of us wants the wetlands disturbed. We don't need the kind of people those condominiums will attract."

Tess looked at her mother. "I didn't know you were so ecologically minded. Since when have you cared about the wetlands?"

Tracy smiled brightly, unable to speak.

"They've been here since the beginning of time," the judge cut in smoothly. "I'm a traditionalist. Change disturbs me."

"Chloe called me," said Tess. "The sale is going through as long as Weber holds off on any construction until the end of the investigation."

Across the smoke-filled room, Tracy Wentworth's eyes met those of her father.

Tess glanced from one to the other. Something

wasn't right. "I'm for a glass of iced tea. Does anyone else feel like one?"

"No, thanks," said her mother. "I'm tired. I think I'll turn in."

"Not for me, either," said the judge.

Barefoot, Tess padded down the hallway to the kitchen. She flicked on the light, opened the refrigerator and poured herself a glass of Verna Lee's spiced tea over ice. Then she stepped outside to the screened porch and sat down, lifting her hair off the back of her neck. Lights twinkled in the distance. Somewhere out there beyond the band of black that was the Chesapeake, normal families went about the business of living. She closed her eyes and imagined them, men and women who sat on either side of their children, playing board games or watching movies. A bowl of popcorn would sit on the coffee table. The dishwasher would be running in the background. A large dog would be splayed on the wood floor, his eyes drooping with contentment. Over the heads of their children, the man and his wife would glance at each other and smile, sharing some kind of intimate communication.

Tess sighed. She wasn't naive enough to believe that her daydream was the norm, but she held on to it anyway, something to believe in, to reach for. She closed her eyes, rewinding to the conversation she'd just heard, and concentrated.

Her mother had called Bailey Jones a chip off the old block. Tess's forehead wrinkled. What did it mean? And what was all that about closing the barn door after the horse had escaped?

Tess didn't believe for a minute that her mother and grandfather had developed environmental principles. They were both steadfast in their contempt for tree huggers, touting profit over conservation every time. Not that her mother was as rabid about her opinions as her grandfather, but then she rarely thought things through the way he did. What could they have been arguing about? She recalled that her own name had come up. Surely it wasn't about her. Tess shook her head and swallowed the last of her tea. Something smelled rotten in Denmark. But what?

It nagged at her, something she couldn't quite put her finger on. She stared out at the dark water. *Everything you have, even Tess...* Her breathing sounded labored in the quiet of the porch. Why was she so anxious? Her grandfather's words were nothing more than his usual refrain about how much they owed him for supporting them. That was it. Nothing more than that.

Pushing down her unanswered questions, she stood up and left the porch, rinsed her glass, set it in the dishwasher and climbed the back stairs to the second story. She hesitated in front of her mother's room, debating whether or not to knock. The space beneath her door was dark. She was probably asleep. Tess continued down the hall to her own room.

Twenty

Verna Lee woke up that morning feeling good. She wasn't what anyone would call happy. Last night's vote had put a solid period to anything close to happiness. But she was a long way from miserable. She was feeling…content. Her rich alto reverberated through the coffee shop, setting the crystals hanging on the display rack into a gentle sway. She was content to be filling the sugar jars, content to be brewing her daily roast of Somalia and Swedish Supreme, content to have found premium Verona chocolate in Salisbury for her chocolate-chunk brownies, content to be alive, here in Marshy Hope Creek, on this beautiful summer morning.

It was after nine. She hadn't turned the Open for Business sign around until eight o'clock, two hours later than she normally did. She'd slept in this morning and even the two cryptic notes of complaint left taped to her door didn't rile her the way they would have yesterday or the day before. Wade's defection didn't bother her, either. The man wasn't born who could spoil her pleasure in a beautiful summer morning.

"My goodness, you have a lot of energy on such a hot day." Libba Jane walked through the door with Gina Marie in tow. "I could use some strong coffee."

Verna Lee raised an eyebrow. "Late night?"

"Yes." She rubbed her eyes. "I've been working on the reports you asked me to work up. I'd hate to put a spoke in Bailey's wheel if he really needs to sell."

"Bailey'll be all right. The vote went in his favor." Verna Lee stooped down so that she was eye level with her niece. "Don't you look cute with your hair pulled back in a pretty pink bow."

Gina nodded gravely. "I like pink."

"Me, too. What can I get you to drink?"

"Chocolate milk," the child said promptly.

Libba groaned. "Verna Lee doesn't have chocolate milk. You know that. Why do you keep asking for it?"

Gina tilted her head. "If I keep asking her, maybe she'll get it."

"Touché!" Verna Lee laughed. "She's got something there, because guess what's in the refrigerator?"

"Don't tell me," said Libba.

Gina Marie clapped her hands. "Chocolate milk."

"Good guess. I have chocolate milk, *regular, pasteurized* chocolate milk from the grocery store."

"Can I have some?"

"May," her mother corrected her. "May I have some?"

Gina's brown eyes widened innocently. "You don't like chocolate milk."

"Stop it, Gina," her mother ordered. "You know exactly what I meant."

Verna Lee lifted Gina to a chair. "Will you sit quietly and let your mama and me talk?"

Gina twisted a dangling curl around her forefinger. "Yes."

Verna Lee set a short glass of chocolate milk, complete with straw, and a slice of banana bread, in front of her. "Be a good girl and eat your snack."

Gina smiled. "I'll be good."

Libba rolled her eyes, poured two cups of freshly perked coffee into colorful mugs and handed one to Verna Lee. "Tell me about the meeting."

"I'm surprised you didn't hear. The sale is going through as long as Weber doesn't hinder the investigation or the crime scene."

"The crime scene is fifteen years old. How much can anyone get from something that old?"

Verna Lee sipped her coffee. "More than you'd think."

Libba frowned. "What are you saying?"

"They called in a forensic anthropologist. I've done some reading," Verna Lee replied slowly. "A forensics team can reconstruct facial features from a skull. DNA from the bone marrow reveals blood type, sex, age, even the type of food a person ate for his last meal. The shape and conformation of the pelvic-area bones shows reproductive history. It's really amazing."

"Do you think Wade has all that information?"

"Definitely."

Libba bit her lip. "I'm worried about my father. If Mama had anything to do with that body, it'll kill him."

Verna Lee had forgotten Cole Delacourte. Ashamed, she rallied quickly. "Your daddy's a good man," she said sincerely. "He's spent his life helping people. Whatever your mother might have done is no reflection on him."

"She was your mother, too," Libba pointed out.

Shrugging her shoulders, Verna Lee shook her head. "Not really. I don't think of her that way. I'd rather that she not be a murderer, but whatever she did is no reflection on me or you. No one will be pointing fingers in our direction."

"I hadn't thought of it like that," Libba said slowly. "I guess leaving for all those years changed my way of looking at things. Mama was her own person, and so am I."

Verna Lee lifted her coffee cup. "Let's toast to that. To us, each her own person."

Gina Marie held up her glass. "Me, too," she shouted. "Me, too."

Libba Jane found her father sitting outside on the back porch reading the paper. "Hi, Daddy. Did you sleep in?"

He looked up, saw her and smiled. "I had trouble sleeping last night so I decided to take it easy. It's one of the advantages of retirement." He held out his arms to his granddaughter. "Hi, sweetie. Do you have a kiss for Granddaddy?"

Obediently, Gina pecked his cheek. "Can I play in the sandbox?"

"Ask your mama."

Gina Marie looked at her mother.

"Go ahead," she said, "but try not to get too dirty." She watched Gina run down the steps and across the lawn to the play area her father had installed just last year. Then she sat down beside him.

"What about you?" Cole asked. "Are you playing hooky?"

"I worked late last night. I'm taking the morning off."

"Care for some coffee?"

She shook her head. "No, thanks. I just came from Perks."

"How is Verna Lee?"

"She's fine. She said whatever Mama might have done, it won't reflect on you. She said you've spent a lifetime helping people."

"That was kind of her. However, this isn't about me."

Libba frowned. "You're still worried, aren't you?"

Cole folded the paper carefully, replacing each section exactly as it was. "Did Verna Lee happen to mention whether or not she's tried to reach her father?"

"I gathered she didn't think it was much of a loss, so I didn't bring it up again. I'm sure she would have told me if she had."

"That's pride talking, and hurt. Verna Lee's childhood leaves a lot to be desired. Neither of her parents was any kind of role model."

Libba slipped on her sunglasses and stared out over the bay. The morning heat was bearable here in the shade, but out on the water only men with a healthy buildup of melanin could manage more than a few minutes. "You made me believe Mama could do no wrong."

"She was human, like the rest of us." He smiled. "Hell, maybe she was more human than the rest of us. She certainly had her weaknesses. All I know is that I met her and then I was done for."

"It's certainly a romantic story."

He nodded. "For me, it was."

A lump rose in Libba's throat. It was hard to breathe. "For half my life I thought she was wonderful."

"I know."

"And for the other half, I thought I hated her."

"*Hate's* a strong word, Libba Jane. I don't believe you hated your mother."

She continued as if he hadn't spoken. "It took coming back to realize that I loved her after all, even if she did banish me for all that time."

"That was all in your head. She was waiting for you to come home. She didn't want you to think she was running your life. She didn't want to be like her parents."

"I had a hard time reconciling what she did to Verna Lee."

"If you're honest with yourself, you might consider that it's what she did to *get* Verna Lee that bothers you more. No one likes to think of her mother as a sexual being."

"Why doesn't what she did bother you, Daddy?"

"It doesn't concern me," he said. "I never doubted that she was faithful to me. What happened before we met had no bearing on our life together. I loved Nola Ruth, her beauty, her intelligence and her mystery. It was all part of her." He smiled at his daughter. "You're very like her."

Libba shook her head. "I don't think so."

"You're saying that because you can't imagine doing what she did, but if you think about it, your lives have parallels. You ran away with an unsuitable man, married him and gave birth to a daughter. The differences are the race factor and the reaction of your parents. We didn't run after you and annul the marriage. Because of how we behaved, you stayed married and raised your child."

"Give me some credit, Daddy," she protested. "I wouldn't have given Chloe away even if my marriage was dissolved."

Cole's blue eyes studied her. "The world is a different place, Libba Jane. Who knows what you would have done in 1962 if you were living in the Deep South and your child was obviously of a different race."

Libba nodded toward Gina Marie, contentedly ladling sand into a pail. "I couldn't have given up my daughter, Daddy," she said firmly. "You can turn it a hundred different ways but, no matter what, I could never have done that."

Cole was quiet for a minute. When she looked at him he was smiling. "I believe you."

She reached across the table and linked her fingers with his. "You should stop worrying. Life is too short."

He nodded. "There is that."

Chloe hadn't meant to eavesdrop. She was lying on the couch in her grandmother's sitting room, the coolest room in the house, reading and willing the temperature to drop. She had every intention of making her presence known right up until she heard the part about her grandmother and Verna Lee's father. Then it was too late.

Shock immobilized her. She'd heard bits and pieces of her grandmother's story, but not all of it. What would they say if she told them about the black man Bailey had seen her argue with on the road outside of town all those years ago?

Not that anyone would realize the body found in the wetlands made any difference to her, but the words paralyzed her long enough for other information to flow, information that was of an infinitely more personal nature to her mother and, therefore, not something she would wish Chloe to hear.

Now the trick was to lie still and hope she wasn't

discovered. Chloe held her breath, hoping that Serena wouldn't seek her out for any of the million and one things she thought were more suitable pastimes than sleeping away the day.

As usual, her thoughts turned to Bailey. Lately, he was strung tighter than a banjo, especially after the town-hall vote and that odd conversation with Tess's mother. He'd laughed off the notion that Nola Ruth, if pushed hard enough, was capable of murder.

Twenty-One

The call from the Oakland School District came just as Wade was about to bite into an egg-salad sandwich, the vending-machine kind that had a shelf life of twenty years, the kind he never would have considered eating at all except for his rift with Verna Lee. He couldn't very well order up something from Perks while he was snooping into her past.

"Our records are confidential," said the woman on the phone.

"Maybe I didn't make myself clear," replied Wade in his most pleasant voice. "This is Detective Wade Atkins from the Wicomico County, Maryland, police department. I'm investigating a fifteen-year-old homicide. I'd hoped it wouldn't take a court order to answer a few simple questions. All I need is a copy of the file."

The silence on the other end was almost palpable.

Wade refused to help her out.

"Do you know what you're looking for, or shall I fax the entire file?" she asked after a minute.

"I'd sure appreciate the whole thing."

"It might take a day or two."

"I'm three hours ahead of you, so tomorrow, before noon, eastern standard time will be just fine."

He anticipated the click that signified a hang-up even before it happened. Wade leaned back in his chair and contemplated the ceiling. Manners sure were different north of the Mason-Dixon. No self-respecting southerner would be so rude as to hang up before saying a proper thank-you, followed by a goodbye. Wade grinned. A southerner would more than likely offer you an afternoon constitutional, shoot the breeze about old times and then talk you up behind your back to anyone who would listen.

A bright blond head opened the door and peeked in. "Hello."

Wade brought his chair forward, a thunk on the floorboards, and stood. "Hello, ma'am. What can I do for you?"

"Actually, I'm looking for Sheriff Carlisle."

"He's not in at the moment. Can I help?"

She shook her head. "No, thanks."

"You're Chloe Richards, aren't you?"

She nodded.

Wade studied her face, analyzing her features the way he had Libba Jane's, looking for signs of Verna Lee. This one with her cat-blue eyes and silvery hair, her petite figure and small bones, was a changeling, except for her smile. They all had the smile.

She wasn't smiling now. Today she was nervous. She tugged at the hem of her shirt and her lower lip was caught between her teeth. "I'd really rather wait for Sheriff Carlisle. It's a personal matter."

He stared at her, nonplussed, marveling once again at the cultural differences that divided the South from the rest of the nation. The ladies he knew would have come bearing gifts followed by questions regarding a number of things, how he was feeling, had he lost weight, what did he think about the new pizza parlor that opened up at the strip mall just outside town, did he think the new football coach from Biloxi was a good choice. Not until all subjects were exhausted and a good half hour wasted would they bring up the real subject of the visit.

Wade pulled out a chair. "Have a seat. He should be back shortly."

"I don't want to disturb you."

"You're not. I was just going over the photos of this crime scene for the hundredth time, hoping something new pops out at me."

Chloe sat, tucking one leg beneath her. "What are you hoping for? I mean, it all happened a long time ago."

"You'd be surprised how the learning curve goes up the longer you look at something."

She looked interested. "What have you learned?"

"We know the victim is a female, middle-aged, Caucasian. We know she was killed with a small pistol at close range. We know her blood type, the extent of her dental work, surgeries, whether she had any broken bones. Very shortly, we'll have a fairly accurate composite of what she looked like."

Chloe stared at him, her mouth slightly open. "You're sure about all this?"

"We are."

"Are there ever mistakes?"

Wade thought a minute. "Maybe. Personally, I've never seen it."

Chloe sat back in her chair. "Why are you telling me all this?"

"It's public record, Chloe. I'm not spilling government secrets."

"Does Bailey know?"

"If he's read today's paper."

She jumped up. "I've got to go. Thanks for your time."

"Whoa. I thought you were waiting for the sheriff."

"I was, but it's not important now. See you later."

Wade watched her leave, a thoughtful look on his face.

Drusilla Washington sucked in her cheeks, pursed her lips, balled her hand into a fist and knocked the side of her head to clear the fog from her brain. Where were her glasses? She was sure she'd left them in the pocket of her apron but they weren't there when she went to look for them. Yesterday her house key wasn't on the shelf by the door and she was a day early for her standing appointment at the beauty parlor. The idea that her mind was dimming terrified her.

She knew what Verna Lee would say. She was too old to live alone, too old to keep ministering to the sharecroppers who came seasonally to harvest peaches and shuck corn, too old to continue the independence she craved as fiercely as the parched piedmont soil lapped up the first rain of the season.

Drusilla walked out to the porch and sat down on a straight-backed chair. It wasn't right the way age crept up on a person. For the first thirty years, she'd been too busy surviving to pay attention to the passing of years. Then another twenty flew by while she raised Verna Lee. By the time she'd stopped to look around and wonder where the time went, she was seventy years old and there was less time ahead of her than behind.

She didn't regret any of it, especially not when it came to protecting Verna Lee. Drusilla never had much to pass along. The child had to find a way to pay for that fancy schooling all by herself. While her classmates had educated parents to help them, Verna Lee had to learn her sums and her spelling and her grammar all alone. But when push came to shove, when it really mattered, Drusilla was there.

Soft lips brushed her cheek. Drusilla's eyelids fluttered. "Verna Lee, is that you?"

"In the flesh." Her granddaughter's tall, lush figure blocked out the setting sun. She held up a basket. "I brought you some dinner. Are you hungry?"

"That depends on what you brought."

"Catfish, a green salad, red-roasted potatoes with rosemary and apple pie. How does that sound?"

"Delicious."

Verna Lee laughed. "Good. Let's eat out here. I'll bring out the TV trays and set it up."

Drusilla leaned back and closed her eyes again. The child was a blessing. At first she hadn't wanted to take on Nola Ruth's half-caste baby girl. Raising a child wasn't easy. She'd managed to avoid the pitfalls of unwed motherhood. It required planning and discipline, but she'd done it. Cleaning up after lily-white Nola Ruth Beauchamp wasn't in her plans. But she'd taken one look at the squalling baby girl, saw the look of pain and horror in the mother's eyes and knew she couldn't walk away. So many years had passed since then. She hadn't asked for or taken money, either, not even when it was offered. Maybe that wasn't fair to Verna Lee, but Drusilla had experience with blood money. It came with strings. It was better to manage on your own. That way no one expected anything. Nola Ruth eventually took the hint and left them alone.

Drusilla frowned. Maybe she shouldn't have told Verna Lee about her birth mother. She didn't give a skunk's stripe about Nola Ruth Delacourte. But she loved Verna Lee. When the girl asked, Drusilla told her. She'd never lied to her, except once. Maybe now was the time to set it to rights.

"All set, Gran." Verna Lee set the brimming plates on the trays. "Dig in."

"My, my. This is fine. Where did you learn to cook like this?"

Verna Lee swallowed a mouthful of salad. "From you."

Drusilla chuckled. "I know. It wasn't much but at least it was something."

Verna Lee's smile faded. She stared at the nut-colored old woman, at her hunched shoulders, her frail arms and matchstick legs, at her face lined with age and experience and the kind of acceptance that comes when life deals mostly setbacks. Her throat closed. She could barely get the words out.

"It was a lot, Gran. I make my living from your cooking. Don't minimize what you did for me."

Drusilla pushed the fish around on her plate. "I got something to tell you. It's about that man."

"What man?"

"The one who came to the store the day you opened, the one who asked about the Delacourtes."

Verna Lee set down her fork. "Are you talking about Anton Devereaux, my father?"

"You know?"

"Yes, but I found out only recently."

"I was wrong not to tell you who he was."

"It's okay, Gran. It happened a long time ago."

"He had fancy clothes and a fancy car. I was afraid you'd leave again. It wasn't easy for me when you were gone. I didn't want it to happen again."

"It's okay," Verna Lee repeated. "I understand. It doesn't matter."

"You're good to say that, Verna Lee, but it does. I was thinking of myself and not you. Maybe your life would've been different."

"My life is fine. Everything turned out. Stop worrying and eat your dinner."

Twenty-Two

Tess Hennessey twisted the cap of the mayonnaise jar until her palm burned. It refused to budge. Frustrated, she cracked the top against the rim of the porcelain sink and tried turning it again. This time it opened. She pulled a knife from the silverware drawer, scooped out a healthy portion and spread it across a slice of soft white bread. Then she repeated the process with another slice.

"Careful," her mother said, coming up behind her. "That stuff puts dimples in your hips."

"I don't have a weight problem," replied Tess.

"No," Tracy agreed. "And you don't want one, either. Mustard tastes just as good."

Ignoring her mother Tess layered slices of roast beef, cheddar cheese, lettuce and tomatoes on one slice and covered it with the other. Picking up the sandwich, she leaned over the sink and bit into it.

"Tess Hennessey, whatever has gotten into you? Did you get up on the wrong side of the bed? What time did you get up anyway? It's after twelve and I haven't seen you all morning."

Tess opened her mouth to answer but Tracy cut her off. "Finish chewing, please."

"There's nothing wrong with me," replied Tess after she'd swallowed her mouthful of sandwich. "I just wish you wouldn't examine everything I do to find something wrong."

"That's ridiculous."

Tess shook her head. "No. You're treating me like Granddad treats you. Do you want me to feel about you the way you feel about him?"

"I love my father," sputtered Tracy.

"You have an odd way of showing it."

Her comment did not have the desired reaction. Tracy folded her arms and raised a quizzical eyebrow. "Is something wrong?"

"You mean, besides what I just told you?"

"Yes. You're behaving very unlike yourself. Sometimes, people who have a problem with someone else pick on the people they're closest to."

"Believe me, it's not that."

"I haven't seen Chloe around lately."

Tess rinsed off the knife and stuck it in the dishwasher. "Since when does Chloe ever hang around here?"

"Has something happened between the two of you?"

"Mama, stop." Tess held up her hands. "Give it up."

Tracy moved to the refrigerator, opened it and pulled out a pitcher of iced tea. "Do you want some?"

"No."

As if she hadn't heard, Tracy filled two glasses and set one in front of her daughter. Then she sat down at the table. "Sit down, Tess."

Reluctantly Tess pulled out a chair and sat.

"I don't want it to be this way between us," Tracy began. "You're my only child and you're not a teenager. We're supposed to be close. I need you to communicate with me. If I've done something to hurt you, tell me. How else can I fix it?"

Tess stared at her mother. She was too logical, too calm. "What if you can't fix it?"

A tiny worried vee appeared between Tracy's eyes. "For heaven's sake, Tess, what are you talking about?"

"I want you to tell me what you and Granddad were talking about the other night."

"What night?"

Was it Tess's imagination, or was there a hint of strain around her mother's eyes?

"The night you went to the town council meeting."

The silence lasted an instant too long. Tracy ran her tongue across her bottom lip. "I don't remember."

"You said Bailey was a chip off the old block. What did you mean?"

This time Tess saw real fear cross her mother's face.

"I don't remember. You must have taken my comment out of context. I probably meant he takes after Lizzie."

"Was Lizzie Jones a good speaker?"

"No. Yes." Tracy faltered and recovered. "What's going on? Why the third degree? What's this obsession with Bailey Jones?" A look of dawning horror crossed her face. "You aren't interested in him, are you?"

Tess leaned forward. "You really should tell me because I'm imagining the worst."

"The worst?" Tracy's hand moved to her throat.

"Yes." Tess spoke slowly, deliberately. "I'm thinking that Bailey and Granddad are related and there's only one way that could have happened."

Tracy remained silent.

Tess continued. "I'm guessing that Bailey is your son and my half brother. You had him with someone when you were really young, someone Granddad hated, so you had to give him up. Maybe the body in the swamp is Bailey's father. Maybe somebody killed him."

Tracy contained herself no longer. "That's absurd. Your imagination is ridiculous. Bailey Jones is not my son. I won't have you thinking that about me. I can't listen to this."

"You're the one who wanted to communicate."

"Not this way."

"You said Bailey was a chip off the old block."

"I wasn't talking about me," Tracy burst out.

Tess stirred her tea with her little finger. Her mother was obviously distraught and just as obviously sincere. If she was telling the truth... Suddenly Tess's eyes widened with understanding. "It's Granddad, isn't it? Granddad is Bailey's father."

"Don't be ridiculous." Tracy's protest was weaker this time.

Tess shook her head. "It won't work, Mama. You may as well tell me. Something's going on around here and I'm the only one who doesn't know."

Tracy stood. "I can't tell you. It isn't mine to tell. Give me some credit for family loyalty."

"What about Bailey? Isn't he family, too? Where's your loyalty to him?"

"He isn't family," Tracy hissed. "Don't you ever say such a thing. He's a mistake, a terrible, terrible mistake."

Tess watched her struggle for control. "I wish you would trust me," she said simply.

"Our conversation is over," Tracy snapped. "I don't want it to leave this room. It *can't* leave this room. Do you understand?"

Their showdown was interrupted by the sound of the doorbell. Tess left her glass on the counter and started up the back stairs, when Camille, their housekeeper, walked into the kitchen.

"A police detective is here to see the judge."

Tracy paled. Her hand moved to her throat. "Have you told him?"

Camille shook her head. "No, ma'am. That's why I came to find you."

"This is ridiculous, Camille," Tracy protested. "Your job description includes answering the door and reporting the name of the visitor."

"I know my job description, Miz Tracy, but I have my limits and telling your daddy the police want to see him is one of 'em."

"Please, Camille," Tracy wheedled. "You know how his temper affects me."

Tess exploded. "I can't believe this. Mama, you are absolutely pathetic. I'll tell Granddad." She continued up the stairs and disappeared into the hallway.

A full ten minutes later, Wade was ushered into the judge's library.

"Thank you, Teresa," said the judge. "That will be all."

"I'd like to stay."

"That isn't advisable."

She looked at Wade. "Can I stay?"

Wade shook his head. "Not this time."

Wentworth waited until the door closed behind her. He waved his hand. "Sit down. What is it this time?"

Wade sat down. "I phoned your sister-in-law."

"Please. That relationship ended with Amanda's death."

Wade ignored him. "I assume you were never on good terms."

"You assume correctly."

"Why not?"

"I beg your pardon?"

Wade waited. He wasn't as versed in loopholes as Wentworth, but he could play a decent game, too.

The judge sighed. "My wife confided in her frequently. As is usually the case, women rarely discuss a husband's assets when they gossip, only his liabilities."

"She said you prevented Mrs. Wentworth from visiting."

"I was never able to prevent Amanda from doing anything she wanted to do."

"In other words, your relationship was difficult."

"Not at all. Amanda was queen under her own roof. I gave her everything she asked for."

"Violet Dixon believes she was unhappy."

"Naturally she would say that. As I explained, women rarely call their sisters when things are going well, which, in Amanda's case, was nearly all the time."

"Tell me about Lizzie Jones's land."

Wentworth blinked. "Excuse me?"

"The Jones land. Tell me about it."

"How would I—"

"Cut the crap, Quentin. Fifteen years ago the Jones wetlands were yours."

"I sold the property. People sell land."

"No money was exchanged. You quit-claimed the parcel back to her. Give me a plausible reason for doing that."

"Am I a suspect?"

"Answer the question."

"I don't think so. Not without my attorney."

"I could place you under arrest."

"I wouldn't do that if I were you."

Wade was contrary enough to consider the possibility, even though he knew Wentworth would be home within two hours. Reason prevailed and he stood. "Nice talking with you, Quentin. Have a pleasant afternoon."

* * *

Tess knocked on the door of the Busby house. A paint-spattered Bailey Jones answered the door. He grinned when he saw her. "If you're here to collect Chloe, she's gone."

"I came to see you."

"I'm flattered."

Tess didn't answer. She was looking at Bailey objectively. He was probably the best-looking male she'd ever seen, but she wasn't in the least bit interested. She never had been. Now she knew why.

"I need some answers."

"What makes you think I have them?"

Tess stamped her foot in exasperation. "C'mon, Bailey. This is important."

"Temper, temper," he chided her. "No one likes a spoiled princess."

"Is that what you think I am? A spoiled princess?"

He shrugged. "If the shoe fits…"

"Well, it doesn't. This won't take long." She pushed past him and stopped, staring in surprise at the walls. "Mrs. Busby is going to kill you."

Bailey closed the door and stood beside her. "I think it's pretty good."

"It's incredible, but no one wants pictures of sharecroppers on her living-room walls."

"I do."

"Like I said, she's going to kill you."

"I'll change it back." He waved her to a drop-cloth covered chair. "Have a seat."

Tess sat. "I had a conversation with my mother."

Bailey lit a cigarette and leaned against an unadorned wall. "Congratulations. That must have taken an act of God."

"I'll get right to the point."

"Please do."

"I think my grandfather is your father."

He drew on the end of his cigarette and blew out a spume of smoke. "Where did you get an idea like that?"

"I heard them talking. I figured it out. Is it true?"

"How would I know?"

"Is he?"

Bailey's eyes narrowed. "I shouldn't be the one telling you this."

Tess's hands shook. "What are we going to do?"

"I'll try not to dishonor the family name," Bailey taunted her.

"I doubt you could make it any worse." She bit her lip. "I'm sorry about the way they've treated you."

"Don't be," he said shortly. "It has nothing to do with you, or your mother."

"How long do you think she's known?"

Bailey shook his head. "You'll have to ask her

that. I don't know much more than you. I don't have question-and-answer sessions with your family."

"They're your family, too," she said in a small voice.

"Don't remind me."

Tess looked down at her hands. For some insane reason she felt like crying.

"Hey." Bailey crouched down beside her. "Don't take it personally. My mother had a reputation. Everybody knows that. Your granddad is a jerk. Everybody knows that, too. We both got screwed when it comes to the maternal side of the family. But you lucked out. You've got Russ and Libba Jane and Chloe. They're fine people." Again he grinned. "The jury's still out on Gina Marie."

Tess laughed. She felt better. "So, what gives with you and Chloe?"

"We're outsiders, both of us."

Tess wondered whether Chloe would tell her the same thing. "I'd like to know you better, Bailey."

She watched the skin tighten across the bladed bones of his cheeks.

"I don't think that's a good idea," he said slowly. "Your mother wouldn't approve."

"I'm over eighteen."

Bailey sighed. "Look, Tess. I don't want you to be in trouble with your family."

"I'm not asking you to move into the extra bedroom. I'm talking about an e-mail now and then."

He studied her face, the trembling chin and hopeful brown eyes. "I guess that wouldn't hurt."

Her relief was obvious. She stood up quickly, before he could change his mind. "That's settled. I'll see you around."

He walked her to the door. "This isn't a promise you have to keep, Tess. Things may get a little uncomfortable around here before they get better. I won't hold it against you if you side with your grandfather."

She frowned. "What are you talking about?"

"I'm warning you, that's all."

She was thinking about his words when the only light in town turned red just as she entered the intersection. Eighty-year-old Agnes Hobbs, driving her 1976 Oldsmobile, caught the tail end of Tess's sporty Mazda coupe in a direct hit so hard that it spun the tiny car around three times before it turned over.

Twenty-Three

Once again, Bailey was interrupted. This time it was Detective Atkins.

He blocked the doorway with his body. "You got a warrant?"

Wade rubbed his jaw. "Don't make this difficult."

"I'm busy right now."

"This won't take long."

Bailey opened his mouth to refuse and changed his mind. "You're not going away, are you?"

"No."

"Do I need my lawyer?"

"That depends on what you tell me."

"Are you reading me my rights?"

"You're not on my list of murder suspects, if that's what you're asking."

Bailey grinned. "Then I won't call him."

Wade followed Bailey into the house, glancing at the brightly colored figures covering the walls. "Nice work."

Bailey raised a skeptical eyebrow. "No offense, but would you know nice work if you saw it?"

"Can't say that I would."

Bailey stopped suddenly and turned, looking Wade up and down. "You're all right here, aren't you, no hidden depths or mixed messages?"

"No one's ever called me deep, if that's what you mean."

Bailey laughed. "Want a beer?"

"Some other time. I'm on duty."

"Suit yourself." Bailey waved his hand. "Sit down." He picked up his brush. "You don't mind if I finish up, do you?"

"Not at all." Wade chose a deep comfortable leather chair. "I need to know why you're so set on developing your mother's land."

"Money," Bailey replied immediately. He added a bit of white to the wall and a woman's head scarf took shape. "And it's my land."

"I was outside during the town-hall meeting the other night. I overheard your conversation with Tracy Wentworth. You don't need money."

"There's no love lost between the Wentworths and me."

"Care to tell me why?"

"Not particularly."

Wade persisted. "She accused you of wanting revenge."

"Really?" He stood back, frowned and changed the shape of an elbow. "I don't remember."

"What did Wentworth do to you?"

Bailey changed tactics, set his brush aside, pulled up a chair and sat down across from Wade. "Why do you want to know?"

The detective surprised him with his bluntness. "I have a gut feeling it has something to do with the body found on your land. There's a missing piece and it bothers me."

"How do you know it isn't some old bum who got confused out there in the marsh and couldn't find his way out?"

Wade chuckled. "I thought by now everybody'd heard our victim isn't an old bum. Don't confuse my lack of depth with stupidity. This is a homicide. Besides, Chloe Richards gave me a heads-up. She's worried about you."

Bailey's eyes narrowed. "Are you trying to tell me something?"

"There's a girl out there who thinks you need a friend," Wade replied evenly.

"And you're volunteering?"

"You could do worse."

The sound of a police siren grew progressively louder. Wade frowned and stood. "You think about what I told you. If you change your mind, you know where to find me."

He reached the intersection at the same time the medics were lifting Tess Hennessey into the ambulance. Red shards of metal and glass littered the street, the smell of burning rubber permeated the air and a mangled, unrecognizable shape that Wade assumed was once Tess's Mazda lay on its side while smoke spewed from the engine. Agnes Hobbs's heavy American sedan appeared unscathed. A crowd of curious citizens had collected on all four corners. Sheriff Carlisle was attempting to gather information.

Assessing the situation in a single sweeping glance, Wade pulled up next to the medic who was climbing into the ambulance. "How bad is she?"

"Concussion and internal bleeding. She's losing blood fast. We're on our way to County General in Salisbury."

Wade backed up, negotiated a three-corner turn, stuck his head out the window and addressed his deputy. "Need any help?"

Carlisle looked up. "We've got plenty of witnesses. The Mazda ran a red. I'd appreciate it if you'd notify the family. I'll meet you at the hospital."

He nodded. "Carry on. I'm headed for the Wentworths' and then County General."

Agnes Hobbs's stricken face smote him. He called out reassuringly, "Don't you worry, ma'am. Everything'll be fine."

"That poor little girl," she said brokenly. "Pray for her. Pray for her family."

"I surely will."

It was a harder promise to keep than it should have been. Quentin Wentworth was a sorry excuse for a human being, although Wade allowed that the thoughts of a man trained as a prosecutor would automatically turn toward negligence and the possibility of a lawsuit, even if it was his granddaughter who was at fault.

Tracy's sentiments were predictable. After her initial hysteria, she accepted Wade's offer of a ride to the hospital. "Stay here," she ordered her father. "Call Russ and tell him to meet us there."

Tracy was silent in the car. Wade dropped her off at the Emergency entrance, pulled into a reserved parking space and followed her inside.

Libba Jane and Chloe sat beside each other in the waiting room. Both women looked up when he approached.

"How is she?" he asked.

Chloe's eyes brimmed with tears. "Not good."

Libba squeezed her hand. "We don't know yet. The doctor is talking to Russ and Tracy now."

Wade nodded. "Mind if I sit with you?"

Libba Jane looked surprised. "If you like. I'm not sure how long they'll be."

Wade picked up a magazine and settled in to wait for Carlisle. As it turned out, it wasn't long. Blake hurried in, the lines of his face deep and serious. He took a seat beside Wade.

"Why are we here?" asked Wade under his breath.

"Be patient. I think I'm onto something."

Russ, white-lipped and silent, came toward them through the double doors leading to the intensive-care unit.

Libba Jane rose and walked into his arms. They closed tightly around her. Together they stood, locked in a private, intimate world of pain.

Wade smiled reassuringly at Chloe. "Where's your baby sister?"

"Granddad has her." Her eyes were on her mother and stepfather. "Tell me what's going on," she pleaded.

Slowly they parted. Russ drew a deep breath. "She has a concussion and she's still unconscious. Her liver was lacerated."

Chloe's lip trembled. "Is she going to make it?"

"It's bad," Russ replied grimly. "It means surgery."

"Can we help, donate blood, or something?"

Libba's eyes were on her husband's face. He

glanced at her and then looked away as if an unspoken message had passed between them.

"Russ?" Chloe started to cry. "I want to do something."

He stepped forward and took his stepdaughter into his arms. "I know you do, sweetheart. Tess has a rare blood type. There isn't anything any of us can do except wait for the doctors to tell us what happens next."

"What is Tess's blood type?" Chloe asked.

Russ's response was terse. "AB negative."

Wade heard Blake's quick intake of breath. He saw Libba's shoulders drop and the brief, sudden closing of her eyelids.

Chloe's face was a white mask, stoic, damp with tear tracks.

Wade looked from mother to daughter and then at Blake. What in the hell was going on here? *AB negative. AB negative.* It meant something. He stood. "If there's anything I can do—" He left the sentence open.

Russ lifted Chloe's chin. "I want you to go home with Sheriff Carlisle. Gina's too much for your granddad. Get some rest and come back in the morning. Your mother and I should know something by then."

On the way to the car, Chloe was silent. Wade glanced at her. She was a dignified little thing, classy, like her mother and her aunt.

Blake touched her arm. "It's tough, isn't it?"

"Yes."

"She's young and healthy, Chloe. More than likely she'll pull through."

"She's got a few things going against her."

Blake nodded. "Her blood type?"

"Yes."

Wade tried to reassure her. "It's just a technicality. Her mother has the same blood type, even if Russ doesn't."

"AB negative is very rare," Chloe explained. "Less than one-half of one percent of the population has it."

"I'm no biologist," replied Wade, "but even I know that you have to have the same blood type as one of your parents."

Chloe turned her cat-blue eyes on him. "Actually, you don't, not if your blood type is AB. You can have an A mother and a B father or the other way around. You can also inherit the AB type from just one parent. It's the negative thing that's difficult. You can't be negative unless one or both parents are."

They reached the police cruiser. Blake opened the door and Chloe climbed inside. He closed it and turned to Wade. "The judge donates regularly when the blood bank comes through. He considers it a point of honor. He's O positive. Nice and normal."

"What's on your mind, Carlisle?"

Blake raised a skeptical eyebrow. "Like you said, you have to have the same blood type as one of your parents."

For a minute Wade continued to struggle for understanding. Then his wires connected. "Son of a bitch."

"Are you thinking what I'm thinking?"

Wade's jaw tightened. All at once everything became completely clear. "The pathology report on the body. The woman's blood type was AB negative."

"We can exhume Amanda Wentworth."

"That would be a last resort. I don't think we'll have to."

Twenty-Four

Quentin Wentworth stood in his library holding back a corner of the curtain to look out the window. He saw the black-haired boy drive up in his silver sports car and knew a moment of fear, nothing compared to the emotion he'd experienced when the sheriff came to tell Tracy about Tess, but fear all the same.

Bailey Jones was bad news. Quentin had had a feeling about the boy ever since Lizzie told him she was pregnant. Before Lizzie, he'd kept his women in Salisbury or Annapolis, still conveniently located, but always outside Marshy Hope Creek where he was well known.

Looking back, Quentin couldn't remember what it was that attracted him to Lizzie Jones. Normally he preferred fair women. Lizzie's eyes and hair were black as sin. Some said she had Indian blood. He hadn't cared about that. She was beautiful and exotic and more important, completely uninhibited. Her legs were long and her breasts—he stopped himself. It was pointless to go down that road again. They had finished with each other years before she died, except for the boy. No one would have suspected anything if it weren't for the boy.

At first, Quentin tried to deny him. Lizzie was a whore. The child could belong to anyone. But when he'd suggested it, she'd asked him to leave. He knew she was telling the truth. Lizzie never lied. It was her penchant for telling the truth that terrified him. He gave her the land back, the land that had once belonged to her father, hoping to buy her silence. They hadn't actually agreed on terms but it was understood between them. Then all hell broke loose.

Wentworth's hands clenched. Lizzie had been careless. He couldn't forgive her for that. If there had been any possible way for him to rescind the land contract after she died, he would have done so. But someone got to Bailey first. Someone helped him, more than likely Quentin's old nemesis, Cole Delacourte.

He watched Bailey step out of the car and climb the porch steps. Then he heard the chime of the bell. Quentin waved away the maid and opened the door himself. He looked down his nose at the boy, at the son he'd sired with Lizzie Jones. "What do you want?"

Bailey grinned. "Is that any way to greet the prodigal son?"

"I'm not in the mood for social calls. My granddaughter has been in an accident."

Bailey's smile faded. "I know. Chloe told me. I'm sorry about that. I like Tess. She takes after Russ."

Quentin snorted. "Is that why you're here?"

Bailey leaned against the porch railing and lit a cigarette. "Are you coming outside or inviting me in?"

Grudgingly, Quentin stepped aside. It wouldn't do for anyone to see Bailey Jones on his front porch. "Put out your cigarette," he ordered.

Bailey took his time finishing his smoke. Deliberately, he dropped the butt on the porch and ground it beneath his heel. Then he followed the judge into the spacious library that served as his office. Quentin waved him to a chair and sat down behind his desk.

"I'll get right to the point," Bailey began.

"Please do."

"Wade Atkins is a smart man. He's headed in the right direction. When he finds out what we both know, you're going to jail for murder."

Quentin sneered. "Am I to assume you're warning me? Why would you bother?"

Bailey leaned back, crossing his arms behind his head, and surveyed the room, the polished floor, the mahogany desk and leather chairs, the original oils and the embossed books lined up behind the glass shelves. "I want you to tell people who I am. If you do, I'll tell my version of how it happened."

"I can do that myself."

"Who would believe you, especially after your cover-up?"

"Are you suggesting that someone would believe your story and not mine?"

"You don't have a story, Quentin. You've lived a lie for fifteen years. You have everything to lose."

"So do you. You already have a criminal record. That'll go against you."

Bailey shook his head. "You're grabbing at straws. I was cleared."

"But you were guilty. The jury was sympathetic and let you go, but you did kill her."

"It's ancient history." Bailey rested his hands on the desk, marring the polished effect of the expensive wood. "Atkins'll figure it out. I'd have a backup plan if I were you."

Quentin swallowed to clear the steel-wool feeling from his throat. "Spell it out. What exactly do you want from me?"

"Full disclosure. A confession admitting that I'm your son. I want the good citizens of Marshy Hope

Creek to know what kind of man you are. I want them to know how you treated my mother and me."

"My family will be ruined. It's not fair to them."

Bailey nodded. "I know what that's like."

"Tracy and Tess are innocent."

"They have my sympathies."

"They haven't hurt you. Why are you doing this to them?" Quentin's voice was a whisper.

"Tess is away most of the year," replied Bailey. "My guess is she won't settle in Marshy Hope Creek. Besides, she has Russ and Libba Jane. As for Tracy, pardon me if I don't shed any tears."

Quentin narrowed his eyes. "Why is this important to you now, after all these years? Is it respectability you want? Are you planning to take my name?"

Bailey's lip curled. "I wouldn't have your name. What I want is vindication. I want to see you humbled."

"So." The judge exhaled and leaned back in his chair. "It's all about revenge."

"Something like that."

"You know," Quentin said after a minute, "Lizzie wouldn't have wanted this. At any time she could have spoken out, but she didn't."

"My mother didn't have high expectations. She was born dirt poor. You know what her life was like. You exploited her."

"Along with half the men in town."

"You were the worst."

"That's absurd. I was decent to her. She wouldn't take my money so I bought her things. You know nothing about it."

"She loved you."

Wentworth looked pained. "And because of that, you're taking me down?"

"You did it to yourself. All I'm doing is enjoying the journey. You made a fatal mistake. Because you didn't want your relationship with a whore to become public knowledge, you killed your wife and then you covered it up." He walked to the door.

"Wait." The judge's voice was raspy. "Maybe we can reach an agreement."

"You heard my terms."

"Lizzie's gone. Amanda's death was an accident." Quentin knew he sounded desperate. "I could make it worth your while if we tweaked the facts just a little."

Bailey's eyes blazed. "You son of a bitch. You want my mother to take the fall for you."

"For God's sake, she's dead. Be reasonable."

"Negotiations are over. You already heard my offer."

"I have to think."

"You don't get it, do you? Wade Atkins is a fingernail away from figuring this out. When he does, your thinking time is over and I'm out of the picture. I don't owe you anything."

"What about the truth? You know I didn't kill her."

"The truth doesn't look so good. Besides, I was seven years old. You're up a creek, Quentin. You made a big mistake when you took matters into your own hands and didn't call the police."

"Your mother benefited. She got her daddy's land back."

Bailey shrugged. "You're an educated man. I imagine you talked her into believing it was for the best."

Wentworth swore. "I wish you'd never been born. I wish I'd never seen Lizzie Jones."

Bailey laughed. "Take it from me. Wishes belong in fairy tales. They never do anybody any good out here in the real world." He sauntered toward the door. "I'll see you around."

Quentin stood. "Is there anyone else who knows about this?"

Bailey turned. "Of course. I'm not stupid and I don't trust you or your daughter. This time history isn't going to repeat itself. What amazes me is that you actually believe being arrested, tried and convicted is less embarrassing than acknowledging I'm your son."

"I don't want Tess to know. No one else matters."

Bailey whistled. "You do have an Achilles' heel after all. Who would have thought it was Tess."

"Tracy knows."

"I've got news for you, Quentin. So does Tess."

The judge's face whitened. "You told her?"

"No. She figured it out after overhearing a conversation between you and her mother. Tess is a pretty sharp girl."

"She came to you?"

"If it's any consolation, I think she tried asking her mother first."

Quentin looked old and broken. For the first time Bailey felt sorry for him. He loved his granddaughter. He hadn't loved his wife and he tolerated his daughter, but he loved Tess and that love had nothing to do with who her parents were. A small burn started in the center of his chest. He recognized the green flame of envy immediately. He'd lived with it most of his life, envious of kids with fathers, envious of their new clothes at the beginning of a new season, envious of their lunches and their spending money and the easy way they gathered in groups, talking, calling out to each other, laughing, making plans that never once included him. Where and when had Quentin Wentworth decided that Tess Hennessey, his granddaughter, should be the recipient of his affections and not Bailey, his son?

"You go on home, Bailey," said the judge at last. "But first let me give you a piece of advice."

"What's that?"

"If you want something badly, don't tell anyone, especially not the person who doesn't want to give it to you. You lose your power that way."

Bailey's eyes met the judge's. "I'll keep that in mind."

"And Bailey?"

"Yes?"

"You're like Lizzie. You don't have it in you to lie. When push comes to shove, you'll tell it like it was."

Bailey shook his head and looked at the floor, a bitter smile twisting his lips. "Don't count on it." Then he left the room, walked past the gallery of Wentworth ancestors framed in wood and silver and let himself out.

Wade needed another look at the fifteen-year-old coroner's report on Amanda Wentworth. A blast of cool air hit him as soon as he opened the door to the sheriff's office. Thank God Carlisle had remembered to leave on the air conditioner.

The blinking light on the fax machine alerted him to a waiting message. He picked up the file and glanced at the subject heading. It was from Marin County, California. He read quickly, not quite believing the printed words. Then he read them once more.

Amanda Wentworth's report slid to second priority now. Folding the faxed pages in half, and then in half again, he slid them into his back pocket, and left the station in search of Verna Lee.

As expected, he found her at Perks, closing up for the evening.

"Wade, how nice to see you." Her voice was warm with pleasure. "Can I get you anything?"

"That depends."

Her tawny-gold eyes widened. "On what?"

"On how this conversation goes."

She filled two glasses with ice and poured in lemonade from a glass pitcher. Handing one to Wade, she sat down on the couch and motioned for him to sit beside her.

Instead, he pulled up a chair from a nearby table and faced her. Steeling himself against the weakness her presence never failed to arouse, he focused on the row of unusual glass bottles on the shelf behind her head. "I don't know where to begin."

Her smile faltered. "What's this all about?"

"I want you to tell me about California."

"California?"

He nodded. "All of it. Don't leave anything out."

"Wade, I—"

He held up his hand. "Before you start, I'm telling you this is important. I'm not proud, Verna Lee. That was whipped out of me before I lost my milk teeth, and there isn't much I haven't seen or couldn't justify after sifting through a wagonload of facts. But this is different. This is the time and place for the truth."

She stared at him, her eyes on his face, her long fingers holding the sweating glass. Finally she swallowed. "How did you find out?"

"I checked you out. Law enforcement has its benefits."

"You had me investigated?" Her voice lowered, assuming a calmness that could only be repressed rage.

"Get mad, Verna Lee. Get as mad as you want, but start talking."

"This is pointless. You've already judged me."

He waited.

"What exactly do you think you know?"

He shook his head. "You don't get to ask the questions. Your job is to tell it like it is, the whole truth and nothing but the truth."

"I don't have to tell you anything. I haven't committed a crime. You have no right to question me."

The blue eyes were stone cold. "Not unless you want me to walk out that door and never come back. Somehow, I don't think so."

"You think mighty highly of yourself."

"Yes, ma'am, I do. I'm also a fairly good judge of character. At least I was. Tell me the truth and prove that I am."

She stiffened, set down her glass on the shelf beside her and rested her hands on her knees. "All right. Have it your way." She smoothed her skirt and closed her eyes as if summoning reserves from somewhere deep inside herself for the ordeal to come.

"I had a job teaching high-school history in the Marin County School District in California. The community demographics were, at the time, white, professional and educated."

Wade knew it well. Marin County had profited from the dot-com explosion. The population was very comfortable, not wealthy enough to rub elbows with old money or Hollywood movie stars, but affluent enough to disregard the bother of balancing their checkbooks.

Verna Lee bit her lip. "I wanted to educate young people. Those kids had everything going for them, including a sense of entitlement that only money can bring. Drugs and cheating were rampant. I wouldn't tolerate it. Pretty soon I had a reputation. Only the best and the brightest were assigned to my classes. At first I didn't realize how much the staff resented me." Her mouth twisted. "I thought they were my friends."

"How long were you there?"

"Nine years."

"So, you were a permanent teacher?"

"There are no *permanent* teachers, Wade. At any time a teacher can be let go, if the reason, or in my case the manufactured reason, is good enough."

"Were you fired?"

"In a manner of speaking. Officially, I resigned at the end of the school year."

"I think you'd better finish your story."

"The last year I was there, one of the star football players showed up in my class. His name was Troy Leland. He was an incredible athlete and his grades, on paper, were outstanding.

"Right away, something didn't add up. He couldn't write a coherent paragraph and his punctuation was atrocious. Normally, in an honors history class, students don't read orally, but we were studying copies of original documents." She shook her head. "He couldn't do it. It was painful to listen to him. I started asking his former teachers about his grades. Most didn't say a thing. A few told me not to rock the boat, that he was scholarship material because of football. I should have listened to them."

"But you flunked him anyway," Wade finished for her.

"At the time I believed it was important to stand on principle. It wasn't fair to the kids who earned their grades honestly."

"Then what happened?"

"He was benched until he pulled up his grade."

"I imagine you were under quite a bit of pressure."

"That's an understatement. I was harassed. My car was vandalized. My tires were slashed and my windows broken. I was threatened by crank calls. My house was tagged." Her eyes blazed. "Can you imagine how I felt? I lived in California, a blue state, one of the most liberal zip codes in the country, and I was right back in pre-civil rights Selma, Alabama."

"Did you cave?"

"Not at first, not until the subpoena."

"The subpoena?"

She threw him a withering glance. "Don't tell me you didn't know."

"Actually, I didn't. Everything you've said so far is new information."

"The Lelands charged me with child molestation. They claimed their son's grade in my class was the direct result of his spurning my inappropriate proposition." She lifted her chin, challenging him to respond.

He met her gaze coolly, without judgment.

"I didn't do it, Wade. I swear I didn't. He was a child."

"It never occurred to me that you had."

She released her breath and the ramrod straightness of her spine sagged. "Thank you for that," she said after a minute. "My husband wasn't as generous. He left me."

The line of his lips tightened. "Go on."

"They pulled my credentials. I was suspended without pay. I hired an attorney. He worked out a settlement. If I passed Troy with a B, no charges would be filed. I could leave the district and seek employment elsewhere."

"But it didn't turn out that way, did it?"

She shook her head. "I came home, moved in with my grandmother and applied for a job here in Marshy Hope Creek. There were openings, but I couldn't get a job anywhere. I requested a copy of my file. It was all there. The charges, my suspension, my letter of resignation, everything."

"Then what happened?"

Color stained her cheeks. "Cecil Edwards, the superintendent, told me I had a job if I agreed to sleep with him. I refused. He told me I'd never work as a teacher again. That's when I cashed in my retirement and bought this place." She looked directly at him. "That's it. You have it, the whole truth and nothing but the truth."

"Why didn't you sue the Marin County School District? You had a court-ordered agreement."

"At first, I was humiliated. I didn't want anyone to know. I'd left here with such high hopes. There were a few who would've been happy to see me humbled. Later, it didn't matter." She lifted her head. "I enjoy working for myself."

Wade shook his head.

"What now?" she demanded.

"When I asked what brought you back here, you wouldn't tell me. Why?"

"It's not something I'm proud of."

"Christ, Verna Lee. We slept together. Why didn't you trust me?"

"I was waiting for the right time, but you beat me to it."

"What's that supposed to mean?"

"It means that you lived up to expectation. You didn't wait for me to confide in you. You went behind my back and spied on me. That's as bad as reading my mail. How am I supposed to trust a man who does that?"

Twenty-Five

Wade swore and kicked the drawer of the file cabinet shut. Marshy Hope Creek wasn't the technology center of Maryland, but surely it warranted a late-model computer. It was too much to expect him to be forensic specialist and homicide detective all at the same time without an adequate filing system.

Sheriff Carlisle had the misfortune of walking through the door at the very moment Wade's temper was uncharacteristically on display.

"Did you file away those folders I told you about in the back room?"

Carlisle reddened. "No," he confessed. "I haven't had time. I put the tabs on the files and stacked them in boxes in the closet."

Wade's face lit up, his bad mood instantly evaporating. "God bless all procrastinators. Blake, I'm so tickled with you right now, I'd kiss you if you weren't so damn ugly."

Blake grinned. "Whatever I did, I'm grateful. What's up?"

"Find the accident report on Amanda Wentworth. I want to see the death certificate and any medical documents."

Blake whistled. "Are we closing in?"

"Could be."

"What about the composite?"

"I'm still waiting on it. A fifteen-year-old murder isn't the coroner's highest priority." Wade stood. "I'll be out for a while. How long do you think it'll take?"

"I'll have it for you in an hour or so."

Wade nodded. "I'm for some lunch. Can I pick up anything for you?"

"Are you going to Perks?"

Wade cleared his throat. "I thought I'd try something different today."

Blake's eyebrows lifted. "Why? You won't get anything better around here."

"I'm sure Verna Lee would appreciate the compliment. I'll see what I can do."

Despite his intentions, Wade found himself standing in front of the Perks Welcome sign. He pushed open the door and walked in. Verna Lee was scooping her freshly made chicken salad into a large plastic container. Her hair was twisted up off her neck and held in place with a clip that looked like a giant claw with a chopstick threaded through the middle. She looked up. "It's a little early for lunch, isn't it, Wade?"

He sat down at the empty counter. "That depends on what time a person has breakfast. I skipped mine this morning, so I figure I'm about five hours overdue."

Her voice was cool. "What can I get for you?"

"I'd like some of that chicken salad you're about to put away, on sourdough bread, toasted. Make one up for Blake, too."

She set a glass of iced tea in front of him. "Coming right up."

"I won't keep you in suspense."

"What makes you think I'm in it?"

"Because I know you."

She wasn't smiling. "I don't think you do."

The apology tumbled from his lips. "I'm sorry, Verna Lee. I should have waited for you to tell me in your own time. I have no excuse for what I did." He frowned. "I don't even know why I did it, except that you frustrated the hell out of me when you wouldn't tell me why you came back here."

"I did tell you."

He shook his head. "I knew there was more to it."

"Why was it important to you?"

"That should be obvious."

"Not to me."

"I've always had a thing for you, even when we were kids. I couldn't believe you were back here. It was too perfect. I wanted to rule out any red flags. I didn't want to fall in love with you if—"

"Stop right there." Angry color stained her cheeks and chest. "Turn around and walk out of here before I throw something at you."

He couldn't have heard her correctly. "I beg your pardon?"

"Leave. Now."

"Verna Lee, I—"

"You have some nerve. You had me checked out to see if I was worthy enough to fall in love with?" She pointed to the door. "Get out."

Sheriff Carlisle picked up the phone and dialed the number of the physician who had served the population on the right side of Marshy Hope Creek for nearly five decades. His receptionist answered. "Nellie, this is Blake." He didn't wait for her reply. "I'm conducting an investigation. If I have to, I'll get a court order, but in the end the final result will be the same, so do us both a favor and just answer one question without passing it by Doc Balieu."

He heard her sigh. "Shame on you, Blake Carlisle. Are you tryin' to get me fired?"

Blake grinned. Nellie had worked in the same office for thirty years. "If that happens, I'll hire you."

Another sigh. "What can I do for you, Sheriff?"

"I need to verify Tracy Wentworth's blood type."

"Hold on."

Blake waited a full three minutes. Finally she returned to the phone. "AB negative."

"I owe you. Thanks, Nellie." The buzz of the dial tone cut off his last word.

His next call was to Violet Dixon, the late Amanda Wentworth's sister. "Mrs. Dixon, this is Blake Carlisle of the Marshy Hope Creek Police Department. I'm calling on behalf of Detective Wade Atkins. You've spoken with him before."

"I remember."

"By any chance, do you remember your sister's blood type?"

"Of course. It was the same as mine. AB negative."

"You're sure."

"Completely sure. We were a perfect match. She gave me a kidney and I'm still alive."

"Thank you, Mrs. Dixon."

"Call me Violet. What's going on?"

"I'll tell you as soon as I'm sure."

Wade appeared in the doorway. Blake held up an envelope. "Bingo."

Wade took the file and flipped through the papers until he found the coroner's report. He began to read. On page two, in the center of the page, he found what he was looking for. Carefully, he closed the file and sat down, stroking his chin. It wasn't conclusive enough for the D.A.'s office, but it might be enough to wangle a confession from Quentin. He had to tread carefully. The judge would demand a lawyer. He needed more evidence, or a witness.

Wade found Bailey in the Busby garage painting over a recycled canvas. There was neither insulation nor air-conditioning in the temporary studio and it was hot enough to make a pig sweat. The boy's forehead and throat were beaded with perspiration. Damp patches stained his shirt and the black hair that fell into his eyes separated into spiky wet strands.

Wade waited until Bailey sensed his presence.

It didn't take long. He set his brushes in an aluminum can and turned around. "What's up, Detective?"

Wade nodded at the canvas. "I would have thought you could afford new ones."

"Old habits die hard."

Wade cut to the chase. "I came to talk to you about your father."

Bailey's expression settled into cultivated indifference. "Excuse me?"

"Quentin Wentworth."

"What makes you think Wentworth is my father?"

"Lucky guess."

"Liar," Bailey taunted him.

Wade thought a minute. "I'll make a deal with you. I'll tell you what I know and then you return the favor."

"You'll tell me everything?" Bailey was clearly skeptical.

"Everything I know," Wade promised.

"All right. What do you know?"

"The fifteen-year-old corpse found on your property was a female, approximately sixty years old, five feet four inches tall, blood type AB negative. The coroner's report on the body of Amanda Wentworth states that her blood type was O positive. Quentin Wentworth's blood type is O positive. Doc Balieu's office confirmed it. The hospital lab verified Tracy Wentworth's blood type. AB negative. An impossibility with an O positive father and mother. Are you with me so far?"

"Yes, sir."

"I confirmed Mrs. Wentworth's blood type with her sister. AB negative. Chloe put me onto it."

"What else did she tell you?"

"That you're worth saving."

Bailey was silent.

"I believe the body found on your land is Mrs.

Wentworth. I need more evidence than I have to arrest Quentin Wentworth for the murder of his wife, if in fact it was murder. I think it was, but I need something to go on, like an eyewitness. My guess is that you're my witness. I could have the body alleged to be Amanda exhumed, but that's a whole lot of trouble, not to mention money that the taxpayers of this county don't need to spend. What's holding you back, Bailey? Has Quentin threatened you?"

"I'm not afraid of Quentin Wentworth."

"Then tell me why you're protecting him."

"It isn't that."

"What is it?"

Bailey shrugged and attempted a laugh. "I don't know. It's tough to explain."

Wade waited.

"I guess you could call it a misplaced sense of loyalty."

Wade ached for Bailey Jones and at the same time he understood completely. The boy was hoping for contrition and acceptance from his biological father. He wanted a fairy-tale ending. Selling out Wentworth would forever prevent it from happening. Wade cleared his throat. "Quentin Wentworth is the meanest son of a bitch in the state of Maryland. His granddaddy was a slaveholder who sold his children. Don't go looking for anything from him. You're doomed to disappointment."

"What'll happen to him?"

"Given his age and his connections, probably a slap on the wrist."

"I was seven years old."

"That'll help him, too."

Bailey drew a long, deep breath. "Sit down, Detective. This'll take a while."

It was twilight by the time Wade called Blake to give him the heads-up. He pulled out of the Busby house driveway, heading west toward the bay and the palatial home of the Cove's first family. The harsh light of a summer afternoon had thinned out, dusting the trees, the roads and the marshlands with a fine coppery glow. It was his favorite time. The mind-numbing heat of late afternoon was gone. Breezes swept across the marshes. The workday was over. It was a time for pretzels and beer on the porch, for soft jazz and bluegrass, for low laughter and hand-cranked ice cream, for long walks and slow, deep kisses and the magic of fireflies dancing just out of reach.

Keeping the air-conditioning turned up, Wade rolled down the front windows and increased his speed, basking in the contrast of damp heat against his face and icy Freon swirling around his legs. He gave himself permission to ignore the speed limit. Here on this side of the Cove he was the law.

Wade had seen his share of crime. Not much surprised him, not even the latest development. The truth of the matter was, if you looked at percentages, Marshy Hope Creek was every bit as mired in scandal as the large cities of Baltimore and Annapolis. It just wasn't as violent and, more importantly, it wasn't printed for everyone to read. The *Island Post* was a newspaper run by an editor who held to an old-fashioned sense of protocol and an abhorrence of sensationalism. Out of consideration for the Wentworths, Tess's accident had been ignored. Wade wondered if the judge's arrest would put a whole new spin on things.

Bailey's story, on the other hand, did surprise him. He wondered why. Not that it mattered, except that Wade liked his questions answered. He had an analytical mind, especially when it came to isolating the problem, weighing his choices, following a particular plan of action, anticipating the outcome. In this case the outcome was hardly satisfying. A seven-year-old boy had kept a secret for fifteen years because he felt he couldn't trust anyone. Somehow that left Wade feeling raw.

Blake was already in position. Wade knocked on the door. Quentin opened it immediately. Wade pulled out the handcuffs. "You're under arrest for the murder of Amanda Wentworth. You have the right to remain silent. You have the right to an attorney. Anything you say—"

"For God's sake, Atkins, come inside and put those away," Quentin said testily.

"I think you'd better call your lawyer and tell him to meet us at the police station. He can post bail and you'll be out by morning."

"Are you serious?"

"I wouldn't say anything right now if I were you, Quentin. You can talk all you want after I've booked you. You'll need your attorney."

"Do you actually believe I'm going with you?"

"With all due respect, resisting arrest isn't gonna help your case." Wade slipped the cuffs around the judge's wrists and snapped them shut. "Do you need to tell anyone you're leaving?"

Quentin paled. "No."

"Let's go."

The ride into town was completed in silence. Blake's police cruiser followed close behind. At the station Wade led the judge into the back room for pictures and fingerprints.

"Are you in the least bit interested in what I have to say?" Wentworth asked icily.

"You'll get your chance."

"I deserve an explanation, Atkins. Goddamn it, I'm a superior court judge. You can't do this to me without an explanation."

Wade nodded. "Fair enough. I guess it wouldn't put me out all that much, as long as you understand that when I'm finished you're gonna march down that hallway, call your lawyer and then the sheriff will lock you into your cell until tomorrow. Is that clear?"

"Perfectly."

"All right. It's like this," Wade began in the same calm voice he used to order a sandwich and lemonade. "You were having an affair with Lizzie Jones. It went on for a long time, long enough for her to bear you a son, a son you never acknowledged. Bailey's not too happy about that, by the way. When Amanda found out, she grabbed your gun, followed you to Lizzie's place and threatened to expose you and kill Lizzie. There was a struggle. You killed Amanda. You dumped her body and further complicated the crime by arranging an accident where an innocent victim burned to death so you could pretend she was your wife."

"That's ridiculous."

"What is?"

"All of it."

"Have it your way." He took his arm. "Let's take a walk."

"Where is your evidence?" Wentworth demanded. "It's my word against Bailey's. He was a child. No one will believe him."

"The body found in the swamp is Amanda's. The woman you claimed was your wife had the wrong blood type. It's in the lab report. That's all the evidence I need to exhume the body. We know a little more about DNA than we did fifteen years ago."

"Wait a minute."

Wade waited.

Quentin exhaled slowly. "I'm no murderer. Amanda's death was an accident. The gun went off while we struggled. Bailey will tell you that. I didn't kill anyone."

"Mighty convenient if you ask me."

"Maybe so," Wentworth conceded, "but it's the truth."

Wade sighed. "Quentin, are you making a full confession?"

The judge sat down on a bench and dropped his head into his hands. "Yes."

"I'll bring Carlisle in here as a witness when we're finished. Meanwhile, speak slowly. I'm no stenographer." Wade flipped open the laptop on his desk. "Tell me what happened."

"It went just like you said, at first. After the gun went off, Amanda died. I buried her in the swamp and brought her car home. At first I didn't know how to explain her disappearance. Then I remembered the county morgue. Deputy Grimes found a Jane Doe for me. He bribed a pathologist. I put the body in the car, drove it out to Highway 39 and set fire to it."

"Silas Grimes went to Florida."

"He wanted an early retirement and a condo on the beach. It wasn't difficult to get Silas to change a few of the facts. It wasn't as if anyone was out looking for a crime. The questions were few and far between. The only one who was skeptical was Amanda's sister. Violet claimed that Amanda hadn't told her she was planning a visit. I explained that Amanda had left the house suddenly because we were having marital troubles. That part was the truth."

"What about Lizzie Jones? Why would she keep quiet all those years?"

"Who would believe her?"

"And Bailey?"

"He was a child, six or seven years old. I don't remember."

"Seven," Wade snapped. "How did you keep him quiet?"

Wentworth reddened. "I didn't have to. He was a child. No one would have listened."

"I think you told him more than that."

"Oh, all right. I told him it would be my word against his, that if he tried to tell anyone, I'd say he shot Amanda while playing with a gun. I said he'd be taken away and his mother would never see him again."

"Not exactly fatherly sentiments, were they, Wentworth?"

"It was my reputation. My life was on the line. I had Tracy to think of. She was recently divorced. Tess was five."

"Interesting," Wade mused, "how you justify blackmailing your own son to protect your daughter and granddaughter."

"I had no choice."

"There was always the truth."

Wentworth shook his head. "I couldn't bear the disgrace. Lizzie was a whore. She was beautiful and seductive, but a whore all the same. My credibility would have been destroyed."

"Four years ago you sat on the bench when Bailey was accused of murdering his mother. You would have sentenced him, your own flesh and blood."

"Yes," Wentworth admitted.

"How can you live with yourself?"

"I had no choice," he repeated.

"I don't see it that way." Wade pressed the print button on the laptop and handed Quentin the phone. "Call your lawyer." He raised his voice. "Sheriff?"

Blake Carlisle walked through the door.

"Wentworth has just dictated a full confession," said Wade. "I need you to witness that it wasn't taken under duress."

Carlisle addressed the judge. "Is that right, sir?"

"I'm not confessing to murder, or even manslaughter," the judge explained. "Amanda was wildly angry. I believed she followed me to Lizzie's to shoot the both of us. We struggled. The gun went off. Amanda was hit. My mistake was in trying to hide it. That's all."

"Not quite," Wade cut in. "You bribed public officials and falsified documents."

"It's still not murder. I didn't kill anyone."

Wade didn't contradict him. His story was nearly identical to the one Bailey relayed to him earlier that day. "We'll let the jury decide. Meanwhile, call your lawyer."

Sometime later, Blake walked back into his office. Wade was still there. "It's been a hard day. I thought you'd be long gone and celebrating by now."

Wade was staring at the computer. "There's just one more thing I'd like to sew up before I go home. It's the least I can do."

Twenty-Six

The next morning Wade rang the doorbell of the Delacourtes' big white house. Chloe answered immediately. She looked surprised to see him.

"Good morning."

"Good morning, Chloe. Is your granddaddy at home?"

She nodded. "We're having coffee in the back. We'd love for you to join us."

Wade grinned. Chloe Richards might be California born, but her manners were definitely southern. He guessed that he was probably the last person on her list to invite over for a coffee break, but no one would ever have known by her polite greeting. "I'd like that."

He followed her through the house, down the long hall, past the kitchen where she detoured briefly for another cup and saucer, and out the back door.

Cole sat facing the bay, protected from the sun's glare by a large oak tree. His newspaper sat on his lap, folded and forgotten. Wade didn't blame him. The panorama before him was difficult to take for granted even when the view was one he'd seen for a lifetime.

It wasn't even eight o'clock but already the temperature was peaking at ninety degrees. Out on the bay, egrets circled above the glittering water. A tardy skipjack chugged its way toward Smith Island, the smoke from its engine circling and disappearing into the cerulean blue of the sky. The lawn, a deep golf-course green, swept down to the water's edge where late-season ducks and plump coots dived for food in the marsh grasses.

Wade pulled his sunglasses from his breast pocket and made his way to where Cole was seated.

The man's greeting was just as gracious as his granddaughter's. "Good morning, Wade. What a nice surprise." He gestured toward an empty chair. "Sit down. Have some coffee, or would you prefer something cold? Iced tea, maybe?"

"Coffee'll be just fine."

Cole nodded at his granddaughter. "Ask Serena to bring out another cup, sugar."

"I'm way ahead of you, Granddad." She set the

cup and saucer on the table, filled it with coffee from the carafe and handed it to Wade. "Enjoy. It's delicious. I don't know what Serena does to our coffee, but you won't find it anywhere else, not even at Perks."

Wade laughed. "Don't tell that to Verna Lee."

"My lips are sealed." She kissed her grandfather's cheek. "I'm on my way to the hospital to check on Tess."

"Give her my love if you see her," said Cole.

Wade tasted his coffee, savoring the strong, rich, chicory flavor. "How is Tess?"

"She's not out of the woods yet, but the surgery went well."

"I'm glad to hear it."

Cole folded his paper. The skin on the back of his hands was paper thin and lined with raised blue veins. "What brings you here so early in the morning?"

Wade looked out at the blue water. "I had a feeling you might be wondering about that body we've been investigating."

"It crossed my mind."

"Quentin Wentworth confessed to the cover-up of his wife's accidental death."

"Good Lord. Is the body Amanda?"

"Yes, sir."

Cole sighed. "The poor woman."

Wade leaned back in his chair and surveyed the

bay. "There's one more thing. Anton Devereaux is alive and well and living in France."

Cole closed his eyes and exhaled. "Thank God."

Wade waited a minute. Then he stood. "I'll see myself out."

Cole nodded. "You'll tell Verna Lee."

"Yes."

"When you see her, give her my regards…and Wade—"

"Yes?"

"Thank you. You've relieved my mind, more than you know."

Wade's eyes met the faded blue gaze of one of the finest old men he would ever meet. "I think I know something of your mind, sir. It's my pleasure to relieve it."

Later that day, Chloe answered the door, took one look at Bailey's face, stepped out on the porch and closed it behind her. "What's wrong?"

He shook his head.

"It's okay," she murmured, pulling him down on the porch swing beside her. "Whatever it is, it'll be okay."

"Atkins knows everything," he said. "I told him."

Chloe closed her eyes. "What did you tell him?"

"I was there when the judge and Mrs. Wentworth were struggling. The gun went off."

"You were there? Where?"

"At home with my mother. Quentin Wentworth was having an affair with my mother. Turns out he's my father." His laugh was a sharp crack, completely without humor. "I thought Tess would tell you."

"Tess knows?"

He nodded. "She guessed. Then I went to Quentin. It's all true."

"How long have you known?"

"I've suspected for years."

"You and Tess are related."

"She won't want anything to do with me, not after she knows I've put away her grandfather."

"You didn't put him away, Bailey. He put himself away. What he did was wrong."

"My mother was a part of it, too."

Chloe didn't disagree. Poor, sad Lizzie Jones. "She's gone. There's nothing you can do about that. As for Tess, she'll understand. I know she will."

Bailey shook his head. "It won't happen. You always think the best of people."

"Why is it so important for you to be accepted by the Wentworths? If they don't want you, why do you care?"

He looked around, at the lush green lawn, at the diamond-bright water, at the gracious old home and attempted to explain. "You've never known a single moment of not being wanted. Wherever you go, whatever you do, you have that security blanket behind you, your mother, your father, your grandfather, Russ and probably a dozen other people I don't even know about. It's different for me. I grew up knowing I wasn't welcome."

"Your mother loved you."

"She loved me, but I wasn't convenient, not until she went blind. After that she needed me. But that's it, Chloe. There's no support group to pick me up when I fall. It's all me. You ask why I want acceptance from them. It's because they're the only family I've got. If your family doesn't want you, nobody does, or at least that's what you believe. How does a person go on, if nobody wants him?"

She wanted to tell him that he would never be in that position, that wherever he went, whatever he did, people would know that he was beautiful and interesting and dangerous and different, but she kept silent. Somehow she understood that it wouldn't be enough. He wanted something more, something intrinsic and fine to hold on to, to take out and examine when she was no longer with him.

She began slowly, finding the right words, gathering momentum as she spoke. "When it comes to family, some people are born luckier than others. But the ones who don't have perfect families aren't doomed, Bailey. They can't be. The way I see it is, you learn from the mistakes your parents make. If you don't, you end up repeating them."

He was silent for a long minute, searching her face. "What did you learn?" he asked.

"Are you making fun of me?"

"I'm asking a serious question."

"I don't know. You're putting me on the spot. I guess I learned that every story has two sides and that gorgeous people sometimes make lousy parents. I learned that people change and that you should never judge them before you meet them just because you've heard stories from someone else. And, I guess I learned that sometimes your first love is the one that counts." She smiled into the night. "I've learned practical things, too."

"Such as?"

"I know how to bake the best peach cobbler in the state of Maryland. I can suck every bit of meat out of a hard-shelled crab. I make a wonderful cup of coffee. I can recite *The Little Engine That Could* from beginning to end without once looking at the words." She looked at him. "So, what do you think?"

His hand settled on her bare leg. "What I think, Chloe Richards, is that I'm lucky to know you."

She nodded, satisfied. "I was hoping you'd say that."

* * *

Libba hooked the back end of the crawfish she was using for bait, lifted her elbow and with a quick flick of her wrist, cast her line just past the shoals of the finger lake. Then she dug the end of the pole into the sand and beckoned to Gina Marie. "Hold on like this," she instructed the child. "When you feel a pull, hang on tight and give a shout. Okay?"

The little girl nodded, straddled the pole, gripped the striped end and planted her bottom in the sand.

"Hang on to her, Libba Jane." Verna Lee pulled her feet into the center of the blanket. "There's a current close to the shore." She muttered under her breath, "Why on earth does a little girl need to know how to fish?"

"I heard that, and it's fun," returned Libba.

"It's fun when you're seven. She's three."

Libba raised her eyebrows. "No one would ever believe you were born and raised right here in Marshy Hope Creek. Fishing is our life."

"Bite your tongue. After those condos go up, none of us will be doing much fishing."

Libba leaned over her daughter. "Are you all right, sugar?"

Gina nodded, her eyes narrow and intent on the churning water, her small fists gripping the pole.

Libba sat down on the blanket beside Verna Lee and brushed the sand from her feet. She looked thoughtfully at her sister's golden shoulders and light brown hair. "Did you bring anything to put on except that halter?"

"No. Why?"

"We'll fry out here. Let's pull this blanket into the shade. I'll pull. You carry the basket."

Comfortably ensconced in the shade of a huge pine, Verna Lee began rummaging through the picnic basket and pulled out a can of beer and a jug of lemonade. "Which do you want first?"

"Lemonade, please."

Verna Lee poured two cups and handed one to Libba. "I was hoping you'd choose the beer," Libba said.

"Why is that?"

"So you'd get just a little bit drunk."

Verna Lee raised her eyebrows. "You want me to get drunk?"

Libba nodded. "Otherwise you won't talk about Wade Atkins."

Verna Lee turned her gaze back to her niece. Gina appeared perfectly and unusually content with her hands on the pole and her eyes fixed on the white chop. She was Russ's daughter without a doubt. "There's nothing to tell," she replied.

"That's not what I heard."

"You can't believe everything people say."

"I know. That's why I want to hear it from you."

"He had me checked out."

"Excuse me?"

"He made it his mission to find out about Marin County."

"Why didn't you tell him?"

"He didn't give me a chance."

Libba stared out at the water and the slow, steady descent of the sun. "You know what I think, Verna Lee?"

Verna Lee sighed. "I imagine you'll tell me anyway."

Libba ignored her. "I think that most people are like ships passing in the night. Sometimes we get close, but not close enough to really connect. There might be lots of Mr. Rights out there for you, but you'll never know it. You won't know because when one of those people gets close, you'll invent something, a fatal flaw you can't get your mind around, a bad habit that's too annoying to forgive, a reminder of the man you married. You'll be glad there's something wrong because God help you if you ended up with someone like him again."

"Are you saying that *Wade Atkins* could be Mr. Right?" Verna Lee's voice rose and cracked.

"You said you liked him, more than you liked anyone else in a long time."

"I haven't been anywhere in a long time."

"My point exactly."

"Am I supposed to turn the other cheek when he couldn't trust me enough to wait until I was ready to tell him about a seriously traumatic event in my life? He spied on me, Libba Jane."

"I don't see it that way."

"Why not?"

"I think Wade has fallen for you. I think it scared him. I think you're a fool to throw away someone you're seriously attracted to because of a mistake in judgment." Libba smiled. "In other words, don't waste years of your life the way I did. Give Wade a shot. If it doesn't work, you won't spend time living with regret."

"You're describing you and Russ."

Libba's hands, long-fingered and brown, clasped her knees. "I waited twenty years to come home."

"I don't think—"

Gina Marie shrieked and leaped to her feet. "I feel it, Mama. I feel it."

Libba moved quickly. "Hold on, sugar. Hold on tight." She gripped the pole just above Gina's hands, knelt in the sand and began reeling in the test. "It's a good one, Gina." She released the clip and the tension eased.

"Where did he go?" Gina asked, disappointed.

"He's still with us. We'll let him take the line. It'll tire him out a bit and then we'll bring him in."

"Don't lose him, Libba," Verna Lee called out.

Once again, Libba pulled back on the pole and reeled in the line. "That's it, baby. Good job. One more time. Hold on, Gina." Alternating between reeling in and pulling back, reeling and pulling, she shortened the line until the fish, a healthy-size bluegill, was close enough to net. "Okay, Gina. Don't let go of the pole, no matter what. I'm going in to get him."

"I won't let go," the child promised, planting her sturdy legs in the sand.

True to her word, she held the pole steady while Libba flipped the fish into the net.

Back on the blanket, Gina proudly held up her prize to show Verna Lee.

"Mighty fine work, sweetie pie," her aunt said admiringly. "Your daddy is gonna be so proud of you. I'll bet he'll cook it up tonight at the barbecue."

"Can we eat it?" Gina asked.

"You bet," her mother promised. She smiled at Verna Lee. "Russ said he'd have everything ready at seven-thirty."

"You're spoiled, Libba Jane."

Libba refused to be baited. "Everyone's coming, except for Tess, of course."

"How is she doing?"

"Better than expected. She'll make a full recovery."

Verna Lee sighed. "Thank goodness."

Libba stood. "It gives us one more thing to celebrate. C'mon help me roll up the blanket."

Twenty-Seven

At seven o'clock the sun was still high enough above the horizon line to keep the mercury at an uncomfortable ninety-two degrees. But it wasn't enough of a deterrent to keep anyone away from a Hennessey party. The deep green lawn was awash with the promise of the evening to come.

Russ had been productive. Colored paper lanterns hung on clotheslines, waiting for darkness. Coal pyramids reeking of lighter fluid filled two commercial-size barbecues. Aluminum buckets, heavy with melting ice, soft-drink cans, wine and beer bottles sat in the shade of the patio. Protected by plastic wrap, platters of luscious fruit weighed down the picnic tables. Freshly picked sweet corn, still in their husks, lined the breezeway. On the kitchen counter, chicken, ribs and Gina Marie's bluegill sat marinating in Russ's secret recipes.

Upstairs in her bedroom, Gina slept the sleep of the innocent, comfortable in the wake of two oscillating fans. Libba, fresh from her shower, stepped into a lemon-yellow shift of cool linen, applied a sweep of mascara to her lashes, glossed her lips, slipped on her kitten sandals and released the clip from her hair. It grazed her shoulders, thick, shining, coffee-colored.

She smiled at her husband who lay on the bed, content to watch the miracle of his wife's transformation. "How do I look?"

"You are one beautiful woman, Libba Jane Hennessey."

She blew him a kiss. "Thank you."

"My pleasure."

"I'll start the salads. We have about thirty minutes. Shelby and Earl are coming. They're never late."

"I'll keep that in mind," he promised.

Downstairs, she moved from room to room turning on the fans, pulling chairs into conversational groupings, laying out fresh finger towels in the bathrooms, setting out the appetizers and cocktail napkins, breathing in the thick, brackish air wafting in from the bay.

Libba smiled. She loved parties. Tonight was special. The mix of people would be eclectic, Verna Lee, their high-school friends Shelby and Earl, a few neighbors, Cole and Chloe, Blake Carlisle and Wade Atkins. Libba's smile faded. Would Chloe invite Bailey Jones? She hoped not, but if she did, Libba refused to let it spoil her evening.

Russ came down the stairs, shower tracks evident in his hair. "I'll start the ribs."

"Russ?"

He stopped, one hand on the refrigerator, and waited.

"Do you think Chloe will bring Bailey Jones?"

"Probably." He pulled out the pan of ribs.

She poured ranch dressing on the cauliflower salad. "I knew you'd say that."

"I like Bailey," Russ said quietly. "He's had a bad rap. He's a hard worker and he's done well for himself."

Libba tossed the salad and returned it to the refrigerator. "I don't think he's right for Chloe."

"I think you're reading too much into this. Let it be and see what happens. Do you really think you can change anything with your disapproval?"

"No."

"It might be best not to offer an opinion. More than likely it'll go against you if she thinks you don't like him."

Libba leaned against the sink. "It isn't that I don't like him, it's just that his upbringing has been so unconventional." She appealed to Russ. "How can he know what to do?"

"People know, honey, sometimes with less than Bailey has."

She sighed. "It's ridiculous. Chloe's young. I'm worrying for nothing."

"That's my girl. Is there anything else you want me to do before I start cooking?"

She shook her head.

Carrying the ribs, he headed out toward the grassy patch where the barbecues were set up, lifted the lid of one, arranged the slabs of meat over the smoldering wood chips and closed it again.

"Yoo-hoo. We're here." Shelby Sloane's shrill voice called out from the road. "Something smells really good." She nudged her husband, a tall balding man with a protruding belly. "Doesn't it smell good, Earl?"

Earl Sloane bent over the ice-filled bucket of drinks and pulled out two beers. He tossed one to Russ. "Mighty good. I heard your little darlin' caught herself a fish the size of Texas."

Russ popped the top of the beer can. "Almost. Libba said she was quiet as a mouse waiting for it, too."

"She's a chip off the old block."

Shelby looked around. "Lordy, it's a hot one. Where's Libba Jane?"

"Did I hear my name?" Libba, balancing two platters of food, opened the screen door with her foot.

Shelby held out her arms. "Hand one of those to me. Why don't you open your mouth and ask for help when you need it?"

She handed a platter to Shelby. "I didn't know you were here."

"Hi, Mom." Chloe walked up the bank, her arm tucked into her grandfather's.

Libba smiled warmly. Chloe looked lovely in a white cotton dress, her tanned shoulders and legs a striking contrast to the delicate material. There was no sign of Bailey Jones. "Hi, sweetie. Hi, Daddy." She kissed both her father's cheek and her daughter's. "Help yourself to whatever you like. I have iced tea inside."

Cole headed for the door. "That sounds perfect."

"Chloe Richards," said Shelby. "You look wonderful. How do you manage to stay so cool in this scorching weather?"

Chloe lifted a delicate eyebrow. "Granddad has air-conditioning."

Shelby groaned. "Don't tell me that. I might just scratch out your eyes I'm so jealous. Do you hear that, Earl? Cole has air-conditioning."

"When I'm as rich as Cole Delacourte, you'll get air-conditioning, too."

Shelby rolled her eyes. "I guess that means never."

"I like the heat," Libba announced.

"That's because you and yours tan up like the trunk of one of those oak trees."

"It's cooler on the porch," said Libba. "Let's have something to drink and get out of what's left of the sun."

Gradually the deep lawn filled with people. Soft laughter floated on the breeze rising off the bay. Alcohol-slurred voices carried across the cut grass. Women in white shorts and skimpy tops clustered on the steps. Men in long, loose shorts and polo shirts gathered around the barbecues, their voices lowering in direct proportion to the crudeness of their jokes. On the porch, Gina Marie held court over three small children, their lips and hands stained Popsicle blue.

Libba, happy with the success of her party, filched a carrot from the vegetable tray in the kitchen.

Shelby followed her inside. "I have some gossip," she announced.

"Oh?" Libba stirred blue cheese into the sour cream. "What gossip?"

"Wade arrested Quentin Wentworth today."

Libba set down her spoon, her vegetables forgotten, and stared at her friend. "What are you talking about?"

Shelby, delighted with the results of her disclosure, climbed onto a bar stool and crossed her legs. Libba's undivided attention was something she relished. "Earl went into town this morning and ran into Blake Carlisle. The body the geologist found in the swamp is Amanda Wentworth."

"You're making this up."

Shelby shook her head. "I'm not. You know Blake Carlisle. He isn't one to keep anyone in jail without a good reason."

"People are innocent until proven guilty, Shelby." She turned away. "I don't want to hear this. Gossip is dangerous."

"You're no fun," Shelby continued. "I never did like Wentworth. Amanda always looked scared to death. Earl says Quentin was having an affair with Lizzie Jones. He says that Bailey—"

The screen door opened. Horrified, Libba recognized the black-haired young man who stood beside Chloe. "Shelby!" she cried out an instant too late.

Shelby turned. Her green eyes widened, but only for an instant. "Speak of the devil. We were just talking about you."

Libba couldn't read Bailey Jones, but she knew her daughter. Chloe was fighting pure, unrelieved rage.

Blindly, Libba stepped into the maelstrom. "Please," she whispered. "This isn't what it seems.

Shelby was telling me about Judge Wentworth's arrest."

Chloe's voice was bitter. "That isn't all she was telling you."

Bailey didn't speak. Instead, he took Chloe's balled fist in his hand.

Libba recognized the gesture, the sheer power of its statement. History, she vowed silently, would not repeat itself. "Please," she said, placing one hand on Chloe's shoulder, the other on Bailey's. "Please, stay. You're welcome here. You're both welcome here."

"Don't fret, Miz Hennessey. I'm not runnin' away."

Shelby slid off the bar stool. She cleared her throat. "Listen, you two. You can think what you like, but the truth is, I mean no harm. If I've offended you, I'm sorry." With that, she picked up the cauliflower salad and left the kitchen.

Libba drew a deep, shuddering breath and forced herself to meet Bailey's gaze. "I apologize. I shouldn't have listened."

"From what I heard, you were trying not to."

"I encouraged her. I have no excuse. It was just so shocking." She pressed her palms against her flaming cheeks. "Never mind. I'm making it worse. Please, stay and enjoy the party."

Chloe hadn't spoken. Her lips were pressed

tightly together. Bailey's thumb moved back and forth across Chloe's knuckles. His voice was expressionless. "You may as well know, she was telling the truth. The sheriff arrested Quentin Wentworth. He's my natural father. He and my mother had an affair. She took money from other people for sex, but not from him. She loved him. He didn't share the sentiment. His wife found out and came after him with a gun. There was a struggle and Mrs. Wentworth died. He took the body away and buried it in the marsh."

Libba didn't think she'd ever heard such painful words spoken with less expression. Her hand moved to her throat. "My God. What about Amanda's funeral? How—who—"

"I don't know about that. I'm sure Atkins does, but I doubt he'll say anything."

"How do *you* know all this?"

Bailey's dark eyes didn't waver. "I was there."

Libba moaned and closed her eyes. Fifteen years ago, Bailey was a little boy.

She felt his hand on her arm and opened her eyes. He was standing directly in front of her. "Take it easy, Miz Hennessey. I've been livin' with this for a long time. Nothing's changed for me except that now other people know."

"All those years you said nothing. How awful for you. Did Quentin know you were his son?"

"He knew."

Libba's eyes filled. "I'm so sorry, Bailey. I'm sorry you had to go through this. Is there anything we can do?"

"Your family's been good to me, ma'am. Your daddy gave me a life. I like your husband and I guess you know your daughter's the best friend I've ever had."

Libba sniffed, searched for a tissue, dabbed at her nose and laughed. "I'm getting the point. Why don't you go outside and socialize until the food's ready. Save me a place at your table. Maybe, after tonight, you'll like me, too."

Bailey grinned. "I'm sure, when you set your mind to it, you can be fairly persuasive."

Chloe wasn't as easily pacified. "We're not staying late."

Libba's heart sank. "You need to eat."

"Granddad doesn't like to stay out late anymore. I made peach cobbler for the three of us at his house."

"I won't complain if you leave after dinner." Libba handed a platter of sliced watermelon to Chloe. "Would you mind putting this on the long table for me? Oh, and say hello to Gina Marie. She misses you."

"She'd rather be with you."

"Of course. I'm her mother, but she loves you, too."

Bailey took the platter from Chloe. "I'd like to see the little terror again myself."

"Gina's not a terror," Libba said indignantly. "She has personality."

"Whatever you say, ma'am."

The door closed behind them. Libba breathed a sigh of relief. It had been a close call, no thanks to Shelby.

Russ poked his head into the kitchen. "The food's ready. Verna Lee's here and she's giving Wade a wide berth. Shelby's sucking down Jack Daniel's like it's lemonade. We need you outside."

Libba shook her head. "Were people always like this around here, or do we notice because we left and came back?"

He frowned. "What are you talking about?"

"Shelby's drama. Quentin Wentworth's hypocrisy."

"I won't disagree with you there. Quentin always was a son of a bitch, but now he's no longer my father-in-law, it doesn't bother me."

"He's Tess's grandfather."

Russ pulled the door shut behind him, walked across the room and took his wife into his arms. "What's going on, Libba Jane?"

"Quentin Wentworth is Bailey's father." The unbelievable words choked her throat. "He killed his wife. The body they found in the marsh is really

Amanda Wentworth. God alone knows who's buried in Amanda's plot in the cemetery."

"Hey, hey, Libba Jane." He stroked her shining hair. "Calm down. It's okay. Wade will have it all under control."

"What about Bailey? He was a little boy. He saw everything."

"Bailey's okay. He's done well for himself. Pull yourself together, Libba Jane. Quentin Wentworth is a horse's ass. He always was. Lizzie's been dead for four years. Bailey's made a success of his life. Everything's fine."

She pressed her fingertips against her eyelids. "I'm worried about how this will affect Chloe."

"Chloe could do a lot worse than take up with a successful artist who can afford to live in New York City. Now come outside. Mingle with your guests. They're asking for you. Verna Lee could use some help with Shelby."

"Verna Lee can hold her own against a roomful of Shelbys."

"It's our party. She's your sister and she shouldn't have to."

"All right." Libba waved him away. "Give me a minute. My mascara's all over my face. Hold them off a little while longer."

"Promise you'll be outside in five minutes."

"I promise."

* * *

It was considerably more than five minutes before Libba joined her guests outside. Russ had found Verna Lee. Wade was seated across from her on an Adirondack chair facing the water. Fireflies lit the air like tiny sparklers around their heads and the moonlight turned the chop on the bay a luminescent silver.

Libba sat beside Russ, leaning against him, grateful that, for her, everything *was* settled.

Wade nodded at her. "It's a great party, Libba Jane."

"Thanks. You got here late. I didn't think you'd make it."

"I had a few things to finish up."

Verna Lee looked at him. "What things?"

"I made a few phone calls, finished up a report, nothing important."

"For pity's sake, Wade, you're the worst liar. Why don't you just tell us what's going on?"

"I can't do that, Verna Lee," he explained calmly. "It comes with the job."

Libba couldn't keep silent. "Does it have to do with Quentin Wentworth?"

His face was smooth and polite. "How would you know that, Libba Jane?"

"You know how this town is, Wade. Even the best-kept secret is one that no one knows about until the next day."

"It's unprofessional to discuss the details of my job at a social gathering. Why don't we grab some of those ribs, a couple slices of watermelon and another beer and settle down with a more interesting topic of conversation."

Libba's eyes met Verna Lee's. "I'll save your seats. Why don't the two of you bring us back a plate."

Wade held out his hand. "Verna Lee?"

There was much more at stake than food. Libba held her breath and didn't release it again until Verna Lee reached out and met him halfway.

Standing beside Wade, Verna Lee smiled. "Chicken or ribs?" she asked.

"Whatever's left," replied her sister.

Later, after peach cobbler and hand-cranked ice cream, brandy and coffee, rum-soaked cigars and lingering goodbyes, groups of two and three collected their belongings and their children and made their way home in the humid, jasmine-scented darkness.

"Did you drive or walk?" Wade asked Verna Lee.

"I walked."

"May I drive you home?"

Riding in the car beside Wade, she spoke very little until he pulled in to her driveway and walked her to the door. "Would you like to come in for coffee?"

"Do you grind your own beans?"

"Of course."

Wade looked up at the star-studded sky. "Are you gonna grill me on why I arrested Quentin Wentworth?"

She turned the key in the lock. "I didn't know you had."

"He's Bailey Jones's natural father."

"I figured that."

"You're kidding."

She shook her head. "Lizzie Jones was my friend. Even if she wasn't, my grandmother knows everything that goes on in this town. People talk. Quentin played around. Lizzie's reputation wasn't exactly a secret and she was beautiful. Isn't that the way it usually works, the powerful and the beautiful?"

Wade followed her into the kitchen. "I wouldn't know about that." He waited while she ground the beans, spooned the granules into the filter and added water. "I suppose you want to know why I arrested him."

"Adultery and fathering a child without benefit of marriage isn't exactly a crime, although maybe it should be," she said as an afterthought.

Wade considered putting her off and decided against it. Libba was right. It would be all over town by tomorrow anyway. "Amanda Wentworth found out about the affair. She came after him with a gun. To make a long story short, she died in the struggle and he hid her body in the swamp."

She closed her eyes briefly and offered up a silent thank-you. Lizzie was innocent after all. "Good Lord! How medieval," she said out loud. "Are you sure?"

"He confessed."

Deep in thought, Verna Lee reached for the mugs and set them on the counter. "What about Amanda's funeral?" Her eyes widened. "He's a superior court judge. Surely he wouldn't have murdered an innocent person to take Amanda's place."

"He claims the woman came from the morgue."

"Do you believe him?"

"Not entirely."

"In other words, you believe some of it, but not all?"

He accepted the mug of thick, rich coffee. "Something like that. I've been thinking about it. Quentin was a powerful man. Still is." He shrugged. "The facts will come out eventually. It's up to the district attorney."

"Quentin rubbed elbows with all of them down there at city hall for a very long time. Do you think there's even the remotest possibility of finding an impartial jury?"

"Probably not," Wade admitted. "The defense

will ask for a change of venue. Whether it will be granted remains to be seen." He sipped the hot coffee. "Excellent."

"Thank you."

"I shouldn't have told you, you know."

"Why did you?"

"My defenses collapse when I'm around you."

"Is that good or bad?"

His gaze rested on her lips, lush and full. He set down the coffee mug and pulled her close. "I'm still evaluating," he said before his mouth came down on hers and he no longer remembered whether it was good or not.

Verna Lee wasn't about to get caught up in the throes of emotion no matter how attractive and available the man happened to be. She'd done that several times already and promised herself that if she ever got another chance at a real relationship she would do things differently. Chemistry would have no place in her decision making. There wasn't a man alive who kept the pheromones hopping more than two years. This time she wanted stability and appreciation, kindness and a sense of humor. She wouldn't be in any hurry, either. She was past the age when she had to think about her biological clock. There would be no children, hence no need to rush into permanence. Marriage was for optimists, or for those who feared growing old alone.

She was neither. In fact, she liked living alone, having control of her own money, liked spreading out in the center of her bed, snuggling under exactly the right number of blankets, reading until the wee hours, liked drinking tomato juice and eating a hard-boiled egg for dinner. Women got comfortable in relationships. They started on cream-filled foods. They gained weight and exercised less. She didn't need Wade Atkins and his Sunday manners and his house of windows on the bay. Her life was going in the right direction. She was making progress at her own pace and it suited her just fine.

Why, then, did her lips part to admit the intimacy of his tongue? Why did she twine her arms around his neck and press against his chest? Why did that involuntary sound, something very like a moan, rise from her throat when he found the pulse point at the base of her throat, and why did she make not a single protest when he lifted her off her feet and carried her to the bed where he proceeded to make love to her so thoroughly that she forgot all about pheromones and chemistry and the fact that the lust factor between a man and a woman could only last, at the most, two years?

Twenty-Eight

Cole Delacourte wasn't a man to turn tail and run from a respectable wager. But he wasn't a fool, either. Lost causes held no appeal for him. Besides, he didn't care for Quentin Wentworth, never had, and, even though it wasn't a charitable thought, he had some stake in seeing justice served.

So, when Tracy Wentworth appeared at his door asking him to represent her father, he refused. Retirement was a reasonable excuse. He was an old man and the rigors of a court battle were sure to shorten what time he had left. He didn't weaken, not even when she pleaded. There were other attorneys, he'd assured her, attorneys, young and ambitious, who would see this case as a challenge. She'd left, pale and chastened but convinced that he wouldn't

change his mind. Cole hadn't counted on her re-
cruiting Libba Jane to the cause.

Several hours later, Libba came calling, Libba,
his daughter, who reminded him more and more of
Nola Ruth, the same dark hair and eyes, golden
skin, slender bones and long spectacular legs. God,
if ever a woman was missed, she was Magnolia
Ruth Beauchamp.

The memory of their first meeting all those years
ago was plain as day in his mind. He was home, on
his first real vacation in much too long. He had
planned to drink bourbon until he was dizzy, dress
in worn shorts and a favorite, moth-eaten shirt, fish
the finger lakes of the Chesapeake and roast his
catch over coals buried deep beneath the sand. He'd
thrown out his line, intent on the test that tightened
the instant it hit the water. At first he didn't notice
the girl with the wind-whipped dark hair and gorgeous legs. But then he did. For the first time in his
life he'd been unable to find words.

Nola Ruth Beauchamp held out her hand. "I've
never seen you here before," she said in her sultry,
delta-flavored voice.

He said something. He must have, or she would
have laughed at him and walked away. Whatever it
was didn't matter. For Cole, in the throes of what
the poets called *love at first sight,* had inadvertently
stumbled across his destiny.

That was more than forty years and a lifetime of compromise ago. She'd returned his love, but not to the same degree, never that. There was always one-half of a couple who cared more, gave more. Nola Ruth wasn't a giver. She was honest and righteous, alluring and mysterious. He'd never doubted her loyalty. Still, she had secrets. They followed her to the grave. Someday soon he would do something about one in particular. Right now, it was Libba Jane, not her mother, who waited for his answer. He loved this only child of his, her mother's daughter, but she wasn't Nola Ruth.

Smiling regretfully, he shook his head. "I'm not up to this, honey. Not anymore."

Disappointed, she'd kissed his cheek and left the house that was no longer hers, the house that had seen five generations of Delacourtes, and was now his alone, except for Chloe, his granddaughter.

In the end it was Chloe who convinced him and if anyone wondered why, it made perfect sense the way she did it. She spoke of values he'd buried deep inside himself in the interests of keeping what he had. She spoke of facing challenges, especially un-pleasant ones. She reminded him that all men run scared and few end up without tallying a regret or two, but they still deserve a competent attorney. She spoke of old age and Bailey Jones and how four years ago Cole had changed his life for the better.

She spoke of her friend and stepsister, Tess Hennessey, and how Quentin had sat by her hospital bed, his eyes closed, head bent, his thoughts his own.

It was the thought of Quentin, Tess's grandfather, that changed Cole's mind. He'd looked at Chloe, petite Chloe, with her small Delacourte bones and her blue Delacourte eyes, and her mind like his own and suddenly, what he must do all became completely clear.

Bailey knew he was not alone long before he saw her walking toward him. The years spent living alone with his mother, surrounded by nothing but swamp, had honed his senses. He heard the snapping of twigs and the slight rustle of decaying leaves under her feet. Then, all at once, she stood right in front of him, a small girl with tanned shoulders, pale hair and the bluest eyes he would ever see.

"Hi," she said softly.

"Hi." He took her hand and linked his fingers with hers. "So, is everything set?"

She nodded. "I got all my classes and reserved my flight. I leave next week." She tilted her head. "Will you drive me to the airport?"

"I'm not much for goodbyes."

"This isn't goodbye."

"Isn't it?"

"I'm not letting you go this easily, Bailey. You

can pretend all you want, but I know how you feel.
I'm not going to let you lose me again."

"Sometimes I think you're too smart for me."

"That doesn't matter, either. I'm going to write
to you and you're going to write back. We'll e-mail
and talk on the phone. I'll come to New York for
Christmas and then we'll both come back here for
food and presents."

He couldn't help laughing. "You have it all figured out."

"You bet I do."

"What do you think your mother'll say when she
hears your plans?"

"My mother knows how it is with us. Besides, it
isn't her life. She has Russ and, for the time-being,
Gina Marie. This is my life and yours. We'll see
how it goes, somewhere else, away from here."

"What if it doesn't work out like you planned?
What if something happens?"

She smiled at him, the smile she'd inherited from
Libba Jane and Nola Ruth. "No matter what, we'll
always be friends."

He relaxed. "I'm rushing things."

"A little."

"Friends." He thought a minute. "That's good."

"It's very good."

"I don't have a lot of friends."

"Neither do I."

He looked at her, his gaze thoughtful, considering. "Do you mind if I hold out for more?"

Chloe's heart lurched. This was a *moment,* the kind people wrote about, one of the ones that no matter how many others she had, or what her future held, this was the one she would come back to. It would stay in her memory to be pulled out and gone over, smoothed out and relived when she was an old woman and the air was quiet and the nights long and all she had left were memories. "I was hoping you would," was all she said.

"I have a surprise for you."

She raised her eyebrows.

"I've decided not to sell the marsh. It's home. Marshy Hope Creek is my home."

She laughed. "I was hoping you'd say that, too. Verna Lee will be pleased."

Wade rang the doorbell and hid the roses behind his back. They were red and long-stemmed, complicated, the kind he associated with Verna Lee. He heard the sound of footsteps on hardwood floors.

She opened the door. He would never get used to how beautiful she was, her wild hair, the golden eyes, the way her clothes fit her lush figure. When he could think again, he presented the flowers with a flourish and enjoyed the sudden widening of her eyes.

"Thank you. They're beautiful. I'm honored."

"You're beautiful."

Her eyes flicked over him, noting the faded jeans and the cotton shirt worn thin at the elbows. "You dressed up for me again," she teased.

"Actually, I did."

"Really."

"Yes."

She rested one hand on her hip. "I have to tell you, Wade, before this goes any further, that your taste in clothing is awful."

"I'm open to suggestion."

She moved aside. "That's a relief. Please, come in."

He followed her into the living room. Her house was like her café, warm, eclectic, artfully arranged with bold colors and interesting artwork. "I like your paintings. Who's the artist?"

"Bailey Jones."

"You're joking."

She poured him a glass of something white in a delicately etched wineglass. "I forgot the beer. I hope this will do."

He tasted it tentatively. As expected, it was perfect, cool and crisp, thirst-quenching.

"I'm not joking," she continued, moving easily, purposefully, toward the kitchen. "I couldn't afford them, of course. These are his rejects."

Wade knew nothing about art. Most modern artists' work didn't appeal to him. But these were paintings, detailed as photographs, of life in the Cove. "He's good."

"Yes, he is." She paused in the doorway. "Do you want to set the table or help with the dishes?"

He held the wine on his tongue for a minute before swallowing. "You don't make it easy for a man, do you?"

"I hadn't thought about it."

"You wouldn't consider trying to impress me?"

She laughed. "Wade, the reason I keep coming back for more is because I don't have to. That's a compliment, by the way."

He nodded. "Accepted. I'll set the table."

It wasn't until they'd finished their meal, cold avocado soup and something with crab and cheese wrapped in a tortilla, washed down with more excellent wine, that he broached the subject he wanted to share. "I did something, Verna Lee. I hope you approve."

"What might that be?"

"Back when I was in the middle of this investigation, I sent out some feelers. One of them came back the other day."

She was all polite attention.

"I asked for the whereabouts of a man named Anton Devereaux."

Her smile froze. "Why would you do that?"

She was too polite, too composed.

"He was seen here in Marshy Hope Creek fifteen years ago when he was arrested for resisting a police officer. Your mother bailed him out of jail. He didn't show up for his trial and she lost her money."

"I know all that. Tell me something new."

"He's alive, Verna Lee. He lives in the Bordeaux region of France. He owns a vineyard."

"I see." She dabbed her mouth with her napkin. "Are you going somewhere with this?"

"He didn't know about you. Nola Ruth never told him she was pregnant."

"That would have been difficult to do. He disappeared."

"It wouldn't have worked out. The timing was wrong."

She crumpled her napkin and left it beside her plate. "I know that."

"He wants to see you."

She frowned. "You've talked to him?"

"His wife died five years ago. They had no children. I told him I'd give you his phone number. Any future contact will be up to you."

No children. She would be the one and only. There would be no competing with Libba Jane. Immediately she was ashamed of herself. Because of Libba, she had a family. "Why are you doing this?"

He reached for her hand. "It's a gift, Verna Lee. You're a beautiful, educated woman. Your parents may not have been of your choosing, but they made you. Because of them you look the way you do, you have talent and interests and accomplishments. How can it be wrong to invite your father into your life? He can't be blamed for never making contact. He didn't know you existed. He came back once, to find your mother. In my book that says he's decent. Why not give him a call? What have you got to lose?"

She was silent for a long time. Her thoughts swirled in a maelstrom inside her head. Nola Ruth Delacourte was her mother. She would never forget the day Drusilla told her the truth. The lady in the big house was her birth mother. For years her father hadn't mattered. She'd barely considered him until Nola Ruth told her story. Anton Devereaux. She'd tested the name on her tongue. He wanted to see her. Wade was right. She had nothing to lose. "He left town and forfeited bail," she said at last. "Does that mean I have to go to France?"

"There are worse things than going to France."

"What about my café?"

"Hire someone."

"You have all the answers, don't you?"

"All except one."

"You've got my attention."

"Do you think you might consider seriously hooking up with me one of these days?"

She shook her head. "Not any time soon."

"I'm not talking about now. Will you marry me someday? Because if I know this will eventually work out, I won't keep pestering you. I can wait."

"All I have to say is someday? You'll accept that?"

"As long as you mean it. You have to be telling the truth."

"I always tell the truth."

"Not always."

"I may not tell you everything, but what I say is the truth."

"I love you."

She smiled. "I believe you."

"Do you love me?"

"I think so."

"When will you know?"

"I think I know."

"When will I hear it?"

"Tomorrow. I'll tell you tomorrow."

He kissed her palm, folded up her fingers and gave her hand back. "In that case, I'll come back tomorrow."

She stared at him. "You're kidding."

"No."

She watched in silence while he cleared his plate,

rinsed his dishes and searched for his keys. She didn't want him to leave. "Saying something doesn't make it so."

"I disagree. If you say it, you believe it. It's like confession. Owning up to something takes courage because it makes it real."

"You're not Catholic."

"I'm a Baptist, same as you. Good night, Verna Lee."

He had pulled the car out of the driveway and was nearly ready to accelerate when she ran after him. He almost missed her. If he hadn't taken a last look out the rearview mirror, he wouldn't have seen her waving, calling after him. He stopped, rolled down the window and waited.

Slowly she approached the car, bent down and rested her arms on the open window. "I'm set in my ways."

"I figured that."

"Where would we live?"

"My house."

"Why not mine?"

"I have the better view."

She thought a minute. He did have the better view. "Okay."

He sighed. "I need the words, Verna Lee. If you can't say them right now, that's okay. I'm not going anywhere except home."

She backed away. "Step out of the car, Detective Atkins."

He turned off the engine, climbed out and leaned against the door. "What now?"

Sliding her arms around his neck, she hid her face in his shoulder. "I don't want you to go," she murmured.

"I won't."

"Do I have to look at you?"

He grinned. "No. Not this time."

Resting her head against his shoulder, she closed her eyes and whispered, "I love you, Wade."

He could feel the pounding of her heart. "I love you, too, Verna Lee."

"Is that enough?"

He laughed. "For now, it's enough."

A NEW VIRGIN RIVER NOVEL
BY ACCLAIMED AUTHOR

ROBYN CARR

When a wounded marine reservist, LAPD officer
Mike Valenzuela, agrees to become Virgin River's first
cop, he does so knowing it's time he settled down.
Twice divorced and the lover of too many women,
he secretly longs for a woman who can tie up his
heart forever. He finds that woman in Brie Sheridan,
a Sacramento prosecutor. Virgin River becomes a safe
haven for Brie after nearly losing her life at the hands of
a crazed criminal. Though tough and courageous, she's
got some fears she can't escape—but now she has someone
who will show her just what it means to trust again.

WHISPERING
ROCK

"The Virgin River books are so compelling—I connected instantly
with the characters and just wanted more and more and more."
—*New York Times* bestselling author Debbie Macomber

Available the first week of June 2007 wherever paperbacks are sold!

New York Times bestselling author

DEBBIE MACOMBER

It was the year that changed everything...

At fifty, Susannah finds herself regretting the paths not taken. Long married, a mother and a teacher, she should be happy. But she feels there's something missing in her life. Not only that, she's balancing the demands of an aging mother and a temperamental twenty-year-old daughter.

In returning to her parents' house, her girlhood friends and the garden she's always loved, she discovers that things are not always as they once seemed. Some paths are dead ends. But some gardens remain beautiful....

Susannah's Garden

"[A] touching and compassionate."
—*Booklist*

Available the first week of July 2007
wherever books are sold!

MDM2444

REQUEST YOUR FREE BOOKS!

2 FREE NOVELS
FROM THE ROMANCE/SUSPENSE
COLLECTION PLUS 2 FREE GIFTS!

YES! Please send me 2 FREE novels from the Romance/Suspense Collection and my 2 FREE gifts. After receiving them, if I don't wish to receive any more books, I can return the shipping statement marked "cancel." If I don't cancel, I will receive 4 brand-new novels every month and be billed just $5.49 per book in the U.S., or $5.99 per book in Canada, plus 25¢ shipping and handling per book plus applicable taxes, if any*. That's a savings of at least 20% off the cover price! I understand that accepting the 2 free books and gifts places me under no obligation to buy anything. I can always return a shipment and cancel at any time. Even if I never buy another book from the Reader Service, the two free books and gifts are mine to keep forever.

185 MDN EF5Y 385 MDN EF6C

Name _____ (PLEASE PRINT) _____

Address _____ Apt. # _____

City _____ State/Prov. _____ Zip/Postal Code _____

Signature (if under 18, a parent or guardian must sign)

Mail to The Reader Service:
IN U.S.A.: P.O. Box 1867, Buffalo, NY 14240-1867
IN CANADA: P.O. Box 609, Fort Erie, Ontario L2A 5X3

Not valid to current subscribers to the Romance Collection,
the Suspense Collection or the Romance/Suspense Collection.

Want to try two free books from another line?
Call 1-800-873-8635 or visit www.morefreebooks.com.

* Terms and prices subject to change without notice. NY residents add applicable sales tax. Canadian residents will be charged applicable provincial taxes and GST. This offer is limited to one order per household. All orders subject to approval. Credit or debit balances in a customer's account(s) may be offset by any other outstanding balance owed by or to the customer. Please allow 4 to 6 weeks for delivery.

Your Privacy: Harlequin is committed to protecting your privacy.® Our Privacy Policy is available online at www.eHarlequin.com or upon request from the Reader Service. From time to time we make our lists of customers available to reputable firms who may have a product or service of interest to you. If you would prefer we not share your name and address, please check here. ☐

BOB07

An abandoned tunnel system beneath a prestigious New England college becomes the stalking grounds of a serial killer...

MICHELLE GAGNON

The crime scenes are grim and otherworldly. The bodies of two female students are found mutilated and oddly positioned in the dark labyrinth beneath the school—haunting symbols painted on the walls behind them.

In her decade tracking serial killers, FBI special agent Kelly Jones has witnessed terrible offenses against humanity. Yet the tragedy unfolding at her alma mater chills her to the bone. Evidence suggests there is a connection between the victims—all daughters of powerful men. And elements of the killings point to a dark, ancient ritual. As the body count rises, so do the stakes. The killer is taunting Kelly, daring her to follow him down a dangerous path from which only one can emerge.

THE
TUNNELS

Available the first week of June 2007 wherever paperbacks are sold!

www.MIRABooks.com

MMG2446